Woman's Part

An Anthology of Short Fiction

By and About Irish Women 1890-1960

Woman's Part

An Anthology of Short Fiction
By and About Irish Women 1890-1960

Selected and Introduced by

JANET MADDEN-SIMPSON

Arlen House
Dublin

Marion Boyars
London & New York

© Introduction, biographical notes, selection:
Janet Madden-Simpson, 1984

ISBN Hardcover: 0 905223 33 0
Paperback: 0 905223 58 6

CIP
Madden-Simpson, Janet
  Woman's Part
  1. English literature—Women authors—History and criticism
  2. English literature—Irish authors—History and criticism
  1. Title
820.9'9287   PR115

Cover Design: Flying Colours
Typesetting: Koinonia Ltd, Manchester.
Printed by: Irish Elsevier Printers Ltd, Shannon, Ireland
Published by Arlen House Ltd, 69 Jones Road, Dublin 3,
in association with Marion Boyars Publishers, 18 Brewer Street, London W1R 4AS.

Contents

For my parents, Harold and Dorothy Madden,
and for Frank Simpson

Grateful acknowledgment is made for the use of the following material:

'By God's Mercy' by Dorothy Macardle. From *Earth-Bound: Nine Stories of Ireland*. Dublin: Emton Press, 1924. By permission of Mr Donald Macardle.

'For Richer, For Poorer' by Edith Somerville. From *The Cornhill Magazine* of October 1933. By permission of Mrs K. Johnston of the Somerville and Ross Estate.

'Bridget Kiernan' by Norah Hoult. From *Poor Women*. London: Heinemann, 1928. By permission of the author.

'Unwelcome Idea' by Elizabeth Bowen. From *Look At All Those Roses*. London: Victor Gollancz, 1941. By permission of Curtis Brown Ltd and Jonathan Cape.

'The Apple' by Elizabeth Connor. From *The Bell* of October 1942. By permission of the author.

'The Proud Woman' by Maura Laverty. From *The Bell* of October 1942. By permission of the estate of Maura Laverty.

'Frail Vessel' by Mary Lavin. From *The Patriot Son and Other Stories*. London: Michael Joseph Ltd, 1951. By permission of the author.

'The Tragedy of Eight Pence' by Geraldine Cummins. From *Variety Show*. London: Barrie and Rockliff, 1959. By permission of Hutchinson Publishing Group Ltd.

'Pilgrimage' by Mary Beckett. From *The Bell* of January 1952. By kind permission of the author.

Permission for 'Virgin Soil' by George Egerton (*Discords*. London: John Lane, 1894) has not been traceable.

Sources for other stories not in copyright:

'Queen O'Toole' by M. E. Frances. From *Freize and Fustian*. London: Osgood, McIlraine and Co., 1896.

'The Snakes and Norah' by Jane Barlow. From *A Creel of Irish Stories*. London: Methuen, 1897.

'The Criminality of Letty Moore' by Erminda Esler. From *The Cabinet of Irish Literature*. London: Gresham, 1902.

'A Rich Woman' by Katharine Tynan. From *An Isle In The Water*. London: A. & C. Black, 1906.

'At The River's Edge' by Violet Martin. From *Stray-Aways*. London: Longmans, Green and Co., 1920.

Preface

THE CONTENTS of this anthology have been selected with the aim of making available – and, in some cases, of making known – a variety of the short fiction written by Irish women between 1890 and 1960. As with the compilation of any anthology, the editor's task has been to choose, from the large body of material which exists, the works which best fit the purpose. In this case, the criterion has been to illuminate some of the ways in which Irish women have written short fiction and how they have used it to explore the conditions of womanhood. Because these stories focus on the lives of women within Irish society, they reveal facets of Irish female experience as it was, and as it evolved, during these years.

Short fiction has been chosen, not only because it yields wide variety, but also because some of the best writing by Irish women has taken this form. The decision to confine this anthology to short fiction, and the further qualification 'by and about Irish women', explains the absence of writers such as Emily Lawless, Molly Keane or Kate O'Brien, among many. And although the desire to practise a kind of literary archaeology makes this very much a book with a slant towards literary history, neither did I wish to abandon aesthetic considerations and the kinds of literary judgments in which I have been trained. This has meant choosing not to reprint stories by writers like Ethna Carbery or Mary E. L. Butler, which seem to me to have historical and sociological interest, but not a great deal of literary quality.

All the pieces included were written originally in English, and they have not been edited with 'improvements' in mind, for though literary fashions may have changed, each story is strong enough to stand as written. Precisely for this reason, I have used the introductory essay as a medium for presenting a sense of historical background to the writing rather than as a place to break down the stories into what might be termed critical components – plot, themes, techniques; the very diversity of the material would have made this approach reductionist. And not all of these pieces are short stories 'proper': anecdotes, sketches, tales, arguments, are here too. Authorial voices and methods are highly individual, but all of the stories relate to, and reflect needs, concerns and crises in the lives of women. The fact that the writers themselves are products of the middle and upper classes is a circumstance of Irish life and Irish history, and yet, on reading the stories, such barriers fall away before the more urgent association of common experience.

No timespan can be entirely natural. Any choice of particular dates, as of particular works, is taken at the expense of others. These stories have not been chosen because they 'typify' a specific period. Taken together, however, they sweep through the formative years of the Irish Free State and of the consciousness of the Irish people. They answer some questions about the position of women in Irish society and raise others; they provide us with a link to the literary and social past. The first selections of this book come out of the influences of Parnellism, the Literary Renaissance and the *fin de siècle*. Others were written over a period of time which included the First World War, the 1916 Rising, the Anglo-Irish War, the Irish Civil War, Partition, the Free State, the Emergency/ Second World War, literary censorship and the post-Emergency move from rural to urban, industrialised society. Yet the stories do not progress in a rigid chronology of ideas and techniques any more than, with one exception, they display hard-line political affiliations. This collection stops just short of 1960, the year which is now seen as the beginning of a period in which women began to look at themselves differently and in which began a corresponding series of changes in editorial, academic, critical and cultural appraisals of women's work and women's writing.

The reasons for this anthology are several. Apart from critical works on some selected and famous Irish women writers, little has been done to analyse trends or concerns in writing by Irish women, or to look at it as an important part of the Anglo-Irish literary traditon. This book is an attempt to bring attention to a part of Irish literary and social heritage that has been too long forgotten and too often dismissed. It also attempts to present a spectrum of writing by women of varying ages and different experiences who have in common the circumstances of sex and nationality, though they may differ in religious, class or political affiliations. As a key to the understanding of the female experience of Irish culture, with its complex, fascinating, and often conflicting variety, I hope that the short fiction in this collection will encourage others to investigate the riches of this largely unknown literature.

I wish to thank the National Library of Ireland, the libraries of University College, Dublin, and Trinity College, Dublin, and the Central Catholic Library, Dublin, for the use of their resources during the research for and the preparation of this work. Their staffs, particularly Miss Lombard of the last-named institution, were unfailingly helpful.

Brian Cleeve's *Dictionary of Irish Writers* provided me with an invaluable starting-point. Meg Castino Gleeson, Antonio Fuentes, Monica Brosnan and, especially, Monica Simpson, offered child-care when it was most needed. Denis Cotter helped by commenting on the earlier draft of the introduction.

Finally, I want to express my appreciation of the loving support of my families. To my mother and father, and to Frank, many thanks for many things.

Janet Madden-Simpson
County Dublin, 1983

Introduction

ANGLO-IRISH LITERATURE has been conventionally understood to be writing carried out by Irish people through the medium of the English language. This conventional understanding is inadequate, distorted by the unvarying concentration that readers, students and critics have lavished upon those perceived to be the major figures of the literature. Meanwhile much else has been dismissed – so much that one can read 'male' for 'major'. The very mention of Anglo-Irish literature conjures up a litany of names from Joyce and Yeats to O'Connor, O'Faolain, O'Flaherty, and from Synge to Beckett. The equation of Anglo-Irish literature with a record of masculine perceptions seems to have been accepted almost without question. Ireland is thought of as a country with an impressive literary tradition from which come great male artists.

These major figures are selected figures, and selected figures are chosen according to a critical code. In the field of Anglo-Irish letters the code as well as the selection has been overwhelmingly biased, resulting in a lop-sided awareness, not only of the literature which is read and studied but of the fabric of Irish life from which the literature has emerged. In *The Lonely Voice,* writer and critic Frank O'Connor remarks that 'the literature of the Irish Literary Renaissance is a peculiarly masculine affair. . . it is in society that women belong.'[1]

Even if one assumes that O'Connor is being facetious in saying that women must be left at home, his failure to mention, much less to discuss, any of the women writers who participated in the 'struggle towards cultural nationalism'[2] is conspicuous. The single exception to O'Connor's interpretation of the masculine Renaissance is Lady Augusta Gregory, but 'it is difficult to think of her as

1. Frank O'Connor, *The Lonely Voice* (London: Macmillan, 1963), p. 202.
2. The definition of Mary Colum, one of the very few Irish female critics, in *From These Roots* (London: Cape, 1941), p. 260.

a typical woman'.[3] As it is, indeed: a woman of Augusta Gregory's energy and ability certainly cannot be thought of as 'typical', though one suspects that the adjective which O'Connor really had in mind was 'ordinary'. Quite apart from her aptitude for literary work and her devotion to the cause of the Renaissance, Lady Gregory did in fact serve the most typical/ordinary of functions; she became an organiser, a literary mother-figure, a midwife to male creativity, putting her social position, her Coole Park estate and herself at the service of the emergent folklore and theatre.[4] Gregory would have to be excluded from what Patricia Meyer Spacks calls the 'relative invisibility of women writers'[5] if only because of her relatively high profile as a collector of folklore, a translator, and a dramatist in otherwise almost exclusively male preserves. Yet O'Connor does not discuss Gregory as playwright, as folklorist, or even as collaborator and contributor. Instead, his full discussion of her consists of two pointedly humourous anecdotes which emphasise her defective pronunciation of English.

The treatment which Lady Gregory receives at O'Connor's hands is interesting for several reasons. An important playwright at a seminal period in the development of a national literature, she

3. O'Connor, p. 202
4. George Moore is one male writer and critic who credits Lady Gregory – mockingly – with 'devotion to literature. Instead of writing novels she had released the poet from the quern of daily journalism.' In addition to the swipe at women's fiction-writing, Moore is less than sincerely admiring about Lady Gregory's dedication: 'As the moon is more interested in the earth than in any other thing, there is always some woman more interested in a man's mind than in anything else and is willing to follow it sentence by sentence. A great deal of Yeats' work must come to her in fragments – a line and a half, two lines – and these are faithfully copied on her typewriter, and even those that his ultimate taste has rejected are treasured up, and perhaps will one day appear in a stately variorum edition.' From *Hail and Farewell. Ave* (London: Heinemann, 1911), p. 275.
   An intriguing aspect of Lady Gregory's part in the Renaissance movement is the implication that, had it not been for her patronage, the entire course of activity may have been quite different. 'Lady Gregory summoned both men [Yeats and AE] to take a look at them before making her decision that Yeats was the right candidate for the national laureate and adopting him and devising a programme of special nourishment to power him for the work.' It is interesting to note the nurturance metaphors that Herbert Howarth uses in this passage from *The Irish Writers 1880-1940: Literature Under Parnell's Star* (London: Rockliffe, 1958), p.20.
5. Patricia Meyer Spacks, *Contemporary Women Novelists* (Englewood Cliffs, New Jersey: Prentice-Hall 1977), p. 1.

is not treated seriously as either a writer or as an influence. Moreover, neither is she given credit for her role as hostess and nurturer, her acting-out of that 'typical' womanly function which O'Connor finds difficulty in ascribing to her. Finally, and most importantly in terms of the material in this anthology, O'Connor's study, like almost every other critical overview of Anglo-Irish literature, shores up a damaging perspective. It is a fallacy that there have been few, or few 'worthwhile', Irish women writers: there have been many. But because commentators who have shaped the Anglo-Irish literary tradition have been concerned with assessing and formulating hierarchical opinions only about selected, usually male, writers, the one-sided cultural imprinting of this literary taste has left readers appallingly ignorant of other writers and their works.

As a result Anglo-Irish literature has come to be associated with an almost exclusively male output. Even a cursory flip through bibliographies, reviews of research, critical studies of the subject,[6] sadder still, a glance at Anglo-Irish literature collections in library holdings and reading lists for courses in Anglo-Irish literature,[7] will confirm that only a very few women – Maria Edgeworth, Lady Gregory, Edith Somerville and Martin Ross, Mary Lavin, Elizabeth Bowen, Kate O'Brien and Jennifer Johnston – have been included, because they have been accorded status and been called 'good' or 'important'. Even these, who stand out by virtue of contrast, are frequently discussed as 'major' writers only in terms of qualifying definitions.

6. A selection of basic sources: *Modern Irish Literature* ed. Raymond J. Porter and James D. Brophy (New York, 1977); *Irish Literature and Drama in the English Language*, Stephen Gwynn (London, 1936); *The Irish Renaissance: An Introduction to Anglo-Irish Literature*, Richard Fallis (Dublin, 1977); *Irish Life In Irish Fiction*, Horatio Sheafe Krans (New York, 1903); *Anglo-Irish Literature: A Review of Research* ed. Richard J. Finneran (New York, 1976); *Modern Irish Literature 1800-1967: A Reader's Guide*, Maurice Harmon (Dublin, 1967); *A Guide to Anglo-Irish Literature*, Alan Warner (Dublin, 1981); *Anglo-Irish Literature* Augustine Martin, (Dublin, 1980).
7. Lady Gregory's *Our Irish Theatre, Cuchulain of Muirthemne*, and *Gods and Fighting Men*, Maria Edgeworth's *Castle Rackrent* and *The Absentee* and Mary Lavin's *Stories* are, apart from Una Ellis-Fermor's *The Irish Dramatic Movement*, the only works written by women included in the seventy-nine entries on the preliminary reading list for the M.A. degree in Anglo-Irish Studies at University College Dublin in 1981-82. This is an internationally known and attended course.

Apart from these few, there has been a general silence on the subject of Ireland's women writers. Daniel Corkery's term 'the hidden Ireland' is as applicable to the state of women writers in Anglo-Irish literature as ever it was to the plight of eighteenth century Gaelic poetry.

Valuable connecting links between those works of Anglo-Irish literature which are known and were read have been lost, and readers remain unaware of much of the material that was written contemporaneously with what is known. The popular concept of Anglo-Irish literature by-passes a rich vein of tradition, which has been ignored and unstudied in all of the theorising about themes, styles, concerns and trends.

The decades since 1960 have seen some pronounced changes in attitudes to the nature of female contributions to the culture. People now profess to think differently about the question of the importance and validity of female experience. Paying attention, even special attention, to writing by women, looking at it again in the light of a new thinking, has been recognised as a valuable critical activity. Yet this re-evaluation of women's writing has, so far, made few inroads into the essentially conservative field of Anglo-Irish literature.

Since about 1960 more women are writing and publishing and being regarded with attentive interest. Best of all, writing by women in Ireland now comes from a wider, more eclectic social range. Deserved critical attention has been focused on Mary Lavin, whose work long suffered comparative neglect. Mary Beckett has been encouraged to write again and to collect her work so that some of it is available to a new generation of readers.

Some scholars, such as Ann Saddlemeyer in her *In Defence of Lady Gregory, Playwright* [8] and Hilary Robinson in her *Somerville and Ross: A Critical Appreciation,*[9] have dealt lovingly and carefully with the work of writers who, although generally acknowledged as important, have been overshadowed or slotted into limiting categories.

8. Ann Saddlemeyer, *In Defence of Lady Gregory, Playwright* (Dublin: The Dolmen Press, 1966).
9. Hilary Robinson, *Somerville and Ross: A Critical Appreciation* (Dublin: Gill and Macmillan, 1980).

But for most Irish women not presently writing and publishing, for Irish women writers of the past, there seems to be little chance of having their works considered in the light of new thinking. The term 'woman writer' is still dismissive, a pejorative epithet in Anglo-Irish literature classes. It is used to shelve writers as diverse in genre and subject as Annie Keary, Janet McNeill, Anne Crone, Teresa Deevy, Emily Lawless, Dora Sigerson Shorter. Writers of fiction, poety and drama are forgotten and neglected. Even the names of many female writers are unknown and if specific unfamiliar names do come up, the description 'woman writer' is taken to imply unimportance, a smaller accomplishment.

This attitude has meant that 'woman writer' unjustly stands for inferiority, rather than for a sense of a difference in experience and perception. Because women writers have had a precarious toehold in the critical hierarchy, many who would be categorised as 'minor' have been entirely overlooked. The important function of the lesser talent (a valuable participation which has much to do with continuing creation, directions, and fashion of a literature) has, of course, been recognised in the cases of many 'minor' male writers. The élitist, masculine-directed critical position does suggest that there is a distinct difficulty in dealing with women's writing. It is also suggestive of problems inherent, not only in male critics or women writers, but in a culture which so obviously reflects this difficulty. The loss is not only to women or to the whole literary tradition but to the basic constituents of culture.

TOWARDS REDRESSING THE BALANCE

Prevailing attitudes towards Anglo-Irish literature are understandable in a critical climate where writers are ranked according to one set of values. There is little room for flexibility or lateral thinking if a single set of prejudiced rules is applied to all. And prejudice is not too strong a word in reference to the consideration of Irish women writers by a masculine-minded body of critics. There are also those intriguing silences by women – when writers or potential writers did not, or could not, speak. They, too, have affected the way in which women have come to be overlooked in the formulation of the Anglo-Irish literary tradition.

It is a fact that Irish women have not written 'great' literature as Yeats, Joyce or Beckett have produced it. Even in masterpieces such as *The Real Charlotte* by Somerville and Ross or *The Death of the Heart* by Elizabeth Bowen, female Irish writers have generally worked within the confines of literary convention, have not experimented in startlingly obvious ways and have, perhaps, been too accepting of sociological and historical limitations. They have also, to their cost, doggedly insisted on writing and exploring as women, and this has not been highly prized. Irish women as a group have produced a large, varied, mostly unknown body of writing that is interesting, informative, sometimes inspired. It is a very human as well as a very feminine – in the widest sense of the word – record of Irish life and imagination. Taken together it gives a distinctive, if sometimes limited, view of the world.

The difficulty with the record compiled by women writers is that the work is sometimes self-annihilating at the same time as it is self-conscious, self-defining and self-illuminating. Just as the writing of Irish women has received negligible critical attention, so the writers have, in general, failed to create a climate for the serious, sustained consideration of their work. Too few Irish women have entered into the fray to construct critical standards, too few have theorised and articulated the kind of critical ideas which can be so influential in establishing an atmosphere for serious appraisal. Too few have taken themselves seriously as artists, too many have failed to stretch themselves. Paradoxically, though not surprisingly, it is often the same writers who achieved astonishing popularity (and extraordinarily high sales figures) and who were so largely prolific in their lifetimes who are now least regarded or altogether forgotten.

No small part of the difficulty in assessing the contributions of women writers to the Anglo-Irish literary tradition is that often, and for complex social and personal reasons, Irish female writers have accommodated themselves to the omnipresent demands of others – families, audiences, publishers. In a world in which the measure of a woman's morality consisted of the 'childlike adherence to the pronouncements of others',[10] women protected personal and literary reputations (which often were taken to be much the same thing) by tending to suppress or redirect ideas or impulses which might be considered unseemly. The pressures of Irish society, the internal divisions and various standards set within it (Catholic or Protestant, upper class or middle class, Irish or Anglo-Irish), meant that the precepts of many women writers included the canon of 'good taste'.

Edith Sommerville considered all her long life that 'good taste' was a cardinal rule of writing and it seems as though many other writers felt likewise. Katharine Tynan was only one woman whose formidable energy was to a large extent kept within the strict bounds of self-censorship. Like M. E. Francis, Tynan was a dedicated, professional working wife and mother. But though her fiction and journalism supported her family, Tynan never encouraged her readers to see her as a role model. On the contrary, like many other women writers, she used her writing to deal with tones and subjects compatible with the conservative stance of middle-class morality.

Her reiterated platitudes about marriage as a woman's noblest and happiest state contrast strangely with a determined silence about her own personal life – and with her habit of killing off the mothers of her fictional heroines. When Tynan does articulate ideas that run contrary to a sentimental angel-in-the-house-convention, she generally does so through a peasant character. The implication is that freedom from expectations and constraints comes only by belonging to a different class. In the writing by Irish women, who did not tend, as did many of their male counterparts, to slough off family ties and leave the country in order to lead independent lives, Tynan's suggestion is neither unusual, nor inexplicable.

As invidious as self-censorship have been self-effacement and self-trivialisation. Many – too many – writers, due perhaps to 'the female necessity of severe restraint',[11] have adopted an exaggeratedly casual attitude towards writing. Elaine Showalter says that

10. Patricia Meyer Spacks, *The Female Imagination* (London: Allen and Unwin, 1976), p. 113.
11. Ibid.

'work, in the sense of self-development, was in direct conflict with the subordination and repression inherent in the feminine ideal'[12] and the attitudes of Irish women to their writing would seem to reflect Showalter's theory. George Egerton is an extremely interesting example of a writer who evinces a deliberate distancing from the notion of writing as work. She prefers instead to take the stance of receptive medium: 'I could not take myself seriously. . . inside ten days I wrote six stories. . . for years they came and said themselves.'[13]

Egerton's foreign travel and bohemian living, as well as her passionate and outspoken fiction, make her unique among her contemporaries. Yet she is representative of the way in which Irish women have collectively, and until very recently, found it difficult either to take the business of writing seriously or to be seen to take it seriously. Symptomatic of the need to appear off-hand, even passive, about writing as work, Egerton ironically placed herself in exactly the same position as sentimental and domestic writers, such as Mrs Alexander, Rosa Mulholland and Mrs Croker, who 'found' their audiences and wrote for them.

The inability or refusal of women to take writing as a serious creative process and to work at it is one reason for the neglect of the writers included in this volume. Few of them saw themselves in the way that contemporary male writers saw themselves: as significant, as expressing, or railing against, the national consciousness and preoccupations.[14] Whether due to propriety or to feelings of

12. Elaine Showalter, *A Literature of Their Own: British Women Novelists From Brontë to Lessing* (London: Virago, 1979), p. 22.
13. George Egerton in 'A Keynote to Keynotes' in *Ten Contemporaries* ed. John Galsworthy (London: Benn, 1932), p. 59.
14. There is a marked contrast here to male Irish writers, many of whom showed no hesitancy in proclaiming themselves prophets of the new Irish literature. Irish women writers have tended not to put themselves forward; in addition they have generally been quick to credit other writers. Katharine Tynan, for example, was thought of as the best and most promising of the Irish poets of her generation until W. B. Yeats came along. Although she entertained him, among many others, at her literary salons and had many serious discussions about their poetry writing with Yeats, in later years she called him 'the onlie begetter of Irish poetry' and dedicated a volume to 'he who taught me'. In point of fact, Tynan was the first Renaissance writer – before Douglas Hyde, AE, or Yeats – to use traditional Irish material in poetry. As early as 1885 she did so in her first published volume. Tynan's 1883 lament on the death of Parnell,

inferiority, this female reticence meant that instead of examining their writings or their functions within the developing literary tradition, women generally preferred to see writing as a personal and private occupation. Yet many Irish women used their writing as a platform for speaking on behalf of others. They wrote powerfully on subjects ranging from white slavery and illegitamacy, to nationalist politics, to the plight of uneducated and untrained women faced with the necessity of earning a living in a society which put little value on the lives of women.

Most female Irish writers have chosen to depict the realities of their lives rather than to work at imbuing those realities with wider frames of reference. The result is that the work of some writers seems to further constrict, concentrate and reflect stereotypical attitudes towards female thought and behaviour. But a second look can reveal a greater depth, especially obvious here in the work of the later fiction writers such as Elizabeth Bowen, Mary Lavin, Mary Beckett and Elizabeth Connor, who allow the currents of feminine revolt to come to the surface. Their stories convey a deliberate sense of claustrophobia, a portent of change as well as a reaction to the frustrations of a parochial Ireland where women still have little formal status but where they no longer submit in as docile a manner to the assigned role.

Elizabeth Bowen, who thought of herself and wrote as a conscious artist almost from the beginning of her literary career, is an exception to the general rule. It is most interesting to look at Bowen's literary criticism and then to consider the way in which she commanded critical respect. But Bowen is an exception

---

was noted , cut out, and kept by Lady Gregory, and was recognised by her as the first manifestation of the new national impulse.

An interesting counterpoint to the whole notion of women's demure approach to literary activity was Amanda McKittrick Ros, unanimously considered eccentric at best, mad at worst. Ros took her writing very seriously indeed and had her works privately published; her weirdly alliterative novels (*Delina Delaney*, 1898 and *Irene Iddesleigh*, 1897) inspired clubs of admirers. Her scurrilous and scatalogical poetry was largely motivated by a desire for revenge against critics who derided her books. Ros herself was convinced of her genius – and certainly, everything about her books is uniquely her own. One of the fascinating aspects of her writing is her word coinage and her appropriation of commonly-used words to mean something entirely different in the context of her stories.

because of her Anglo-Irish background and her long residence in England. In the male-dominated society of post-Famine Ireland,[15] where male writers busily created male, often impossibly idealised, images of womanhood,[16] and where in any case male writers received the bulk of serious critical attention, 'lady' poets, novelists, and short-story writers were judged by a separate set of rules and assigned a definite literary place.[17] The position of women – on the

15. For a perceptive and enlightening essay on male-dominated Ireland see 'Women and the Church since the Famine' by J. J. Lee in *Women in Irish Society: The Historical Dimension* (Dublin: Arlen House–The Women's Press, 1978). Lee's essay is a detailed and convincing account of the way in which the Great Famine of 1845-49 and its aftermath affected and weakened the position of women in every aspect of Irish society. It helps to explain the milieu in which women were universally regarded as inferior and imperfect and in which, also, the scope of women's lives steadily diminished.

16. Not only did Yeats, Moore, Synge, and many others rework mythological heroine figures such as Gráinne, Emer and Deirdre; allied to their contemporary re-stereotyping of already stereotyped figures was the general nationalist revival of the notion of Ireland incarnated as a romantic female figure. The *aisling* tradition of Gaelic poetry (in which Ireland is seen as a dream-vision of a beautiful young girl), the figures of Dark Rosaleen, Caithlín ní Houlihan and even the hag of the Shan Van Vocht – all are traditional, conventional manifestations of the concept of Ireland as a passive female in distress, helpless and waiting for a male hero-figure to come and rescue her. Significantly, apart from retelling Ossianic material and some romantic love stories, women have not tended to use extensively mythological material. Fiction writers, in particular, have concentrated on modern settings and characters and have looked for inspiration to the rural peasantry rather than to the wealth of Irish myth and folklore. Perhaps the frankness of much of the original material has had something to do with their avoidance of it: the idea of Niamh as a siren, or Maedbh as an unwomanly warrior, or Deirdre and Gráinne as adultresses almost certainly would not have attracted literary women who had to worry both about their own reputations and the business of audience. Most male writers, too, of course, have avoided the reality of women from the Celtic past and have romanticised or sentimentalised them.

17. Ernest Boyd (whose *Ireland's Literary Renaissance*, last revised in 1922, is still one of the standard works on the period) was an early and influential commentator who firmly placed women writers by consistently using a specialised critical vocabulary distinct from that used in his discussion of male writers. 'Innocent tenderness', 'delicacy', 'gentle', 'charming', and 'unassuming' are used to describe and praise female writing. But he calls Jane Barlow's conception of the Irish peasantry 'decidedly unnatural' and does not shrink from categorising the poet Dora Sigerson Shorter as 'ignorant' and 'careless'. The message seems to be that praise of female writing is done in the tones of polite society but that negative reactions can be expressed as bluntly as one pleases. Boyd is certainly unrestrainedly negative about fiction writing (most of it done by women) in the Renaissance period. His chapter on

fringes of the literary arena – was no more than a mirroring of what was taking place in other areas of Irish society.

Women writers at the time of the Literary Renaissance, and for a long time after, are often mistakenly thought of as writers of popular and sentimental verse and fiction. It is a serious under-estimation. The leaning towards realistic, even 'social-problem', fiction is pronounced. Some women, like some men, wrote nation-alistic myths or romances, but even these are apt to include some surprisingly down-to-earth details about the day-to-day lives of women. A reading of the women who facilely transmitted the orthodox attitudes about women's place and woman's function reveals that they were as intimately aware of the difficulties of being a woman as were writers who approached their subjects from a more crusading and analytical angle. This common awareness is a bond which to some extent makes most Irish female writing feminist; that is, in the sense that the reader is almost without exception expected to identify with the heroines and to participate in their stories.

Few of the writers represented in this volume, however, had much to do with feminist or suffragist activities;[18] if they did, they tended, like Geraldine Cummins, Edith Somerville and Violet Martin, to espouse a moderate and 'rational' approach to the

---

'Fiction and Narrative Prose' is subtitled 'The Weak Point of the Revival' and he dis-misses much of the fiction written by saying that it is mostly 'circulationist'. Whether this is genre-snobbery or misogyny is difficult to say. The only two female fiction writers whom Boyd discusses at length are Jane Barlow and the Hon. Emily Lawless. He ultimately finds neither of them important.

18. Edith Somerville and Martin Ross were involved with the Munster Women's Franchise League and served as officers; Geraldine Cummins was actively associated with the same group.

Margaret MacCurtain's essay on 'Women, The Vote and Revolution' in *Women in Irish Society* documents Irish women's organised political activity. Groups ranged from Anna Parnell's Ladies' Land League (joined by Katharine Tynan and the novelist Hannah Lynch) to the Irish Suffrage Society, Cumann na mBan, the Irish Women Workers' Union and Inghinidhe na hEireann. For those who think that Irish women were not concerned with feminist and suffragist activities, or took little part in revolutionary movements, this well-documented essay will come as a revelation. Margaret Ward's *Unmanageable Revolutionaries* (Dingle: Brandon, 1983) is a recent book which illuminates the subject.

problem. The 'woman question', so explosively evident in so much of world fiction from 1880 to 1920 is, with the exception of Sarah Grand's and George Egerton's writing, largely difficult to find in the writing of Irish women. The urgent problem of national identity at this crucial period of Irish history swamped the 'woman question' and sapped its vitality. But although feminist views are not generally treated explicitly in the earlier writing of Irish women, there is evidence that an innate and universal sense of feminism came within the scope of fiction.

In spite of – or perhaps because of – the prevailing forment of Anglo-Irish Literary Renaissance and Irish nationalism, 'there was only one small part left to tell: the *terra incognita* of herself, as she knew herself to be, not as men liked to imagine her. . .'[19] Without articulating this idea even as George Egerton did, in retrospect, most Irish women have generally tended to write about women and 'women's subjects'. Yet the themes which the writers have chosen are universal. Friendship, work, hatred, loyalty, jealousy, scruples of conscience, temptations, joy, fear, desire, love: all of these things are consistently treated and explored from the point of view of the personal, from the perspective of female experience. In telling of the *terra incognita,* even obliquely, the writers tell of these things in the context of Irish womens' lives, and tell also of the limited female control of those lives – tell more, in some cases, than the writers intended. In writing of what they know, of what they themselves feel, observe, learn and experience, Irish women not only produce their best writing but also construct a unique sociological and literary record.

19. Egerton, in *Ten Contemporaries,* p. 58. The journalist and satirist Susan Mitchell expressed the same idea in characteristically wry, inverted terms: 'For the most part, we look to men to reveal us to ourselves. Man is our *logos,* articulate on our behalf.' Her irony is a turning of the tables – it appears in her study *George Moore* (Dublin: Maunsel, 1916), p.28.

THE WRITERS AND THE WRITINGS

Beneath any analysis of how Irish women approach the writing process, beneath any investigation of individual styles and concerns in writing, lie some fundamental questions. Why did they write? For whom, and in what circumstances, did they write? Why did Irish women turn so firmly to the writing of fiction and why is it so much better, in the main, than their poetry or drama?

It was not a woman who suggested that the short story form is a vital tool for expression because it is a form peculiarly suited to the narrative expression of a 'submerged population'.[20] It was, however, a woman writer who pointed out ironically that women turned to writing because it was a 'respectable and harmless occupation. The family peace was not broken by the scratching of a pen. No demand was made upon the family purse.'[21] Both comments about writing apply to the authors included in this volume. They were attracted to the medium of short fiction for many different reasons. Some, such as Katharine Tynan, found story-writing convenient for periodical publishing. Elizabeth Bowen felt that story-writing was not only a relief from novel-writing but had an advantage over it.[22] Dorothy Macardle in prison was able to fuse revolutionary propaganda with story-telling; Edith Somerville and Violet Martin wrote stories when they could not find the time for a novel and needed an immediate source of income.[23]

But common to all of the writers included here – and to many, many others not included – is the consistent, even insistent, concern with the portrayal of female characters. This circumstance

20. O'Connor, The Lonely Voice, p. 20.
21. Virginia Woolf, 'Professions for Women' in Virginia Woolf. Women and Writing, introduced by Michele Barrett (London: The Women's Press, 1979), p. 57.
22. Elizabeth Bowen's comments about the art of short-story writing and her own approach to, and feelings about, the nature of the genre and her own writing processes are fascinating. They are contained in the essay 'Truth and Fiction' in her Afterthoughts: Pieces About Writing (London: Longmans, 1962).
23. A very interesting account of the frustrations encountered by Edith Somerville and Violet Martin, whose collaboration was frequently disturbed by distance and family duties, can be found in Hilary Robinson's Somerville and Ross: A Critical Appreciation. See especially pp. 46-47.

cuts across religious, political and social differences. It would seem to be an obvious reflection of authors' own experiences as women and their recognition of those experiences as a source for writing. It is also an acknowledgment of their substantial reader-ship and the demands of that readership.

The nineteenth century in Ireland saw the establishment of the National School system. This regulated form of education – avail-able to a large part of the population for the first time – coupled with the virtual obliteration of the Irish language after the Great Famine,[24] meant that reading and writing in the English language came to play an increasing part in the lives of many Irish women who had formerly been excluded from such pursuits. Concurrent with the growing Irish reading audience of the middle and late nineteenth century came the great ascendancy of fiction as a liter-ary form. The long-honoured and well-maintained oral traditions of rural Ireland formed a ready-made mine of stories, folklore and legends which were quickly taken up by the Renaissance writers in particular.[25]

Fiction-writing, somewhat strangely, gathered momentum only gradually. It is not unexpected, though, given the circumstances of women in relation to professions and higher education, that many of the earliest fiction writers were women and that fiction provided them with an accessible and highly flexible form, not nearly as overtly male-dominated or with such established traditions as other literary forms. Fiction, at any rate, has always been strongly associated with women. From its inception, the novel, especially, quickly proved itself to be a medium for the exploration of female characters and predicaments.

24. The decline of the Irish language in Ireland and its replacement with English is a still largely unexplored field of study. One of its most intriguing aspects is the develop-ment of Hiberno-English, the form of the English language which is spoken in Ire-land today; I am indebted to Professor Alan Bliss of University College, Dublin, for my understanding of the subject. His essay 'The English Language in Ireland', although unpublished and not widely available, is the best general introduction that I have seen.

25. See Ernest Boyd, *Ireland's Literary Renaissance* (Dublin: Figgis, 1966). Chapter XV, 'Fiction and Narrative Prose', contains his opinion on the subject and did much to form the subsequent view, contained in books such as *Modern Irish Literature* by Maurice Harmon.

Not surprisingly, then, Irish women turned in large numbers to fiction as the genre through which they could express themselves, though some, like Katharine Tynan and Jane Barlow,[26] first made their names as poets and others, like Dorothy Macardle, Elizabeth Connor and Geraldine Cummins, also wrote drama. Often denied or limited in their opportunities for formal education and a subsequent career, women have been encouraged to be keen observers of detail and taught to be sensitive to nuances of behaviour. Even requisite social conversation has historically provided women with the opportunity for fusing the minutiae of daily life with imaginative ways of describing it, and because of the complex social conditions in Ireland, Irish women, more than most, have been provided with excellent opportunities for observation and verbal awareness.

The writers represented in this volume come almost without exception from the upper and middle classes and yet, because of the several strands of Irish tradition and culture, they have been by no means ignorant of, nor isolated from, aspects of Irish life which differed from the Ireland into which they were born. Edith Somerville and Violet Martin learned Irish and made their own dictionary and phrasebooks in order better to understand the soul, as well as the sense, of the dual English-Irish linguistic influences which surrounded them. Jane Barlow's poems and stories explicitly demonstrate her interest in language. Anglo-Irish Elizabeth Bowen captures the peculiar voice of middle-class suburbia while Norah Hoult uses the silent thoughts of Bridget to give voice to the country girl. Dorothy Macardle and Geraldine Cummins emphasise speech rhythms for dramatic effect; Mary Lavin's curiously flat dialogue and Mary Beckett's marvellously comic recreation of the distinctive Belfast accent have in common an intrinsic awareness of language which immediately marks their work as Irish and provides one of the most interesting avenues for the investigation of the writing of Irish women.

26. Jane Barlow's first book, *Bog-Land Studies* (1892), is described by Boyd as 'an experiment'; what Barlow was attempting, and was the first Renaissance writer to attempt seriously, was the conveying of Hiberno-English dialect. Her poetry was regarded as novel, but in danger of belonging to the stage-Irish tradition. Barlow continued, more restrainedly, to experiment with language and began to write fiction.

Facility for language and sensitivity to the hybrid Hiberno-English linguistic peculiarities of Ireland are obviously not confined to one sex in Ireland, but the interest taken by female writers in the matter of language is everywhere evident in their works, at least as evident as the interest shown by male writers. It may frequently be less developed in an experimental sense, but it is rarely absent. Even diaries and letters, those two traditionally highly important forms of female self-expression, abound with examples of just how closely Irish women have been involved with the verbal representation of the life around them.

The diaries of Violet Martin[27] are the most outstanding examples of the connection made between story-telling, reportage and fiction-writing. Similarly, the letters of Edith Somerville and Violet Martin emphasise the relationship between epistolary writing and fiction and reflect the involvement of the writers in the world around them. But significantly, considering that those two women closely collaborated on their writing efforts through the Somerville and Ross partnership, there are almost no mentions of work in progress and few instances of specific ideas to be incorporated into the writing. Instead, the letters are filled with evidence that for these busy women, as for so many women, there was a split between the woman and the writer.

Writing had to be relegated to a place that came after family duties, social obligations and financial considerations. The letters of Somerville and Martin were not written as practice-pieces for fiction, but descriptive turns of phrase, character sketches, amusing and unusual bits of dialogue appear constantly. The letters do reveal that even at times when the collaborators were unable to work actively at their literary partnership, they maintained a lively interest in the materials for fiction. Indeed, the Somerville-Martin letters are classic examples of the way in which private writing by women not only gives an occasion for self-expression but often contains the skeletal elements of fiction.

27. The diaries of Violet Martin are unpublished. The first was kept in 1875, when she was thirteen years of age, the last in 1915, the year of her death. Thirty-seven volumes of her diaries are held at Queen's University Belfast, as are Edith Somerville's manuscript diaries.

Journals and letters have always served an important literary function: they provide a testing-ground where the solitary act of writing can find a base and from which it can be launched into a more social sphere. The notion of writing stories and sketches to pass the time, to entertain a circle of family and friends or to present a picture of Irish life to English and American audiences was not new to the Anglo-Irish; at least since the time of Maria Edgeworth it had been set as a precedent. By the middle of the nineteenth century, Lady Morgan had made her mark and fortune and Anna Maria Hall had gained wide popularity abroad as an interpreter of Irish life. By the time of the Irish Literary Renaissance, in a country which had always made much of traditions of literature, clever daughters like Katharine Tynan were being encouraged to express publicly their political and literary ideas and to contribute to the many and diverse periodicals which flourished in the atmosphere of the late-nineteenth-century Celtic Revival.[28]

Apart from the national impetus towards the expression of mythological, religious and nationalist sentiments – entered into enthusiastically and in fact spearheaded by the Anglo-Irish Protestant middle and upper classes – the general interest at home and abroad made Celtic-flavoured material a valuable commodity. The depiction of Irish life by Irish writers was eagerly desired by Irish readers, by foreign readers and by Irish readers living out of Ireland. Because, as in Ireland itself, a large part of this newly-discovered audience was composed of the female sex, there was an upsurge of interest on the part of editors and publishers for 'suitable' material written by Irish writers. It was also considered desirable that there be Irish female writers who could write to female readers and provide points of contact in subject matter and sentiment.

28. *Twenty-Five Years: Reminiscences* (London: Smith Elder, 1913), *The Middle Years* (London: Constable, 1916), and *The Years of The Shadow* (London: Constable, 1919) are three of Tynan's five books of reminiscences. They are filled with anecdotes, literary gossip, letters, and a general sense of the revival period. Tynan's memories are often dismissed as being highly subjective, but they are valuable for several reasons. Living in both Ireland and England she knew an enormous number of writers whom she tells us about. They include Hannah Lynch, Rose Kavanagh, Dora Sigerson Shorter, Yeats, Alice Meynell and many others. She also gives a sense of the difficulties in being a mother, a wife, a breadwinner, and a professional journalist and author.

Short fiction is the form of imaginative writing that is most
naturally a progression of story-telling, letter-writing, diary-keep-
ing and even school essay-writing. It was a form highly suited to
newly advanced publication techniques. And so, apart from questions of social responsibility and the functional advantages of dis-
seminating particular political, cultural and religious values, women
discovered that the writing of short fiction could be a practical
proposition. Erminda Esler, May Laffan, Margaret Hungerford,
Annie French Hector, M. E. Francis, Rosa Mulholland, Mrs Rid-
dell and Somerville and Ross were just a few of the writers who
found that their fiction appealed to British, Irish, and American
audiences and to people in places as far-flung as Poland, France,
Germany, Hungary and Denmark. Following the example of Anna
Maria Hall half a century earlier, women like Katharine Tynan
(who made particularly good use of market possibilities; she herself
reckoned that she had at one time or another written for almost
every periodical and newspaper published in both England and Ireland),[29] learned to make writing viable economically, and so, viable
as a pursuit.

The large sales figures of these writers indicate a high degree of
reader identification. Tynan, for example, carefully exploited the
facts of her life and made her successive roles of daughter, wife and
mother into the raw material for poetry, short stories, novels, reminiscences and thousands of words of journalism. For Tynan, as
for many Irish women who turned to writing, literary efforts provided an outlet which could also be slotted into the constriction
and demands of family life. Writing presented an opportunity for a
compromise; it did not necessarily involve absences from the home,
it did not involve a loss of social standing, it could be carried out
with a minimum of time, space and expenditure, it could be paced
according to the pressure of other activities and it could be the
means to a personal income and some measure of independence.

29. Tynan has, under her name, the second largest series of entries in the *British Museum*
    Catalogue of Printed Books. She is out-distanced only by the prolific L. T. Meade,
    another Irish woman. The bulk of Tynan's work remains uncollected and there can
    be no doubt that excessive productivity was the fatal flaw both of her work and her
    talent.

Yet, like other women, Irish women have frequently found writing a frustrating occupation; Edith Somerville once had to hide herself in a wardrobe in order to gain some writing time. Writers with dependents or other responsibilities have had to struggle with the temptation to churn out quick, profitable work, as well as with the frequently uneasy meshing of private life and life within the family. Mary Lavin's and Mary Beckett's problems of continuing to write while raising families were no more easily overcome in the last twenty years than were other writers' similar difficulties a century earlier. They have kept on writing, however, and Lavin, like Elizabeth Bowen, has been internationally hailed as a fine writer. But the interest in some writers has, curiously, done nothing to provoke interest in, or to call attention to, the value of rediscovering and re-reading the writing of Irish women of the past. That there is value in so doing seems incontrovertible.

The immediate impression short fiction by Irish women writers gives is of a sympathetic communion entered into by writer and reader. Because so many of the women represented here were unable to devote themselves to writing as a full-time activity, because many had to break through the multiple submergence of nationality, class and sex, their writing is perhaps not always as artistic in execution as it might be. But it is always accessible, always vital. One measure of its success is the extent to which the reader can enter into Irish female experience. Themes, language, and particularly characters draw the reader into worlds other than those usually portrayed in Anglo-Irish literature. Reading these stories, one thinks of Kate O'Brien saying, 'We have made a literature, slowly and in some pain and confusion.'[30] These stories offer a share in that literature, a sense of that pain and confusion. The ideas, emotions, and experiences which inform them bring the reader to a new perspective on woman's part in Irish life and literature, and so to a more profound participation in both.

30. In an essay called 'Imaginative Prose by the Irish 1820-1970' in *Myth and Reality in Irish Literature* ed. Joseph Ronsley (Ontario: Wilfred Laurier University Press, 1977).

Virgin Soil

George Egerton

Mary Chavelita Dunne, who wrote under the name George Egerton, was born of Irish parents in Australia in 1859, but grew up in Ireland. She spent two years in Germany, eloped with a married man to Norway and became involved with the literary revival which was taking place there. In Norway Egerton met Knut Hamson and translated his *Hunger* into English. After the death of her companion, she returned to England and married. It was while living in Millsteet, County Cork, that Egerton began to write; her *Keynotes* (London: John Lane, 1893) was the first appearance of the New Woman in English-language writing. The sensuality and outspokenness of *Keynotes* and *Discords* (London: John Lane, 1894) caused a sensation and made Egerton an immediate success. But none of her subsequent books, including her autobiographical novel *The Wheel of God* (London: G. Richards, 1898), or her later plays, were successful. She died in 1945.

'Virgin Soil' is almost more a tract than a story – an indictment of the hypocrisy of the middle classes and a study of the conventionally brought-up girl who encounters harsh realities in her married life. It is a unique story both emotionally, and in that it deals with a subject which does not otherwise appear in Anglo-Irish literature.

Like Ella D'Arcy, the Irish short-story writer with whom she is often bracketed, Egerton is now read only by those interested in the literary 1890's, the 'Yellow Book' period. Terence de Vere White has edited her letters and diaries in *A Leaf from the Yellow Book* (London: The Richards Press, 1958).

THE BRIDEGROOM is waiting in the hall; with a trifle of impatience he is tracing the pattern of the linoleum with the point of his umbrella. He curbs it and laughs, showing his strong white teeth at a remark of his best man; then compares the time by his hunter with the clock on the stairs. He is florid, bright-eyed, loose-lipped, inclined to stoutness, but kept in good condition; his hair is crisp, curly, slightly grey; his ears peculiar, pointed at their tops like a faun's. He looks very big and well-dressed, and, when he smiles, affable enough.

Upstairs a young girl, with the suns of seventeen summers on her brown head, is lying with her face hidden on her mother's shoulder; she is sobbing with great childish sobs, regardless of reddened eyes and the tears that have splashed on the silk of her grey, going-away gown.

The mother seems scarcely less disturbed than the girl. She is a fragile-looking woman with delicate fair skin, smoothly parted thin chestnut hair, dove-like eyes, and a monotonous piping voice. She is flushing painfully, making a strenuous effort to say something to the girl, something that is opposed to the whole instincts of her life.

She tries to speak, parts her lips only to close them again, and clasp her arms tighter round the girl's shoulders; at length she manages to say with trembling, uncertain pauses:

'You are married now, darling, and you must obey' – she lays a stress upon the word – 'your husband in all things – there are – there are things you should know – but – marriage is a serious thing, a sacred thing' – with desperation – 'you must believe that what your husband tells you is right – let him guide you – tell you –'

There is such acute distress in her usually unemotional voice that the girl looks up and scans her face – her blushing, quivering, faded face. Her eyes are startled, fawn-like eyes as her mother's, her skin too is delicately fair, but her mouth is firmer, her jaw squarer, and her piquant, irregular nose is full of character. She is slightly built, scarcely fully developed in her fresh youth.

'What is it that I do not know, mother? What is it?' – with anxious impatience. 'There is somthing more – I have felt it all these last weeks in your and the others' looks – in his, in the very atmosphere – but why have you not told me before – I –.' Her only answer is a gush of helpless tears from the mother, and a sharp rap at the door, and the bridegroom's voice, with an imperative note that it strikes the nervous girl is new to it, that makes her cling to her mother in a close, close embrace, drop her veil and go out to him.

She shakes hands with the best man, kisses the girl friend who has acted as bridesmaid – the wedding has been a very quiet one – and steps into the carriage. The Irish cook throws an old shoe after them from the side door, but it hits the trunk of an elder-tree, and falls back on to the path, making that worthy woman cross herself and mutter of ill-omens and bad luck to follow; for did not a magpie cross the path first thing this morning when she went to open the gate, and wasn't a red-haired woman the first creature she clapped eyes on as she looked down the road?

Half an hour later the carriage pulls up at the little station and the girl jumps out first; she is flushed, and her eyes stare helplessly as the eyes of a startled child, and she trembles with quick running shudders from head to foot. She clasps and unclasps her slender, grey-gloved hands so tightly that the stitching on the back of one bursts.

He has called to the station-master, and they go into the refreshment-room together; the latter appears at the door and, beckoning to a porter, gives him an order.

She takes a long look at the familiar little place. They have lived there three years, and yet she seems to see it now for the first time; the rain drips, drips monotonously off the zinc roof, the smell of the dust is fresh, and the white pinks in the borders are beaten into the gravel.

Then the train runs in; a first-class carriage, marked 'engaged,' is attached, and he comes for her; his hot breath smells of champagne, and it strikes her that his eyes are fearfully big and bright, and he offers her his arm with such a curious amused proprietary air that the girl shivers as she lays her hand in it.

The bell rings, the guard locks the door, the train steams out, and as it passes the signal-box, a large well-kept hand, with a signet ring on the little finger, pulls down the blind on the window of an engaged carriage.

*   *   *   *   *

Five years later, one afternoon on an autumn day, when the rain is falling like splashing tears on the rails, and the smell of the dust after rain fills the mild air with freshness, and the white chrysanthemums struggle to raise their heads from the gravel path into which the sharp shower has beaten them, the same woman, for there is no trace of girlhood in her twenty-two years, slips out of a first-class carriage; she has a dressing-bag in her hand.

She walks with her head down and a droop in her shoulders; her quickness of step is due rather to nervous haste than elasticity of frame. When she reaches the turn of the road, she pauses and looks at the little villa with the white curtains and gay tiled window-boxes. She can see the window of her old room; distinguish every shade in the changing leaves of the creeper climbing up the south wall; hear the canary's shrill note from where she stands.

Never once has she set foot in the peaceful little house with its air of genteel propriety since that eventful morning when she left it with him; she has always framed an excuse.

Now as she sees it a feeling of remorse fills her heart, and she thinks of the mother living out her quiet years, each day a replica of the one gone before, and her resolve weakens; she feels inclined to go back, but the waning sun flickers over the panes in the window of the room she occupied as a girl. She can recall how she used to run to the open window on summer mornings and lean out and draw in the dewy freshness and welcome the day, how she has stood on moonlight nights and danced with her bare white feet in the strip of moonlight, and let her fancies fly out into the silver night, a young girl's dreams of the beautiful, wonderful world that lay outside.

A hard dry sob rises in her throat at the memory of it, and the fleeting expression of softness on her face changes to a bitter disillusion.

She hurries on, with her eyes down, up the neat gravelled path, through the open door into the familiar sitting-room.

The piano is open with a hymn-book on the stand; the grate is filled with fresh green ferns, a bowl of late roses perfume the room from the centre of the table. The mother is sitting in her easy chair, her hands folded across a big white Persian cat on her lap; she is fast asleep. Some futile lace work, her thimble, and bright scissors are placed on a table near her.

Her face is placid, not a day older than that day five years ago. Her glossy hair is no greyer, her skin is clear, she smiles in her sleep. The smiles rouses a sort of sudden fury in the breast of the woman standing in her dusty travelling cloak at the door, noting every detail in the room. She throws back her veil and goes over and looks at herself in the mirror over the polished chiffonnier – scans herself pitilessly. Her skin is sallow with the dull sallowness of a fair skin in ill-health, and the fringe of her brown hair is so lacking in lustre that it affords no contrast. The look of fawn-like shyness has vanished from her eyes, they burn sombrefully and resentfully in their sunken orbits, there is a dragged look about the mouth; and the keynote of her face is a cynical disillusion. She looks from herself to the reflection of the mother, and then turning sharply with a suppressed exclamation goes over, and shaking the sleeping woman not too gently, says:

'Mother, wake up, I want to speak to you!'

The mother starts with frightened eyes, stares at the other woman as if doubting the evidence of her sight, smiles, then cowed by the unresponsive look in the other face, grows grave again, sits still and stares helplessly at her, finally bursting into tears with a:

'Flo, my dear, Flo, is it really you?'

The girl jerks her head impatiently and says drily:

'Yes, that is self-evident. I am going on a long journey. I have something to say to you before I start! Why on earth are you crying?'

There is a note of surprised wonder in her voice mixed with impatience.

The older woman has had time to scan her face and the dormant motherhood in her is roused by its weary anguish. She is ill, she thinks, in trouble. She rises to her feet; it is characteristic of the habits of her life, with its studied regard for the observance of small proprieties, and distrust of servants as a class, that she goes over and closes the room door carefully.

This hollow-eyed, sullen woman is so unlike the fresh girl who left her five years ago that she feels afraid. With the quiet selfishness that has characterised her life she has accepted the excuses her daughter has made to avoid coming home, as she has accepted the presents her son-in-law has sent her from time to time. She has found her a husband well-off in the world's goods, and there her responsibility ended. She approaches her hesitatingly; she feels she ought to kiss her, there is something unusual in such a meeting after so long an absence; it shocks her, it is so unlike the one she has pictured; she has often looked forward to it, often; to seeing Flo's new frocks, to hearing of her town life.

'Won't you take off your things? You will like to go to your room?'

She can hear how her own voice shakes; it is really inconsiderate of Flo to treat her in this strange way.

'We will have some tea,' she adds.

Her colour is coming and going, the lace at her wrist is fluttering. The daughter observes it with a kind of dull satisfaction, she is taking out her hat-pins carefully. She notices a portrait in a velvet case upon the mantelpiece; she walks over and looks at it intently. It is her father, the father who was killed in India in a hill skirmish when she was a little lint-locked maid barely up to his knee. She studies it with new eyes, trying to read what man he was, what soul he had, what part of him is in her, tries to find herself by reading him. Something in his face touches her, strikes some underlying chord in her, and she grinds her teeth at a thought it rouses.

'She must be ill, she must be very ill,' says the mother, watching her, 'to think I daren't offer to kiss my own child!' She checks the tears that keep welling up, feeling that they may offend this woman who is so strangely unlike the girl who left her. The latter has turned from her scrutiny of the likeness and sweeps her with a cold criticising look as she turns towards the door, saying:

'I *should* like some tea. I will go upstairs and wash off the dust.'

Half an hour later the two women sit opposite one another in the pretty room. The younger one is leaning back in her chair watching the mother pour out the tea, following the graceful movements of the white, blue-veined hands amongst the tea things – she lets her wait on her; they have not spoken beyond a commonplace remark about the heat, the dust, the journey.

'How is Philip, is he well?' The mother ventures to ask with a feeling of trepidation, but it seems to her that she ought to ask about him.

'He is quite well, men of his type usually are; I may say he is particularly well just now, he has gone to Paris with a girl from the

Alhambra!'

The older woman flushes painfully, and pauses with her cup halfway to her lips and lets the tea run over unheeded onto her dainty silk apron.

'You are spilling your tea,' the girl adds with malicious enjoyment.

The woman gasps: 'Flo, but Flo, my dear, it is *dreadful!* What would your poor father have said! No wonder you look ill, dear, how shocking! Shall I – ask the vicar to – to remonstrate with him? –'

'My dear mother, what an extraordinary idea! These little trips have been my one solace. I assure you, I have always hailed them as lovely oases in the desert of matrimony, resting-places on the journey. My sole regret was their infrequency. That is very good tea, I suppose it is the cream.

The older woman put her cup on the tray and stares at her with frightened eyes and paled cheeks.

'I am afraid I don't understand you, Florence. I am old-fashioned' – with a little air of frigid propriety – 'I have always looked upon matrimony as a sacred thing. It is dreadful to hear you speak this way; you should have tried to save Philip – from – from such shocking sin.'

The girl laughs, and the woman shivers as she hears her. She cries –

'I would never have thought it of Philip. My poor dear, I am afraid you must be very unhappy.'

'Very,' with a grim smile, 'but it is over now, I have done with it. I am not going back.'

If a bomb had exploded in the quiet, pretty room the effect could hardly have been more startling than her almost cheerful statement. A big bee buzzes in and bangs against the older woman's cap and she never heeds it, then she almost screams:

'Florence, Florence, my dear, you can't mean to desert your husband! Oh, think of the disgrace, the scandal, what people will say, the' – with an uncertain quaver – 'the sin. You took a solemn vow, you know, and you are going to break it –'

'My dear mother, the ceremony had no meaning for me, I simply did not know what I was signing my name to, or what I was vowing to do. I might as well have signed my name to a document drawn up in Choctaw. I have no remorse, no prick of conscience at the step I am taking; my life must be my own. They say sorrow chastens, I don't believe it; it hardens, embitters; joy is like the sun, it coaxes all that is loveliest and sweetest in human nature. No, I am not going back.'

The older woman cries, wringing her hands helplessly:

'I can't understand it. You must be very miserable to dream of taking such a serious step.'

'As I told you, I am. It is a defect of my temperament. How many women really take the man nearest to them as seriously as I did! I think few. They finesse and flatter and wheedle and coax, but truth there is none. I couldn't do that, you see, and so I went to the wall. I don't blame them; it must be so, as long as marriage is based on such unequal terms, as long as man demands from a wife as a right, what he must sue from a mistress as a favour; until marriage becomes for many women a legal prostitution, a nightly degrada-tion, a hateful yoke under which they age, mere bearers of children conceived in a sense of duty, not love. They bear them, birth them, nurse them, and begin again without choice in the matter, growing old, unlovely, with all joy of living swallowed in a senseless burden of reckless maternity, until their love, granted they started with that, the mystery, the crowning glory of their lives, is turned into a duty they submit to with distaste instead of a favour granted to a husband who must become a new lover to obtain it.'

'But men are different, Florence; you can't refuse a husband, you might cause him to commit sin.'

'Bosh, mother, he is responsible for his own sins, we are not bound to dry-nurse his morality. Man is what we have made him, his very faults are of our making. No wife is bound to set aside the demands of her individual soul for the sake of imbecile obedience. I am going to have some more tea.'

The mother can only whimper:

'It is dreadful! I thought he made you such an excellent husband, his position too is so good, and he is so highly connected.'

'Yes, and it is as well to put the blame in the right quarter. Philip is as God made him, he is an animal with strong passions, and he avails himself of the latitude permitted him by the laws of society. Whatever of blame, whatever of sin, whatever of misery is in the whole matter rests *solely* and *entirely* with you, mother' – the woman sits bolt upright – 'and with no one else – that is why I came here – to tell you that – I have promised myself over and over again that I would tell you. It is with you, and you alone the fault lies.'

There is so much of cold dislike in her voice that the other woman recoils and whimpers piteously:

'You must be ill, Florence, to say such wicked things. What have I done? I am sure I devoted myself to you from the time you were little; I refused' – dabbing her eyes with her cambric handkerchief – 'ever so many good offers. There was young Fortescue in the artillery, such a good-looking young man, and such an elegant horseman, he was quite infatuated about me; and Jones, to be sure he was in business, but he was most attentive. Every one said I was a devoted mother; I can't think what you mean, I –'

'Perhaps not. Sit down, and I'll tell you.'

She shakes off the trembling hand, for the mother has risen and is standing next to her, and pushes her into a chair, and paces up and down the room. She is painfully thin, and drags her limbs as she walks.

'I say it is your fault, because you reared me a fool, an idiot, ignorant of everything I ought to have known, everything that concerned me and the life I was bound to lead as a wife; my physical needs, my coming passion, the very meaning of my sex, my wifehood and motherhood to follow. You gave me not one weapon in my hand to defend myself against the possible attacks of man at his worst. You sent me out to fight the biggest battle of a woman's life, the one in which she ought to know every turn of the game, with a white gauze' – she laughs derisively – 'of maiden purity as a shield.'

Her eyes blaze, and the woman in the chair watches her as one sees a frog watch a snake when it is put into its case.

'I was fourteen when I gave up the gooseberry-bush theory as the origin of humanity; and I cried myself ill with shame when I learnt what maternity meant, instead of waking with a sense of delicious wonder at the great mystery of it. You gave me to a man, nay more, you told me to obey him, to believe that whatever he said would be right, would be my duty; knowing that the meaning of marriage was a sealed book to me, that I had no real idea of what union with a man meant. You delivered me body and soul into his hands without preparing me in any way for the ordeal I was to go through. You sold me for a home, for clothes, for food; you played upon my ignorance, I won't say innocence, that is different. You told me, you and your sister, and your friend the vicar's wife, that it would be an anxiety off your mind if I were comfortably settled –'

'It is wicked of you to say such dreadful things!' the mother cries, 'and besides' – with a touch of asperity – 'you married him willingly, you seemed to like his attentions –'

'How like a woman! What a thorough woman you are, mother! The good old-fashioned kitten with a claw in her paw! Yes, I married him willingly; I was not eighteen, I had known no men; was pleased that you were pleased – and, as you say, I liked his attentions. He had tact enough not to frighten me, and I had not the faintest conception of what marriage with him meant. I had an idea' – with a laugh – 'that the words of the minister settled the matter. Do you think that if I had realised how fearfully close the intimacy with him would have been that my whole soul would not have stood up in revolt, the whole woman in me cried out against such a degradation of myself?' Her words tremble with passion, and the woman who bore her feels as if she is being lashed by a whip. 'Would I not have shuddered at the thought of *him* in such a relationship? – and waited, waited until I found the man who would satisfy me, body and soul – to whom I would have gone without any false shame, of whom I would think with gladness as the father of a little child to come, for whom the white fire of love or passion, call it what you will, in my heart would have burned clearly and saved me from the feeling of loathing horror that has made my married life a nightmare to me – ay, made me a murderess in heart over and over again. This is not exaggeration. It has killed the sweetness in me, the pure thoughts of womanhood – has made me hate myself and *hate you*. Cry, mother, if you will; you don't know how much you have to cry for – I have cried myself barren of tears. Cry over the girl you killed' – with a gust of passion

– 'why didn't you strangle me as a baby? It would have been kinder; my life has been a hell, mother – I felt it vaguely as I stood on the platform waiting, I remember the mad impulse I had to jump down under the engine as it came in, to escape from the dread that was chilling my soul. What have these years been? One long crucifixion, one long submittal to the desires of a man I bound myself to in ignorance of what it meant; every caress' – with a cry – 'has only been the first note of that. Look at me' – stretching out her arms – 'look at this wreck of my physical self; I wouldn't dare to show you the heart or the soul underneath. He has stood on his rights; but do you think, if I had known, that I would have given such insane obedience, from a mistaken sense of duty, as would lead to this? I have my rights too, and my duty to myself; if I had only recognised them in time.'

'Sob away, mother; I don't even feel for you – I have been burnt too badly to feel sorry for what will only be a tiny scar to you; I have all the long future to face with all the world against me. Nothing will induce me to go back. Better anything than that; food and clothes are poor equivalents for what I have had to suffer – I can get them at a cheaper rate. When he comes to look for me, give him that letter. He will tell you he has only been an uxorious husband, and that you reared me a fool. You can tell him too, if you like, that I loathe him, shiver at the touch of his lips, his breath, his hands; that when he has turned and gone to sleep, I have watched him with such growing hatred that at times the temptation to kill him has been so strong that I have crept out of bed and walked the cold passage in my bare feet until I was too benumbed to feel anything; that I have counted the hours to his going away, and cried out with delight at the sight of the retreating carriage!'

'You are very hard, Flo; the Lord soften your heart! Perhaps' – with trepidation – 'if you had had a child –'

'Of his – that indeed would have been the last straw – no, mother.'

There is such a peculiar expression of satisfaction over something – of some inner understanding, as a man has when he dwells on the successful accomplishment of a secret purpose – that the mother sobs quietly, wringing her hands.

'I did not know, Flo, I acted for the best; you are very hard on me!'

Later, when the bats are flitting across the moon, and the girl is asleep – she has thrown herself half-dressed on the narrow white bed of her girlhood, with her arms folded across her breast and her hands clenched – the mother steals into the room. She has been turning over the contents of an old desk; her marriage certificate, faded letters on foreign paper, and a bit of Flo's hair cut off each birthday, and a sprig of orange-blossom she wore in her hair. She looks faded and grey in the silver light, and she stands and gazes at the haggard face in its weary sleep. The placid current of her life is disturbed, her heart is roused, something of her child's soul-agony has touched the sleeping depths of her nature. She feels as if scales have dropped from her eyes, as if the instincts and conventions of her life are toppling over, as if all the needs of protesting women of whom she has read with vague displeasure have come home to her. She covers the girl tenderly, kisses her hair, and slips a little roll of notes into the dressing-bag on the table and steals out, with the tears running down her cheeks.

When the girl looks into her room as she steals by, when the morning light is slanting in, she sees her kneeling, her head, with its straggling grey hair, bowed in tired sleep. It touches her. Life is too short, she thinks, to make any one's hours bitter; she goes down and writes a few kind words in pencil and leaves them near her hand, and goes quickly out into the road.

The morning in grey and misty, with faint yellow stains in the east, and the west wind blows with a melancholy sough in it – the first whisper of the fall, the fall that turns the world of nature into a patient suffering from phthisis – delicate season of decadence, when the loveliest scenes have a note of decay in their beauty; when a poisoned arrow pierces the marrow of insect and plant, and the leaves have a hectic flush and fall, fall and shrivel and curl in the night's cool; and the chrysanthemums, the 'good-bye summers' of the Irish peasants, have a sickly tinge in their white. It affects her, and she finds herself saying: 'Wither and die, wither and die, make compost for the loves of the spring, as the old drop out and make place for the new, who forget them, to be in their turn forgotten.' She hurries on, feeling that her autumn has come to her in her spring, and a little later she stands once more on the platform where she stood in the flush of her girlhood, and takes the train in the opposite direction.

Queen O'Toole

M. E. Francis

M. E. Francis was the pen name of Mary Sweetman, Mrs Francis Blundell. Born in 1859 of Anglo-Irish family at Killiney Park, near Dublin, she grew up in Queen's County (present-day County Laois). As a child, Francis and her sisters (two of whom also became writers) wrote fiction and founded their own family magazines. Francis' first published story appeared in *The Irish Monthly,* and throughout her long career she wrote many religiously influenced stories. Her *A Daughter of the Soil* (London: Osgood, McIlraine, 1895) was the first novel to be published serially in the weekly edition of *The Times*. Besides many novels and short stories, Francis also wrote her reminiscences, *The Things of a Child* (London: Collins, 1916). She died in 1930; her work has been forgotten.

'Queen O'Toole' is, like much of Francis' writing and much of the writing of the time, a story intended to present a slice of Irish life to English audiences. It is also a portrayal of an unusual passion combined with a very evocative celebration of motherhood. Like her other fiction, it takes up themes which are distinctly, resoundingly feminine, and, if melodrama intrudes, Francis' ability to appeal to her readers' emotions explains her great popularity during her writing career. Several of her novels, particularly *The Story of Mary Dunne* (London: John Murray, 1913) and *Miss Erin* (London: Methuen, 1898) are serious examinations of the evils of Irish society, especially as they affect the lives of women.

'HAVE YE all now, ma'am?'

'I have, alanna, God bless ye! Make haste home, an' don't get buried in the snow. Lord save us, what a night!'

The snow came driving through the door as the child opened it, and in the dim light without, the trees looked black and ghostly, and the long white vista of road uninviting to travellers. But Maggie did not pause to consider it; with a blithe little backward nod she skipped across the threshold pulling the door to, after her, and Queen O'Toole was alone.

It was not very large, this palace of hers; just one room about eight feet square, which contained a bed covered with a rug and a patchwork quilt, a dresser ornamented by sundry bright-coloured cups and plates, a chair without a back and a three-legged stool. A little shelf ran along the wall parallel with the head of Queen O'Toole's couch, which, as Her Majesty was bed-ridden, came in handy for her needs throughout the day. A cup of milk stood there now, flanked by a tin candlestick, in which burned a lanky 'dip', occasionally snuffed in primitive fashion by the old woman's finger and thumb; behind these lay a pair of lazy-tongs, the comfort of her life, as she frequently declared, recently presented by one who had compassion on her helpless condition. With their aid and that of Maggie and her mother, who ran round – a matter of a mile or so – two or three times a day to see if she wanted anything, Kitty O'Toole got on very well indeed. She had a shilling a week from the parish and eighteenpence and permission to live in this queer little box of a lodge from the Lord of the Manor – the latter favour the more appreciable as Kitty was absolutely incapable of opening the gate for man or beast. Indeed it generally stood hospitably ajar, but being a back entrance and little used it did not so much matter. Four years before, the old woman, till then the most active of her kind, had lost the use of her lower limbs and ever since had been dependent on the bounty of her neighbours. In spite of their kindness, and of constant visits from friends among the gentry, Kitty spent many long hours by herself, and had she not possessed resources of her own would have found the time heavy and tedious. But she was usually very busy when alone, and could scarcely get through all she had to do in the day. She said interminable rosaries, and duly read certain prayers in her dog-eared 'Garden of the Soul', repeating the words half aloud, sucking in her breath at the end of a sentence in a manner which betokened much unction, and wetting her thumb religiously when about to turn over a fresh page. Then, alongside her bed, as far as she could reach, was a perfect gallery of pictures (stuck up by her own hands) which had to be looked at, and dusted, and talked to, each in their turn. There were a few photographs, but Kitty's works of art were chiefly of the pious order, highly coloured and effective, the blues and reds of the framed masterpiece in the middle being crude enough to set one's teeth on edge. Kitty kept under her pillow, however, the greatest treasure of all, that which afforded the happiest moments of her life; and now that Maggie had departed for the night she proceeded to enjoy it at leisure. Having snuffed the candle and smoothed the counterpane she drew forth from the companionship of the prayer-book, the rosaries, a handkerchief or two, and old tobacco-pipe and a daguerreotype of her husband – all of which reposed under her head – a small square box and unlocked it by means of a key which hung round her neck on the same string as her crucifix. This box contained money: sixpences, threepenny bits, a few shillings and a good many coppers – in all, eighteen shillings and ninepence. Kitty ranged coins in rows on her counterpane and chuckled.

'There's very near enough, now,' she said. 'Very near! Glory be to God.'

The skinny fingers went into the box again and took out a folded paper, which was opened and inspected with a triumph touched with melancholy. It was a curious document; an oblong piece of note-paper on which the following inscription was printed as well as Kitty knew how:–

OF YOUR CHARITY
PRAY FOR THE SOLE OF
DANIEL O'TOOLE
THE LAST DESSENDINT OF THE ANSHANT
KINGS OF ERIN
WHO DIED
MARCH 15TH, 1873.
†
When this you see
Say R.I.P.

This, Kitty's own unaided production, was an epitaph composed by her for her deceased husband, and destined to be engraved on a large flat tombstone as soon as she should have scraped together enough money to pay for it. To understand her great anxiety on this score a little story must be told. Kitty O'Toole had loved this husband of hers with all her heart and had been not a little proud of him. He was a lovely man, as she said many a time, the quietest and good-naturedest in the country – and he had bourne his honours very meekly. Nevertheless he *was,* as every one knew, one of the real old O'Tooles, lineally descended from the famous king of that ilk, and for all that Kitty could make out to the contrary the very last of the true line. Had not his mother told her so, often and often when she was a slip of a girl and Dan had first begun 'to put his comether on her?' Was not his father's name Kevin (or, as she pronounces it, Kavin), and did not everybody know the 'Laygend' of St. Kevin and King O'Toole? There was proof positive if any one was disposed to doubt her word – and in sooth the neighbours did not trouble themselves to gainsay it, and when the poor man was laid under the sod, and they saw how it comforted his widow to talk of his pretensions, they were wont to listen with kindly interest and amusement. 'Queen O'Toole' they called her sometimes, and Kitty, when she heard them, would nod and sigh and say, 'Well, if everyone had their rights!' It was her delight to point out the spot where this scion of royalty was taking his rest (after working for many years like any commoner), and to show the little thornbush at the head which she had trimmed into the shape of a cross, and which did quite as well as a stone – so she said. But when her poor old legs were 'whipped from under her,' and she was no longer able to clip her cross, or to saw at the rank grass with her blunt scissors, she grew sad and thoughtful.

The churchyard lay about the ruins of an old abbey, an historical place where the bones of many Irishmen, more celebrated even than the last of the O'Tooles, were hidden away. Funerals came from all parts to the famous spot, and, to say the truth, this city of the dead was sadly overcrowded. The graves were sown so thickly that there was scarce footway between; and here and there the paths led right across the neglected hillocks, beneath which lay the forgotten dead. Kitty O'Toole's soul grew sick within her when she thought that the last resting-place of her beloved might meet with such desecration. Even now she could no longer attend to it, and soon, when she too was tucked up under the daisy-quilt, there would be no one to speak of the grave, to tell how there, and nowhere else, was buried Daniel O'Toole; and how he was the last of his race, and descended from the mighty king of that name. They would make short cuts across the sacred mound, and flatten it down till it was indistinguishable amid the lush grass; people would forget who lay beneath, and the name of O'Toole would be remembered no more. It was after many nights of wakeful anguish that the inspiration came to Kitty to 'save up', so as to procure a tombstone for her lord. Twenty-five shillings she had found on inquiry to be the lowest price at which she could obtain her heart's desire, and now after much pinching and scraping she had accumulated the money which lay outspread on her patchwork quilt. One may imagine the privations necessary to save an amount out of a weekly income of two shillings and sixpence. No 'baccy' – a luxury dear to her soul – very little tea, the smallest modicum of butter which she could manage to scrape on to her bread – no wonder that it was a lean and shrivelled old woman who counted her money so joyfully this winter's evening! The composition of the epitaph had cost her much thought and trouble. Kitty's knowledge of history was vague, and when or where King O'Toole had lived seemed immaterial to her; the important point was to put forward Dan's claims to honour in the most impressive manner possible. This, she flattered herself, she had accomplished; but it was the couplet at the end which most caused her heart to swell with innocent pride. It had been suggested by an old valentine which formed part of her artistic collection, and on which was set forth a large scarlet heart surrounded by roses, with the legend on a scroll beneath:

'When this you see
Remember me.'

Queen O'Toole had altered the last line to suit her purpose, and so it ran:–

'When this you see
Say R.I.P.,'

which was at once neat, terse, and devotional. Her Majesty smiled as she folded up the paper, and restored it to its place. She was gathering the coins together with the like intention when a slight noise without made her glance hastily towards the window. Lo! a face was pressed against the narrow panes – a woman's face, pale and strange in the dusk. It was almost immediately withdrawn as

Kitty turned her head, and presently there came a knock at the door. The old woman hastily bundled her money into the box, locked it, pushed it under her pillow, and called out tremulously, 'Who's there?'

'For the love o'God, let me in,' said a voice without. 'It's gettin' dark an' the child's perishin.'

Queen O'Toole pulled a string which raised the latch – her door was constructed on the same principle as that of Red-Riding-Hood's grandmother; and a woman entered the room, a tall woman wrapped in a dripping black cloak, beneath which she seemed to carry a rather large bundle. Her wet boots squeaked on the tiled floor, and from under her battered bonnet had escaped long streamers of black hair which were blown across her pale face as she stood on the threshold.

'Come in, come in, and shut the door, for goodness' sake!' cried Kitty. 'What brings ye out thravellin' on such an evenin'?'

The woman closed the door, and shook off the loose snow from her shoulders. Then throwing back her cloak she disclosed the form of a child of about two, who uttered a wail as she did so, and turned a little wan, pitiful face to the light.

'God help it!' said Kitty, 'is it sick?'

'He's dying', I think,' said the mother, speaking for the first time. 'An' he's all I have in the world.'

'Ah, look at that, now!' returned Kitty with a well-meant attempt at consolation; 'an' here's myself left all alone, without ere a wan at all.'

'He's dying, I tell ye,' said the woman fiercely. 'What good'll he be to me when he's gone? An' him the finest an' beautifullest little fellow you could set eyes on till he had that fall.'

'God help ye!' said Kitty. 'Sure maybe he won't die on ye afther all. There's a power o' life in childer. Sit down there by the fire and dry yerself. There's a sup o' milk in the cup there, ye might warm for the child, an' the kettle'll boil up in a minute if ye'll put it on. I can't stir these ould legs o'mine or I'd do it for ye.'

'Wait till I tell ye,' returned the woman, her voice tremulous with suppressed excitement. 'I want to tell ye what the docther up at me own place said about Billy. Says he – "Ye should have brought the child to me before," he says – "he's hurted in his inside an' 'pon my word I'm afraid to touch him now." "Is there no way of savin' him?" I says, for my heart was broke. "Well, the only chance at all 'ud be to take him to Dublin to the childer's hospital," he says, "they'd do what's needed for him there, an' take good care of him. He'd want the best o' care an' food, if he's to recover at all." Well, I set out that same day walkin' – an' I've thramped thirty miles an' more since, carryin' him – but Dublin's long way off yet, an' the cold is killin' him. He'll never hould out – he'll die before my eyes on the way' – she stopped, choking with tearless sobs.

'Sure, why don't ye go on the train?' cried Queen O'Toole. 'That'ud bring ye there in a few hours, so it would. Haven't ye the price of a ticket?'

'I haven't wan penny in the whole world,' said the woman, and then she suddenly fell on her knees by the bed.

'Oh, for the love of heaven, give me some o' the money in your little box,' she cried. 'I seen ye countin' it through the window. Give it to me in the name o' God! – you that has only yourself – an' save my darlin' child.'

'Ye crathur, you should have it an' welcome,' she said, after a pause, in shaky tones, 'but sure this I can't spare. I've been savin' it bit by bit this long while, an' I'll tell ye what for.' Thereupon she related her story with pleading eyes fixed on the stranger's face.

'Sure, what signifies it, when your husband's dead an' gone?' cried the latter, impatiently.

'Isn't he in heaven with the angels, an' what does he want with gravestones? But my boy's alive yet, an' maybe wouldn't die if he was cared in time. It's easy seein' ye never had a child o' your own, or ye wouldn't be that hard.'

'Then beggin' your pardon, I've had four,' put in Kitty, irate at the imputation, 'the finest childer in the whole place, God bless them. I know what it is to have them, an' I know what it is to bury them too, so ye needn't be goin' on as if no wan had any feelin' but yerself.'

'Did ye bury them all?' asked the other, slowly rising from her knees.

'Everywan o' them,' sighed Queen O'Toole. 'The last lived to be two year old. Ah sure,' with a sudden change in her voice, 'isn't it well for them? I niver fretted for any of them the way I fret for the good name o' my poor man.'

'Ye haven't a mother's heart in ye at all,' cried the strange woman. 'I'll talk to ye no more.'

She turned her back and crouched down by the fire, unfolding the poor babe's ragged wrappings and holding his attenuated limbs to the warmth.

'Heat up that sup o' milk for him,' urged Kitty. 'Do, it'll put life in him. An' make yerself a cup o' tay.'

'No, I don't want bite or sup from ye for myself, thank ye; but I'll give the child the milk. I wouldn't if I could help it, but I can't see him die before my eyes.'

She stretched out her hand for the cup, the little fellow moaning as she moved.

'Let me hould him for ye,' pleaded Kitty, putting out her lean old arms.

The mother, with an odd look in her face, consented, and Queen O'Toole sat bolt upright, proud, if rather fearful, rocking the child and crooning a queer little song – 'Hush-sh-sh-sh honey! Hush-sh-sh, my darlin' honey, hush-sh-sh!'

The warmth of the withered bosom, the montonous ditty, the soothing motion had the looked for effect. The child fell into a doze, one tiny hand grasping Kitty's forefinger.

'Now, maybe I didn't hush as well as ye could yourself!' whispered the latter triumphantly.

The woman drew near, a new agony of entreaty in her eyes.

'In the name o' God, save him for me!' she groaned.

'I can't!' answered Kitty, and fell a-sobbing.

The stranger drew back, and looked at her hostess with a long wicked look. Then she turned away and again sat down by the fire.

The night wore away slowly; the baby awoke, and cried, and slept again, swallowing with difficulty a few drops of milk now and then. The woman roused herself when he stirred, and ministered to his wants, but between whiles sat staring into the embers with gloomy eyes. At dawn, Kitty, waking from an uneasy doze, found her standing by her bedside.

'Give me the child,' she said. 'I'm goin'.'

She took the little creature from the old woman's cramped arms, and then stooping over her, made a sudden dive beneath the pillow. Queen O'Toole yelled as she beheld her treasury in the hands of the enemy.

'Aye, ye may look an' screech,' cried the other savagely. 'It's the price o' me child's life that ye have here. I begged an' prayed ye for it on me knees, so I did. An' ye'd rather spend it on an ould stone. But I'm goin' to take it now, an' may God forgive us both – for you're as bad as me.'

The key of the poor little box hung, as has been mentioned, on a string round Kitty' neck; but its present possessor stopped at no such trifle. The flimsy woodwork flew apart under the pressure of her sturdy finger and thumb, and the woman tossed it on the bed while she transferred its contents to her own pocket. Then without another word, another look at the helpless old woman, she made for the door, and was gone almost before Kitty had time to realise what had occurred. Poor Kitty! It would be impossible to describe her feelings. Gone, every penny of her savings; gone her castle or rather her tombstone – in the air; gone her cherished plans for making Dan's name and memory immortal! She could not hope to live long enough to scrape together the required sum now.

'I'll be dead first!' she moaned. 'I'll soon die now – ah, my heart's broke entirely.'

She lay there sobbing, with the patchwork quilt drawn over her head, while the pale rays of daylight filtered gradually in through the tiny casement.

After a time she sat up, pushing the straggling grey hair off her face which was glazed and swollen with tears. Her eyes fell on her beloved picture, the frame of which was now glittering in the sun.

'Ah, Blessed Virgin, darlin'!' she cried, apostrophising that brilliantly tinted print. 'Isn't it the sorrowful ould woman you're lookin' at this day – you an' your Blessed Son? Holy Mary, jewel, me heart's broke!'

A vision of Dan's grave rose before her mind's eye. Dan's grave unkempt, neglected, an ever-broadening brown path crossing its middle, and with a cry she fell back on her pillow again.

After some time there came a violent knock at her door, and a hasty rattling of the latch.

'Whisht, Maggie asthore, I'm rale bad this mornin'. Don't go frightenin' me that way,' murmured the old woman querulously, as she languidly pulled the string that raised the latch.

But it was not Maggie who burst into the room, it was the strange woman again, with her face livid and drawn in the searching morning light, and great drops standing on her brow.

'I'm back,' she cried breathlessly, approaching the bed with rapid but uncertain steps, and flinging Kitty's treasure into her hand. 'Take it – it's the unluckiest money ever I touched: it has brought a curse on me an' the child. He was convulsed altogether a while ago. I'm a wicked woman, an' the Lord's chastisin' me. The child's goin' – me darlin's goin'! It's no use, I'll have to give him up now.'

Queen O'Toole had caught the coins eagerly and was hugging them to her breast. She scarcely heard the other's words, so great was her transport of joy at this unexpected good fortune. But glancing up presently the utter despair in the mother's face struck her.

'Is he that bad?' she said gently, drawing aside one of the flaps of the black cloak.

The child was not actually dying, but was absolutely exhausted by his recent seizure; the little face had that aged look so pitiful to see in a babe, the little hands were clenched.

Queen O'Toole glanced from him to the mother, and then back again, her hands tightened over the coins; her mouth quivered. In the half-minute that ensued she went through strange experiences. Baby voices sounded in her ears, touches of little fingers fluttering about her face; upon her heart she seemed to feel the pressure of a tiny form. She too – she too, was a mother – the mother of dead children – she knew the joy and the agony! Fifty years of life's wear and tear had caused her to forget for a while, but the look in that woman's face brought it all back to her.

With a groan she leaned forward, holding out the money in her trembling palm.

'Take it,' she said. 'I'll give it to ye. Take it in God's name, an' go. Go quick. Maybe ye'll catch the ten o'clock train if ye make haste.'

The other burst into a passion of tears. She, who had been so glib to plead or to revile, had now no words to express her gratitude; she, who had not wept in her fury and despair, could only find tears in this sudden unlooked-for joy.

'Go, alanna, go for the love o' God!' sighed Kitty, withdrawing her empty hand. But the strange woman seized it and pressed it feverishly to lips and bosom. Then she went out swiftly into the wintry sunlight; and Queen O'Toole took up the broken money box, and turned her face to the wall.

The Snakes and Norah

Jane Barlow

Jane Barlow, the daughter of a dissenting Church of Ireland minister who was also vice-provost of Trinity College, Dublin, was born in 1857 at Clontarf, County Dublin. She lived almost all her life in nearby Raheny, then a country district.

Barlow's first published poems appeared in the *Dublin Magazine* but it was a book of narrative poems, *Bog-Land Studies* (London: Unwin, 1892) which launched her writing career. *Irish Idylls* (London: Hodder and Stoughton, 1892) consolidated her popularity and she subsequently published many volumes of verse, stories and sketches. Barlow's work is almost exclusively concerned with the Irish peasantry; her quiet, studious life was spent in observing the countryside and the people who inhabited it and her much-misunderstood attempts at re-creating peasant speech are only the most superficial aspects of her sincere interest in the 'native' Irish.

'The Snakes and Norah', like so much of Barlow's writing, is intended to move beneath the surface of peasant experience, with its hidden complexity. It is specially interesting for the moral response to Norah's 'unnatural' desires.

Jane Barlow was a member of the National Literary Society and was awarded a D.Litt. by Dublin University. She disapproved strongly of the events of 1916 and died in the following year. Once extremely popular, Barlow is mentioned in most of the early critical studies of the Irish Renaissance. There has been no critical study of her work, and few modern assessments of her contribution to Anglo-Irish literature.

THE KENNY'S little farmstead was a somewhat amphibious one, occupying the southern end of the isthmus which keeps the Atlantic foam from riding into Lough Fintragh, a small, dark-watered nook niched in the shadow of steep mountain slopes. Another murkier shadow brooded over it in the opinion of the Kennys, who, like most of their neighbours, at least half-believed that its recesses harboured a monstrous indweller. Their thin white house stood fronting the seashore, with a narrow grazing strip behind, while their yard and sheds lay along the dwindling isthmus, which becomes a mere reef-like bar of boulders and shingle before it again touches the mainland. In calm weather Joe Kenny might see his unimposing ricks reflected from ridge to butt, with gleams of ochre and amber and gold in both salt and fresh water; but in stormy times, which came oftener, it might befall him to witness a less pleasing spectacle of hay-wisps and straw-stooks strew bodily, floating and soaking on the wasteful waves. So he was not surprised to find that this had happened when he walked out one December morning after a wild night whose blustering had mingled menace with his dreams. Despite its close-meshed roping and thick fringe of dangling stone weights, the more exposed haystack had been seriously wrecked and pillaged. 'Och, bad cess to the ould win' and its whillaballoos!' said Joe, as he surveyed the distorted outlines, and made a rueful estimate of the damage. 'If I got the chance to slit its bastely bellows for it, 'twould be apt to keep its huffin' and puffin' quiet for one while – it would so.' This was not, however, the limit of his losses. Presently he stood looking vexedly over the door of a half-roofed shed, which contained a good deal of sea-water and weed; also a very small red calf, and a large jelly-fish. The calf was drowned dead, but the jelly-fish seemingly lived as much as usual. 'Eyah, get out wid you, you unnathural-lookin' blob of a baste!' said Joe, giving this unprofitable addition to his stock a contumelious flick with his blackthorn. 'There's another good fifteen shillin's gone on me. I'd never ha' thought 'twould ha' tuk and slopped over the wall that way. Sorra the bit of a Christmas box I'll be able to conthrive her this year, and that's a fac'; and to-morra fair day and all – weary on it!'

'Her' was Rose O'Meara, Joe's sweetheart; and since he had long looked forward to the opportunity of the Christmas gift as likely to bring about a favourable crisis in his courtship, the falling through of his plan made him feel dejectedly out of humour, in which unenjoyable mood he strolled on towards the pigstye. Traces of the spent storm lay all around him. The tide had receded some way, but the waves were fast by, still hissing and seething, and flinging themselves down with hollow booms and thuds. They had evidently been beating high against the yard-wall, for all along it they had left great masses of brown sea-wrack tossed in bales and clumps, as if loaded out of a cart; and these were connected by trails of green and black weed, skeleton branches, shells, clotted forth, driftwood, and other debris, all in an indescribable tangle. As Joe stumped through it, he struck his foot sharply against something hard, and nearly tripped up. When he recovered his balance, he saw that the obstruction was not the boulder which he had already execrated in haste. It was a wooden box. In much excitement Joe picked it up, and set it on the top of the wall for exacter scrutiny. The tides were constantly sweeping in with miscellaneous fringes on the Kennys' demesne, but seldom did they bring anything that might not be justly termed 'quare ould rubbish.' During all the course of Joe's life, and he was not in his first youth, no waif had been washed up so promising in appearance as this box. About ten inches square it was, and made of a fine grained wood, which seemed to have been very highly polished. The corners were clamped with bronze-like metal, elaborately wrought, and plates of the same inlaid the keyhole and hinges. So strong was the lock, that when he tried to wrench off the lid he seemed to have a solid block in his hands, and it shut so tightly that the lines of juncture were almost invisible. Its weight was considerable enough to increase his conviction that it held something very precious.

Joe's first impulse was to rush home with his prize, exhibit and examine it. Immediately afterwards, however, it flashed across him like an inspiration that here was Rose's Christmas box; and upon this followed a more leisurely resolve to keep it a secret until he should present her with it intact on Christmas morning, still distant three whole days. This course would cost him the repression of much impatient curiosity, but it was recommended to him by a sense that it would enhance the value of the gift. He would be making over to Rose all the vague and wonderful possibilities of the treasure-trove, which in his imagination were more splendid than any better-defined object, as they loomed through a haze of unseen gold and jewels. Disappointment had scanty room among his forecasts. 'Sure, I'd a right to give it to her just the way it is, wid anythin' at all inside it, for amn't I axin' her to take meself in a manner like that, whether good, bad, or indiff'rint comes of it? – on'y it's scarce as apt, worse luck, to be any great things as the full of a grand lookin' box is. But she might understand 'twas as much as to say I'd be wishful she had every chance of the best that I could git for her, the crathur, if it was all the gold and silver and diamonds that ever were dhrownded under the say-wather, and'd never think to be lookin' to reckon them, no more than if they were so many handfuls of ould pebbles off of the strand.' Thus reflected Joe, who had a vein of sentiment, which sometimes outran his powers of expression. And thereupon, leaving the box atop of the wall, he went to look after the pigs. He found them all surviving, though the storm had caused some dilapidations in their abode, which obliged him to do a little rough carpentry, and kept him hammering and thumping for several minutes. And when he returned to the place where he had left the box, the box was gone.

He searched wildly for it among the litter on both sides of the wall, and nowhere could it be seen. Yet at that hour what man or mortal was there abroad to have stirred it? Then he thought that the weeds looked wetter than they had been, and he said to himself that 'one of them waves must ha' riz up permiscuous and swep' it off in a flurry while his back was turned; and a fine gomeral he'd been to go lave it widin raich of such a thing happenin' it.' So as no more satisfactory explanation was forthcoming, he turned homeward, empty-handed and crestfallen. But before he had taken many steps, he saw sitting under the lee of the yard-wall Tom O'Meara, Rose's brother, who was generally recognised to be courting Mary Kenny, Joe's youngest sister. The O'Mearas lived a good step beyond the other end of the isthmus, and Joe had begun to speculate what so early a visit might signify, when the greater wonder abruptly swallowed the less as he became aware that Tom had the twice-lost box in his hands.

'Look-a, Joe, at what I'm after findin',' he called jubilantly.

'Findin'? Musha moyah! that's fine talkin',' said Joe. 'And where at all did you find it, then?'

'Where it was to be had,' said Tom, promptly adjusting his tone to Joe's, which was offensive.

'Then it's sitting atop of our wall there it was,' said Joe. 'Whethen, now, some people has little enough to do that they can't keep their hands off meddlin' wid things they find sittin' on other people's yard-walls.'

'And suppose it was sittin' on anybody's ould wall,' said Tom, 'what else except a one of them rowlin' waves set it sittin' there wid itself, and it all dhreepin' wet out of the say? Be the same token it's quare if one person hasn't got as good a right to be liftin' it off as another. Troth and bedad, I'd somethin' better to do than to be standin' star-gazin' at it all day, waitin' to ax lave of the likes of yous.'

'I'll soon show you the sort of rowlin' wave there was, me man, if you don't throuble yourself to be handin' it over out of that, and I after pickin' it up this half-hour ago,' said Joe, with furious irony.

'Come on wid you, come on!' Tom shouted, jumping to his feet with a general flourish of defiance. At this point the dispute bade fair to become an argument without words, and would probably have done so had it not been that the two young men were the brothers of their sisters. As it was, a sort of Roman-Sabine complication fettered and handcuffed them. 'Divil a thing else I was intendin' to do wid it, but bring it straight ways in to your sister Mary,' said Tom, 'that you need go for to be risin' rows about the matter.'

'It's for Rose's Christmas box; that's what I think bad of,' said Joe.

'Let's halve it between the two of them, then, whatever it is,' said Tom, feeling that a compromise was the utmost he could reasonably expect from the circumstances.

And so it was arranged, rather weakly on Joe's part, he being the better man of the two, and well within his rights, if he had chosen to claim the box unconditionally. The joint presentation should take place, they agreed, on Christmas Eve, the next day but one, when Rose O'Meara would be visiting the Kennys; and then Tom departed whistling, with the pick he had come to borrow the loan of, while Joe consoled himself as best he could for this arbitrary subtraction of more than half the pleasure and romance from his morning's find.

Late on Christmas Eve, when the Kennys' kitchen was full of glancing firelight, and the widow Kenny, with her son and daughters and her guests, Tom and Rose O'Meara, had all had their tea, Joe and Tom were seen to often whisper and nudge one another, until at last Joe got up and produced the box from its secret hiding-place. But Tom hastened to forestall him as spokesman, placing considerable confidence in his own perspicacity and grace of diction. He said –

'See you here, Mary and Rose. This consarn's a prisint the two of us is after gettin' the two of yous – I mane it was Joe found it aquilly the same as me, that picked it up somthin' later. And it's he's givin' the whole of his half of the whole of it to Rose; but he's nothin' to say to the rest of it; and it's meself that's givin' Mary the half of the whole of the half – och no, botheration! it's the whole of the – it's the other whole half of it –'

'You've got it this time,' Joe remarked in a sarcastic aside.

'– I'm givin' Mary. So that's the way of it, and when we've got the lid prized off for yous, you'll just have to regulate it between yous, accordin' to what there is inside.'

'And if it's all the gold and diamonds in the riches of the world,' said Joe, 'you're kindly welcome to every grain of it, Rose jewel – ay, bedad, are you.'

'To the one half of it,' corrected Tom, with emphasis. But his sister tapped him with the pot-stick, and said, 'Whisht, you big omadhawn, whisht.'

'It's a pity of such a thing to be knockin' about and goin' to loss,' said Mary, rubbin' her finger on the embossed metal-work; 'and I wonder what's gone wid whatever crathur owned it. Under the salt say he's very apt to be lying this night – the Lord be good to him!' The rustle of the waves climbing up the shingle outside seemed to swell louder as she spoke.

'For anythin' we can tell, he might be takin' a look in at us through the windy there this minute to see what we're doin' wid it,' said Joe.

Everybody's eyes turned towards the dark little square of the window, and Mary left off handling the box as suddenly as if it had become red-hot.

'Oh, blathers!' said Tom. 'Just raich me the rippin'-chisel that's lyin' on the windy-stool, Norah, and we'll soon thry what it is at all.'

Norah, the elder sister, made a very long arm, and secured the tool with as little approximation as might be to the deep-set panes.

She had neither sweetheart nor Christmas box, and was disposed to take a rather languid and cynical view of affairs.

'There's apt not to be any great things in it, I'm thinkin',' said the widow Kenny from her elbow-chair by the hearth. The truth was that she had been reflecting with some bitterness how not so many years since Joe would have 'come flourishin' in to her wid any ould thrifle of rubbish he might ha' picked up outside,' whereas now he had kept this valuable property silently in his possession for three days, for the purpose of bestowing it upon the O'Mearas' slip of a girl. Consequently, Joe's mother held aloof from the eager group round the table, and uttered disparaging predictions of the event. Tom and Mary did make a prudent attempt to fend off their collision with the disappointment which might emerge from the mists ahead by repeating, as the chisel wrestled with the stubborn hasps and springs, 'Sure, all the while belike there's on'y some quare ould stuff in it, no good to anybody.' Joe and Rose, on the contrary, chose to run under crowded sail towards the possible wreck of their hopes, and talked of sovereigns and bank-notes and jewels while the lid creaked and resisted.

But when at length it yielded with a final splinter, it disclosed what no one had anticipated – namely, nothing. The box was quite empty. Daintily lined with glossy satinwood, as if for the reception of something delicate and precious, but bare as the palm of your hand. There was not even so much vacant space as might have been expected, for the sides were disproportionately thick. Very blank faces exchanged notes with one another upon this result. Almost any contents, however inappropriate and worthless, would have been their 'advantage to exclaim upon,' and more tolerable for that reason than mere nullity, about which there was little to be said. Rose was the first to rally from the general mortification, observing with forced cheerfulness that 'sure 'twould make an iligant sort of workbox, at all ivints, and 'twas maybe just as handy there bein' nothin' in it, because 'twould hould anythin' you plased.' To which Mary rejoined, dejectedly refusing to philosophise, 'Bedad, then, you may keep it yourself, girl alive, for the lid's every atom all smashed into smithereens.'

The young people were not, however, with one exception, in the mood for dwelling upon the dark side of things. Their depression caused by the collapse of the Christmas box was superficial, and soon passed away. When in course of the evening the two young men went out to feed the pigs, Rose and Mary accompanied them to the back door, where they all loitered so long that the patience waiting round the empty trough must have been sorely tried. Sound of their talking and laughing came down the passage and were heard plainly in the kitchen, whence Mrs Kenny had slipped up her ladder stairs to say her rosary, so that Norah was for the time left quite alone. She was decidedly out of humour, albeit by no means on account of the others' rapid reverse of fortune. Rather, we may apprehend, she had viewed that incident as a not regrettable check to a tide of affairs which was unduly sweeping all manner of good luck her neighbours' way, and unjustly leaving her high and dry. This grudging spirit had forbidden her to appear interested in the examination of the box, but now she could satisfy without betraying her curiosity. As she drew her fingers aimlessly round its smooth inner surface, there was a sudden snap and jerk, and out slid a secret drawer, which had been concealed by a false bottom. It was filled with rose-pink wadding, amongst which lay the coils of a long gold snake necklace. She lifted it out amazedly, and held it up in the firelight, with jewelled head gleaming and enamelled scales, a far finer piece of worksmanship than she knew, though the flash of brilliants and rubies assured even her uninstructed eyes that she had come on something of much value.

While she was still looking at it she heard steps returning up the passage, and forthwith tried hastily to replace it in the box. But at a clumsy touch the drawer flew back into its former invisibility, and her flurried fumbling failed to press the lurking spring. Then, as the steps came very near, she thrust her ornament into her pocket, and moved away from the table on which the box stood. In doing so, she was conscious only of a proud perversity which made her loth to be found meddling with what she sullenly called 'no consarn of mine.' Presently, however, other motives for concealment grew clearer and stronger. Of course, the longer she retained it the more difficult would the restoring of it be. Her crossness made it impossible for her to imagine a joke as a natural explanation of her conduct. Moreover, a covetous wish to keep the beautiful thing for its own sake sprang up, and had a swift growth. She said to herself that 'she didn't see why she need have any call to be givin' it up, after all. Wasn't she after findin' it in the quare little slitherin' tray, and the rest of them wid no more notion of it bein' there at all than ould Sally the goat had? It might be lyin' where it was till the world's end on'y for her? And sure, for the matter of that, the ould box itself was no more a belongin' of the lads to give away than of any other body that might ha' happened on it tossin' about the shore. So if it wasn't theirs be rights, she thought she'd be a fine fool to not keep what she'd got.' Sophistical arguments such as these convinced her reason easily enough, but her conscience was less amenable to them. They were reinforced by some further considerations which possessed no ethical value at all, and which she had the grace to be ashamed of putting into clearly outlined thoughts. She allowed herself to have only a vague sense of grievance at the fact that Rose and Mary had 'presents, and people to be makin' fools of them, and all manner,' whereas none of these desirable things were bestowed on her. Yet it formed a mental atmosphere which made the propect of yielding up her discovery seem incongruous and odious, in the same way that a bitter wind blowing makes us loth to throw open our doors and windows.

'Cock them up to be gettin' everythin',' she said to herself, as she sat in a corner with her hand in her pocket, and drew through her fingers the cold, smooth coils, remembering how the gem-encrusted head had blazed in the firelight. She wished that she could venture to take it out and proudly display it as her property; but she was far from daring to do so. On the contrary, she felt herself laden with a guilty secret, and was presently beset by all the misgivings, suspicions, and surmises which infest people who carry about such a burden. Whenever anyone went near the box her heart thumped with terror lest the drawer should be detected, and its rifled condition somehow traced to her. Then she trembled to think that the lads perhaps knew all the time of the necklace's existence, and were just reserving it for a grand suprise; or she imagined herself letting it drop accidentally and being unable to account for her possession of it. These speculations so pre-occupied her that she was obliged

to explain her absent-mindedness by declaring herself 'intirely dis-
thracted wid the toothache'; upon which the condolences and sympathy of the others aggravated her uneasiness with remorseful
gratitude. Her conscience nipped her shrewdly when Rose said,
'Ah, the crathur, I'll run over to-morra early and bring you the
bottle ould Matt Farren gev me mother; it's the grandest stuff at all
for the toothache,' – Rose whom she was defrauding of a share in
that golden marvel! At length she had resource to a plan which
promised her temporary relief from urgent fears and self-
reproaches. This was to hide away the necklace in some cranny of
the rocks on the shore, where, if it should be rediscovered, nothing
would implicate her in the matter. She said to herself, indeed, that
they would have just as much chance of finding it there as in the
mysterious drawer; but beneath that soothing reflection lay a
resolve to minimise the chance by choosing the most unlikely
chink possible. Since the evening was by this time far spent, and
the O'Mearas had already taken leave, she knew that she must
hurry to execute her design before Joe came in from seeing after
the cattle, when the house would be shut up. So she slipped quietly
out of doors.

It was a dark, gusty night, and the waves still turbulent after
their late uproar, were clattering noisily up the shingly ridges of the
beach. As Norah ran along she could barely discern the glimmer-
ing of pale grey stones and white foam-crests. She kept on by the
lough side of the isthmus, because the walking there was smoother,
but when she thought she had come a safe distance she stopped, intending to cross over and seek a hiding-place for her spoil among a
small chaos of weeded boulders. Looking for a moment athwart
the black water, she saw a dim streak of light in the sky above it.
The moon was glimpsing out of an eastern cloud-rift, and throwing down a meagre web of rays, which the unquiet dark surface
caught fitfully and shredded into the broken coils of a writhing
silver serpent. Perhaps it was this, or perhaps the golden snake-
chain in her hands, that suggested the thing, but at any rate Norah
suddenly bethought her of the *Piast*. For Lough Fintragh is
haunted by the terror of one of these monsters, a huge and grisly
worm, dwelling down in the shadowy end of the lake, where the

water is said to have no bottom, and to wander in labyrinthine caverns about the roots of the moutains. The creature had not been very often seen, but Norah well knew what a direful fate had over-taken every soul to whom its shag-maned, lurid-eyed head and rood-length of livid scales had disastrously appeared. One of its least appalling habits, ran report, was to glare fixedly at its victim, until fascinated and distraught he leaped wildly into the jaws gap-ing for their prey. In the lonesome, murmurous dimness by the shore, Norah did not care to linger over such incidents, and she was turning away quickly, when a shock of fright almost paralysed her. Within a few yards of her feet she saw two reddish amber eyes glowing through the gloom, and from the same place came a sound of something in rustling, flapping motion.

It was, in fact, only a harmless and rather bewildered seal, who, during the past night's turmoil, had somehow got into the lough, and who now, instinctively aware of the rising tide, had set out eager to quit the insipid fresh water for his strong-flavoured Atlan-tic brine. But Norah naturally jumped to the conclusion that no-thing less fearsome than the *Piast* itself was flopping towards her, and she fled away before it in a headlong panic, which culminated a moment afterwards when she ran against some large moving body. This, again, was simply her brother Joe, returned from setting his friends on their way; but Norah, with a wild shriek, gave herself up for lost, and did actually come near putting an end to herself by tumbling in frantic career over one stone, and striking her head violently on another. She had to be carried home insensible, and Christmas Day had come and gone before she found her way back gropingly to consciousness.

Meanwhile conjectures, of course, were rife as to the origin of her mishap, and the antecedents of the 'iligant gold snaky chain' that she was grasping. 'Sclutched that tight she had it in her sclenched fist, we were hard set to wrench it out of her hand,' Mrs Kenny volubly told her neighbours. The favourite theory held that she 'was after pickin' it up on the shore, and would be skytin' home wid it in a hurry, not mindin' where she was goin' and that was the way she got the ugly toss.' And when Norah had recovered from the effects of it sufficiently to be asked for her own account of the matter, she could throw but little light thereon. Her accident had left, as so often happens, a strange misty gap in her memory, which it was vain to scan. The space between her first sight of the box and her blinding crash down on the shingle was all a confused blank. However, two results of the affair emerged, and, though their cause remained untraceable, had a distinct influence upon her future. One of them was, that she would on no account permit the snake necklace to be regarded as her property. She persistently asserted that it belonged to Mary and Rose; and when Dr Mason, who had undertaken to dispose of it in Dublin, remitted an incredible number of pounds, she would hear of no arrangement save dividing them between her sister and sister-in-law elect. The other had more important consequences to the whole course of her life. It was an abiding dread of their connecting isthmus, which had become so horrible a place to her that never again would she cross over it, even when promised the protection of the most stalwart escort. Now, as the isthmus is very much the nearest way from the Kennys' farm to any other habitations, this peculiarity of Norah's cut her off greatly from whatever society the neighbourhood afforded, besides gaining her a reputation for 'quareness' not likely to increase her popularity. Probably, therefore, it may have been part of the reason why the years as they came and went that way found her rooted fast and growing into a settled old maid.

Those glowering yellow eyes being blurred out of her recollection, the *Piast* did not occur to her as the object of her fear. But some people were not slow to connect it with the uncanny inhabitant of the lough, and in process of time their various imaginations hardened into a circumstantial narrative of an especially terrific appearance of the monster. To this day, indeed, so current is the story, that many a wayfarer along the bleak shingle strip goes the faster for a doubt whether such an awful experience as befell Norah Kenny may not be writhing towards him beneath the sunless waters of Lough Fintragh.

The Criminality of Letty Moore

Erminda Esler

Erminda Esler was born in Donegal in about 1860, the daughter of a Presbyterian rector. She graduated from Queen's University in 1879 with honours, married and went to live in London. While there, she first began to contribute short stories to English magazines and then began to write books, of which the most famous were *The Way of Transgressors* (London: Sampson Lowe, 1890) and *The Way They Love at Grimpat* (London: Sampson Lowe, 1894). Not only was Esler a very popular writer: she was also in demand as a critic and as a speaker to groups such as the Irish Circle of the Lyceum Club and the London branch of the Irish Literary Society. Her home place of Tyrconnell was the background which Esler used for all of her stories, and she was always very conscious of Ireland and of the Irish literary movement.

'The Criminality of Letty Moore' is of interest, not merely because of Esler's northern Protestant subject, but because of her portrait of an independent working woman – an unusual character in Anglo-Irish literature. Erminda Esler died in 1924. Her work has been completely forgotten.

MARY WILLETT had decided to emigrate. As this is not her story, it is unnecessary at this juncture to explain why.

It was an October afternoon, but chilly. The frost had come too soon, and the leaves were too russet and too brown for the time of year, and the breath of the north wind was cold.

Mary stood by the window of Letty Moore's kitchen, looking out. One takes a careless attitude sometimes when not quite at ease with the topic under discussion. Letty sat facing the light, which fell fully on her small-featured, large-eyed face and showed the anxiety there.

'I wouldn't go, if I were you,' Letty said.

'If you were me you just would,' Mary answered with a short laugh.

'You are so young,' Letty went on wistfully.

'That is a fault one outgrows with time.'

'And you are so pretty.'

'That should help me.'

'I don't know that it does, always, when a girl has her way to make.'

'It is decided that I am going, anyway, so there is no use in seeing the worst side of things now.'

Letty began to cry. 'Does John approve?' she asked. John was Mary's brother.

'Of course he does. But for him I couldn't go. He will find the money; he says it is only fair, since I am set on it.'

Letty wiped away her fast-falling tears. 'I wish – I wish –,' she said miserably.

'If there was any good in wishing,' Mary interrupted in a hard tone, 'I should wish that home was a happier place for us young ones and that John might marry you.'

'That has been nothing but your fancy ever,' Letty said firmly and for the moment the bright flush of colour in her face made her almost as pretty as her friend. 'Because you like me you think he does, it's nothing but that.'

'I don't know that he'll ever tell you of it,' Mary went on, 'having so little to offer you as things are, but he has always been fond of you.'

A current of thought ran, like slow and harmless flame, through Letty's mind. She had not a fortune, it was true, but she had her industry – that meant money, and a home of her own, in case John thought the paternal home was too full already. But girls do not enunciate thoughts of this kind, even to their closest intimates. Letty seemed to think in lightning flashes, but when she spoke her words were measured, and quite irrelevant to the subject of her thoughts.

'When do you mean to go?' she asked.

'Next week, if I am living.'

'Oh, dear,' Letty said with a bursting sigh, 'and the weather growing colder every day, and – everything!'

Mary shrugged her shoulders.

'I'll give you my fur cloak,' said Letty, hurriedly. 'It'll not need much altering to fit you, and it's that warm it'll keep the life in you and I'll make you a hood for the journey, a lined one, to fit close round your face.'

Mary threw her arms about her friend's neck, and burst into tears. All her wounded pride, her resentment, perhaps her dread of the enterprise before her, finding utterance thus.

Letty Moore was a professional, that is to say, she had been trained to dressmaking and lived by it exclusively, in which respect she differed from several others at Grimpat, who worked at the business fitfully, and had some income apart from it. But there was not a fortune in the industry even to a professional. No Grimpat woman ever thought of more than one new dress in the year and where that was a good one, such as silk, why it did for several subsequent years, of course. But this involved few changes of fashion, and on the whole, was for the peace of mind of dressmakers.

There were times when Letty wished that she was not the best dressmaker, which goes to prove that she was a little more of a woman and a little less of an artist than might have been believed, and that was where accident brought her now and then a sudden rush of work and responsibility. It was on the very evening of Mary's visit to her that old Mr Tedford died, and as he was very well-to-do, and of the highest respectability, it seemed as if the whole neighbourhood claimed kindred with him and went into mourning. Letty stitched and stiched, and fitted, and altered, and sent home parcels all day long so that the eve of her friend's departure had arrived before she found time to make in her fur cloak the few alterations she had spoken of. When these were completed she locked up her house and took the carrier's cart to Nutford. She was bound to supply the hood she had promised and there was no suitable material to be procured nearer home. Owing to work and preoccupation, Letty had forgotten that the day was Thursday, and that the Nutford shops closed early on Thursdays. When she found the windows all shuttered and the doors all barricaded, Letty's natural conclusion was that Nutford was also in mourning for Mr Tedford. But after a moment the reasonable explanation occurred to her and she sped from house to house and from street to street in vain. Such shops as remained open offered nothing better than could be found at Grimpat.

Letty went home in a kind of despair. She had promised that hood, and Mary was depending on it, and to present herself before Mary in the morning without it was a prospect she had not the moral courage to face. Arrived at her own house, she opened every trunk, and drawer, and receptacle. She studied the possibilities of every remnant, but there was nothing that would be of the slightest service. Scarlet satin, stripped yellow and black silk, and patchwork were equally out of the question. She could not send her friend out into the world barred like a zebra or gay as a parrokeet.

'To think of disappointing her, and her so fond of me!' said Letty, with a sob. She recalled Mary's quick rush of rapture at the mention of the hood, her half-whispered words, 'If only everybody was as good as you!' and felt that to break her promise was too grievous to think about.

'I don't know how I'll face her, and that's the truth,' she said.

The floor was littered with scraps, cuttings, and odds and ends. She began to sort them mechanically, putting the larger pieces back whence they had been taken, gathering the smaller bits into a covered basket that she kept for refuse, opening and shutting the drawers mechanically, scarcely knowing what she did.

Suddenly she paused, and a kind of tremor stole over her. In one of the drawers was a piece of silk which she had been commissioned to keep till the spring. Old Mrs Smith had bought it as a present for her niece, and had entrusted it to the dressmaker pending her niece's next visit. Letty withdrew the silk from its wrappings of tissue paper and laid it on the bed. On the outer cover was the vendor's name, 'John Marshall, Nutford'.

'If only I had been in time,' said Letty, 'I could have got a bit of that. It's the very thing.'

She drew forth a fold of the silk and touched it with caressing fingers. The ground was black, with a pattern of triangular patches of pink, a quaint, old-fashioned pattern, the mode of an hour, a pretty but ephemeral thing, but Letty did not know that. She took her yard-measure and ran along the length of the piece. 'Nine yards,' she said. Those were not the days of voluminous sleeves or bouffant skirts. 'Three-quarters of a yard would make the hood, and I have the lining, and the wadding, and black strings that would do, and I could match the silk tomorrow at Marshall's and put it back. It wouldn't be a sin; I don't think it would be a sin. It is for Mary's sake, not to disappoint her, and her so fond of me. Oh, dear! I hope it's not a sin. I wouldn't do a sin for anything.' But she had taken the scissors, and had cut off the length of silk required, even while she protested.

Until late in the night she sewed feverishly. When the hood was finished, she tried it on herself. 'It makes me just bonnie!' she said with a gay little laugh. And truly at the moment her eyes were as bright as stars and her cheeks like roses. Letty did not know that the fever of a first misdoing was in her veins.

She slept little that night, because she had Mary and the hood and John Willett and all the others to think about. The thought that when Mary had gone she would scarcely hear of John, and certainly never anything intimate concerning him, added a conscious element to her depression.

There was much excitement at the Willett's when Letty arrived there, almost as much as if the occasion had involved a marriage or a funeral. The neighbours had come to say goodbye. A few of the more intimate would remain to speed Mary's departure, the others left their little gifts and good wishes and went away.

To dispose of gifts at the last moment, when one is starting on a journey to another continent, involves trouble. Mary was very busy and excited, half-laughing, half-tearful, her sisters disposed to envy her and to promise that they would join her as soon as she advised them to do so, while Mrs Willett moved about like a large and solemn Minerva, talking mournfully of wilful children and the dangers that awaited those who were ungrateful for a home.

Letty had determined to go with Mary to Nutford. She wanted her to wear the cloak on her journey to Liverpool, but she did not want her to wear it at Grimpat where it would be recognised. When she had said goodbye to her friend she would go to Marshall's and match the silk. She did not acknowledge this even to herself, but it is possible that amid her sorrow and her fears she found it not altogether unpleasant to travel half an hour side by side with Mary's brother.

The leave-takings were over at last, and Mary, a little despon-

dent, a little elated, steamed away towards the New World. Letty
watched her out of sight, wiped her tears, and then took her way
briskly towards the draper's. The practical trod hard on the heels of
the dramatic, as always happens in this mixed life of ours.

Mr Marshall could not match the silk. He said it was useless
even to attempt to do so, that the dress was one of a set purchased
in lengths and so retailed, that he bought the lot at a clearance sale
and had not the faintest idea where they had been made.

Letty thought she would faint when she received this information. Floating darkness seemed to shut the man's unimaginative
face away from her, and the breath on her lips felt cold. Mr
Marshall was frightened – he caught at her hastily across the
counter, and helped her to seat herself. 'You are not well,' he said.

'Not just too well,' she answered dully. 'I have been working very
hard lately, owing to Mr Tedford's death, you know, and then to
see Mary Willett go away has been a kind of trial. She was my old-
est friend.'

'The world is full of trouble,' said Mr Marshall. The occasion
demanded speech, and he could not think of any more apt or
apposite. Letty said nothing; she leaned her arms on the counter
and contemplated him in pale dismay.

'You don't know even if that bit of silk was French or English?'
she asked, after a pause.

'I don't know a thing about it but what I have told you. Is it very
important that it should be matched?'

'The dress length is a bit short for what I want. I can't make it
the way it was intended, unless I get three-quarters of a yard more.'

'Then you'll have to make it some other way,' the man answered
pleasantly. 'What would you say to a bit of black or a bit of pink for
trimming?'

Letty shook her head as she rose. 'No, no,' she said, 'it wouldn't
be a bit of good; nothing will be any good but just the silk itself.'

Mr Marshall looked after her as she went down the shop. 'She
works too hard,' he said, 'and she is a nice little body – getting on
too when one comes to think of it. She has been a regular customer
of mine for seven or eight years.' Then Mr Marshall sighed, though
neither he nor anyone else could have told why.

Letty went down the street like one in a dream. The cold north wind ruffled her hair and fluttered her trim skirts and blew coldly into her distended eyes. 'I am a thief,' she was saying to herself, 'a thief!' Taking the silk when she believed she could put it back scarcely seemed a liberty, much less a crime; now its aspect was altogether different.

'I wonder what I'm to do!' the girl said to herself. There were women to whom she would have gone immediately and made confession and offered anything in compensation for the missing material; but in Mrs Smith's case this was not to be thought of. Mrs Smith would simply tell the whole parish that Letty Moore was not honest or to be trusted, because she had stolen a piece of her silk gown. Then the thought of John Willett came into Letty's mind, and of how he would receive this tidings. 'What will become of me, any way?' she said.

'I'll not charge her for anything but the bare making,' said Letty. 'I'll put in all the lining and bone free, and give her value that way, and I'll line the bottom of the skirt with a bit of silk. If she notices it, I'll say I had it by me, and she is welcome to it.' Then she sighed again. It struck her already that the path of the wrong-doer is a tortuous one and Letty was very fond of plain dealing and straight ways.

When she reached home, she took out the piece of silk and looked at it. Then she began to cry in a tired way. 'To think of me being a thief; but it's just what I am. I suppose it's the way people begin to rob banks and get sent to prison. I wonder will she find out? If she doesn't I'll –' she did not know what wild condition she wanted to offer to destiny, she only knew that she was ready to promise anything provided she escaped the consequences of this one misdoing.

Meantime, Mrs Smith had also been to Nutford, and had also had an errand to John Marshall's, and thus, by one of the evil chances which overtake certain unfortunates, she sat down in the very chair poor Letty had vacated, and was welcomed by Mr Marshall with just the same smile and the same insinuating movement of the hands. Mrs Smith laid her reticule on the counter, opened it, took out her list, and spoke first of bombazine.

While Mr Marshall waited on her, she picked up abstractedly

the strip of silk Letty had left behind and wound it absent-mindedly round the finger of her cotton glove. When her purchases were effected, and she was about to open her purse, the bit of silk caught her attention for the first time.

'Another bit of my silk, Mr Marshall,' she said, unbending. 'Have you got a new consignment of them dress lengths? I wouldn't mind a black one for myself, if you have a black as good a bargain.'

Mr Marshall shook his head. 'It's a rare chance to get such goods as they were, so cheap. One doesn't do that twice in half a dozen years. I could sell them ten times over if I had more. There was a young lady in to match one of them a while ago, and she is just distracted that there is not more to be had. That's her pattern round your finger.'

'Mr Marshall,' said Mrs Smith impressively, 'you told me you had just one pink and black, and that you sold it to me, yet here's another pink and black of somebody else's!'

'Whatever I told you at the time was the truth,' said Mr Marshall, with dignity. 'There is no need to say what isn't to sell my goods.'

'But here's another pattern of the same,' Mrs Smith persisted. 'Who brought this pattern?'

'It was Miss Moore.'

'Letty Moore the dressmaker! Well, now, to think of that! Fancied my silk for herself, I suppose, and thought to match it. But you haven't another, you say? Well, I'm glad of that; set her up, indeed, with a gown like my niece's. Now she's cut this pattern off my piece. I don't call that dealing on the square, do you?'

'Miss Moore is a very respectable young woman, and wouldn't do anything she couldn't stand over, I'm sure,' said Mr Marshall with decision. 'I have done business with her for a very long time, and I have a great regard for her.'

'That's as may be, Mr Marshall; but if she's cut a pattern off my stuff, I don't call it on the square, and so I'll tell her.'

Letty was not feeling at all well that afternoon. There are mental shocks that try the sensitive as much as a period of illness. In town communities the filching of a small piece of material would not

seem a very serious matter; the culprit would regard it with indifference and the defrauded person would probably not take it very
much to heart. But Grimpat morals were very rigid; neither Letty
nor anybody else regarded a breach of the eighth commandment
lightly.

'She'll not want the gown till the spring, and in that time, maybe,
the Lord will somehow give me a chance of putting things right,'
the girl said, but she was not hopeful. Letty meant to pray very
hard and to practise divers good deeds in anxious desire of a
miracle. But instead of a miracle from the sky, came Mrs Smith up
the garden path, reticule, umbrella, and widow's weeds complete.

'I called to speak about that bit of silk that you took charge of for
my niece,' said Mrs Smith, after an interchange of greetings. She
had not failed to observe Letty's start of dismay and the sudden
pallor that followed it.

'Yes, Mrs Smith.'

'I'm not sure when my niece will be coming and so I thought I'd
as well send her the bit of stuff, and let her have it made up at
home; so I'll take it.'

'I'll send it,' said Letty, 'it's too much for you to carry.'

'Not a bit,' said Mrs Smith, 'the weight of nine yards of silk is
neither here nor there. I gave you no linings, did I?'

The girl answered 'No,' faintly.

'Then it will be lighter to carry.'

Letty went upstairs and took out the piece of silk, and folded it
neatly with hands that were as cold as ice. She knew she was going
to be found out and ruined. At the moment she wished that she
could die; if she were dead, her misdeed and Mrs Smith's comments thereon would matter less. She stood with her hands resting
on the folded parcel, waiting for some merciful miracle of this
kind, but none came. Her heart beat slowly and faintly, but it kept
on beating. When Letty saw that help would not come from this
quarter, she went downstairs.

'You've tied it up, have you?' said Mrs Smith, a little suspiciously. 'You mightn't have done that without measuring it, for
fear you might give me somebody else's piece instead of my own.'

'That's your piece, right enough,' said Letty dully. 'There was only one of that sort.' Then she clutched at her terror with desperation. 'I'll measure it for you, if you like, Mrs Smith.'

This offer reassured the elder lady. 'Not at all, Miss Moore,' she said with some cordiality. 'It's been all right in your hands, I'm sure.' Then she took her leave graciously enough.

Letty looked after the old woman's rigid figure as she walked away. 'Maybe she won't open it for a while and in the interval I will make her a present worth twice the value of what I've took. Then she'll know, if she thinks about it at all, that I've paid her back.'

But Mrs Smith was not the type of person to act in such an irrelevant manner. She took off her bonnet and shawl and gloves when she reached home, but she measured the silk before she put them away, and the silk was three-quarters of a yard short.

'One never knows people,' said the lady, nodding to herself. 'I would have thought Letty Moore as honest as the sun. Well! I'll show her up.'

Drama was rather remote from Mrs Smith's experience, but she saw a good many dramatic possibilities in the present situation, and they exhilarated her. Herself as a confiding and defrauded person, Letty Moore as an abashed culprit, who had long traded on the good faith of the community, and the whole of Grimpat for an admiring audience, afforded a striking situation. Mrs Smith banked up the fire with ashes, because she intended to be absent some time; then she went back to Letty Moore's.

Letty was sitting behind the geraniums by the window. She did not feel able to work that evening, and so was thankful that work was rather slack. Thus it happened that she saw Mrs Smith come in at the little gate. At the moment she was not able to meet her; like a terrified child she ran upstairs and hid her face in the pillow of her little bed.

Mrs Smith knocked till she was tired, then she lifted the door latch and entered. The kitchen was empty, but the worthy woman concluded that Letty was at home, otherwise she would not have left the door on the latch. She therefore sat down to await her appearance.

Letty had heard the knocking. The lifting of the latch was a softer sound, and did not reach her. In the protracted silence which followed she concluded that Mrs Smith had gone away, and so, after a time, she picked up courage to descend the stairs. But Mrs Smith was sitting in wait for her at the stair-foot.

The good woman had rehearsed every form of accusation in the interval, and had thought of saying, 'You stole my silk, give me back my silk,' but at sight of the girl, a milder mood came over her, and she said, politely enough, 'I called about that silk, it seems shorter than when I left it with you.'

'It couldn't be shorter, Mrs Smith,' said Letty, looking at her antagonist with terrified eyes. 'What could make it shorter?'

'That's what I don't know,' said the visitor firmly. 'I only know that I gave you nine yards of silk, and that you gave me back eight and a quarter. I know, too, that you were trying to match it, for I found the pattern at Marshall's.'

Letty sat down, her hands lying listlessly in her lap, her face pale and stricken. People have committed a murder and felt less over-whelmed, at the moment of arrest, than did honest, upright little Letty Moore, in the face of the knowledge that she was discovered to have 'conveyed' three-quarters of a yard of cheap silk.

'I needn't deny that I took it, Mrs Smith, since you know all about it, she said slowly. 'I didn't know it was a dress length. I thought it had been cut off the piece and that I could match it, I knew it came from Marshall's.'

'And what did you want with my silk – what had you to do with it?' said Mrs Smith, her anger rising. 'It was stealing, whatever you say.'

'I had promised Mary Willett a hood, but with Mr Tedford's death and all, I was kept busy until the last minute. When I went to buy the silk the shops were all closed. If they had been Grimpat shops, I would have knocked and made them open, but I couldn't do that at Nutford. I felt as if I couldn't break my word to Mary. Your silk was here in the house and when I was looking for some-thing that would do I came on it. I thought if I took what I wanted off it I could put it back the next day, but Mr Marshall says it can't be matched. I am quite willing to make it good to you in any way you like.'

'I'll have my bit of silk or nothing,' said Mrs Smith frigidly. 'I don't want your money or your trimmings or your matchings. I just want my material back again, and I'll have it or I'll know why.'

Letty said nothing, but her silence and her stricken attitude, instead of mollifying Mrs Smith, goaded her to fury.

'If there's law in the land or in the Church,' she went on, her voice rising, 'I'll take the mask off your face – a meek, pretentious, whited sepulchre. To think of the gowns and cloaks, and linings folk have entrusted to you, Letty Moore, believing in you as if you were the Gospel. It's easy to see now how you came to be so well-to-do, with three-quarters off here, and a yard off there, but I'll open people's eyes.'

Letty rose and stood before her accuser.

'You'll have to do what you think right,' she said, in a suffering, toneless voice. 'I never took a thread or a hook-and-eye belonging to living woman in my life before. I have told you just the truth of how I came to do it this time.'

Mrs Smith gave a snort of infinite scorn.

'Every thief who is caught says it was the first time. We'll see how many folks have missed things when I show you up. And you teaching in the Sabbath School, too! Well, next Sabbath you can teach the eighth commandment. To think of such a – a whited sepulchre!' In her vocabulary Mrs Smith could not at the moment find another term as scathing. As she spoke she went out and banged the door heavily behind her.

Letty resumed the seat she had quitted and leaning her elbows on the table, took her face between her hands. She felt quite cold and her pulse beat in languid throbs. Mrs Smith would tell everyone that she had stolen her silk and one and another would come to think in time that she had always been dishonest. It would ruin her business, but a hundred times worse than that it would ruin her good name. To think of all the people who trusted her learning that she was a thief! To think of the minister and John Willett and his mother, who in her own way had been disposed to favour her! The talk would creep to Nutford, too, and Mr Marshall, who had always thought so well of her as a customer, would probably set someone in future to watch her when she entered, lest she should secrete the reels of cotton or remnants of ribbon that were lying loose.

At this thought two slow tears of bitter suffering ran slowly the length of her pale cheeks.

'God knows I didn't mean to steal,' she said aloud and the tones fell curiously on the still air. 'God knows I never defrauded man or woman before of anything in all the days of my life.' Then after a long pause she added, 'There is always God.'

She faced the position with despairing patience. Even God could not bring her blamelessly through it, because she had taken the piece of silk. She *was* guilty. Had she been wrongly accused, she would have met whatever followed, confidently foreseeing her ultimate justification. But for the guilty justification was impossible. 'I can never hold up my head again,' she said blankly.

After a little, the sense of physical prostration passing away, she rose and resorted to her needlework mechanically. But it dropped from her limp hands – she felt too tired, too stupid, and uninterested.

It was towards dusk when the door opened and the minister came in. The moment she saw him Letty knew what he had come to speak about.

Mr Witherow was a tall, slim man with a clearly-cut and rather rigid face, a face to which anxieties about his congregation had added as many lines as the years had done. In creed Mr Witherow was a Calvinist, of the Calvinists, whose idea of Heaven and Immortality and the Day of Judgment were as clearly defined as his knowledge of weekday and sacrament services. Mr Witherow had never doubted once in his whole lifetime that at the Day of Judgment he would be called by name to answer before the assembled nations for each individual member of the congregation committed to his charge.

In his dreams Mr Witherow frequently heard himself asked in a voice that was like a thunder-peal, 'Richard Witherow, what of Andrew Wilson? Richard Witherow, what of William Dart, committed to you in the long past?' This made him thankful for his congregation was small. It made the attendant anxieties less and showed him a shorter period of reckoning on the Dread Day. But he kept his life here very strenuous, and it loaded him with a sense of personal responsibility that is not generally felt in the profession.

'I have had a visit from Mrs Smith,' the minister began simply. 'She is in a terrible state about three-quarters of a yard of silk that she says you cut off her dress length.'

'I took it,' said Letty slowly. 'I told her I took it.'

Mr Witherow inclined his head sorrowfully. 'I did not mean to steal and she knows that,' Letty pursued steadily. 'I offered her any compensation she would accept.'

'She wishes to have you made an example of. She says you ought to be excommunicated,' said Mr Witherow. And his thought was as serious as his words.

'If you will sit down, sir, I will tell you how it happened,' said Letty, 'and then if you think well to cut me off from the means of grace – I sha'n't complain.' Then she told all the story over again, amid slow, unheeded tears.

'It is very unfortunate,' Mr Witherow said, with a sigh, when she had concluded. 'To borrow a piece of silk without leave was a very small thing in itself but it is an opening of the door of evil. When people borrow money in that way, meaning to put it back, the act sometimes brings them penal servitude.'

Letty gave a shudder. 'I have been thinking it all out,' she said, 'in old times people were hanged for as little as this.'

'Indeed yes,' said the minister thoughtfully, 'people were hanged or transported for the merest trifles. A man got fourteen years' penal servitude once and died under sentence, for stealing a potato-pie. We have reason to thank God we are not so cruel nowadays.'

'I suppose she could have me arrested?' said Letty in a dreary voice.

'I dare say she could, and fined, but I don't think she will though I hold her to be a rather bad kind of Christian; she only wants to expose you, and she will do that, talking among the neighbours.'

'I think the best thing I can do is to restore sevenfold and then go away from here,' the girl said huskily. 'I'll make as good a living among strangers as I can do at Grimpat, once I have lost my character and I would rather not wait for the old neighbours to give me the cold shoulder. I meant no harm, God knows, but I'll have to take the consequences of doing harm, all the same.'

'When Mrs Smith came I reasoned with her,' said the minister slowly. 'I told her she was showing a very bad spirit, even if you were guilty, which I did not believe. I talked to her very seriously.' Then he rose to go. 'I will talk to her again,' he said. 'Have you any objection that I should offer to restore sevenfold? The Scriptures do not speak of more, and fourfold was generally held to be sufficient.'

'A hundredfold,' said Letty with a sob. 'I have a little money saved in all these years. I'll give her anything she asks.'

Mr Witherow felt very depressed as he walked down the road, not so much by the thought of Letty's individual suffering as at the thought of all the suffering that so often follows inadequate causes. 'No doubt it is because she belongs to the elect that her first step astray is punished so sĕverely,' he said with a sigh. Mr Witherow firmly believed that the path of the elect here was thick with thorns, but in compensation he held that these made for the safety of pedestrians towards the Kingdom. Then his thoughts reverted to Mrs Smith. She certainly was an unlovely Christian, but she had been placed in his care, and he was responsible for her. Her unloveliness would not justify him if he had one day to answer 'I do not know' to the question 'Richard Witherow, what has become of Sarah Smith?'

'I'll tell her of Letty's offer,' he said. 'If she declines to accept it, I'll excommunicate her for her lack of charity, and that will surprise her more than losing her silk,' he added, smiling for the first time.

Mrs Smith was having tea when Mr Witherow called on her. She was looking bright and animated, because she anticipated interesting results from the several calls she intended to pay before bed-time.

Mr Witherow took off his hat as he entered, but he did not accept the seat Mrs Smith indicated, not intending to unbend to the intimacy implied in a sitting attitude.

'I have been to see Miss Moore,' he began gravely, 'and I have learned all particulars regarded your loss. Miss Moore is willing to restore the value of the silk sevenfold. What is its value?'

'The piece cost twenty-seven shillings.'

'Then let us assume that what she took, borrowed under a misapprehension actually, is worth half-a-crown. In lieu of that, she authorises me to offer you seventeen-and-sixpence.'

'I won't take it,' said Mrs Smith triumphantly. 'I would rather show her up than have the price of twenty silk dresses.'

'If you don't accept Miss Moore's offer,' said the minister imperturbably, 'I will summon you before the Session. A woman who would want to destroy the character and prospects of a girl who has lived in our midst since childhood and is a credit to the community –'

'A canting publican,' interrupted Mrs Smith.

'A credit to the community,' Mr Witherow repeated firmly. 'The woman who would want to destroy her and her prospects for a half-a-crown matter, is not only a bad Christian, but a bad woman.'

'Me!' said Mrs Smith, with a shriek.

'If the matter comes before the Session, we shall have no option but to excommunicate you,' Mr Witherow went on. 'It will be a great grief to your children in America to learn that the church in which their father was an elder has been obliged to excommunicate their mother. It will be a blot on the family history.'

'I want nothing but my own again, I have a right to that,' Mrs Smith maintained stoutly, but the usual colour of her cheek looked thin and veinous, and her breath came hurriedly.

'To restore your own little bit of silk is impossible under the circumstances. Miss Moore acknowledges that she took it. The Bible exacts nothing but confession and fourfold restitution. Miss Moore offers sevenfold. You had better accept her offer.'

'She's got you on her side,' said Mrs Smith bitterly. 'A sleek, canting. . .'

'Mrs Smith,' said the minister, 'I hope I shall always be found on the side of the merciful. I desire nothing better either now or at the Last Day. The wish to ruin a poor young friendless girl could only be prompted by the devil and as a minister of the Gospel I will oppose it in every corner of the parish. This is my last word. I am very sorry that a woman of your age, so long held in esteem by the neighbours, should have ever wished to act such a cruel and evil part. Good evening.'

Mr Witherow had scarcely reached the little gate outside the cottage ere Mrs Smith was after him. 'I will take that seventeen-and-sixpence.'

Mr Witherow turned. 'Do you understand what that binds you to?' he asked. 'If you accept restitution and subsequently talk of your loss you will be guilty of slander, a serious offence in the eyes of the law of the land.'

'I wouldn't be bothered with it,' said Mrs Smith fiercely. 'To tie one hand and foot and tongue, and everything, and call this a free country too!'

Mr Witherow laid his hand on the old woman's trembling shoulder. 'Mrs Smith,' he said, 'your husband was one of the elders of my congregation when I was ordained. His was a gentle and beautiful nature. He was one of the Elect, his memory is yet fragrant in our midst. You are yourself a woman, the mother of other women. You have been young. Possibly that experience is not so remote that you are unable to recall it.

'Try on that account to feel generously and, because of all that is honourable in your life-history, to act generously towards a sister woman. No one ever regrets a good deed, while a deliberate cruelty cannot fail to plant a sharp thorn in that last pillow on which each of us must ultimately lay his or her dying head. You have now an opportunity of behaving nobly and making me proud of you. I will leave it to yourself to think whether or not you will embrace the opportunity.'

Towards eight o'clock Letty Moore was reading her Bible; there are times when people find that the only refuge. 'I will lift up my eyes unto the hills, from whence cometh my help,' she read aloud. She did so, she turned her face involuntarily towards the window, but it was night and the blind was down. At that moment there came a peremptory knock to the door. Letty opened it, and Mrs Smith came in. To see the girl quail at her approach gave the old woman her last moment of evil pleasure.

'I came to speak about the silk,' she said.

Letty did not answer. She only waited for the terrible announcement that was likely to follow. 'I was thinking that maybe you might like to buy the whole of it,' she went on. 'It cost twenty-seven shillings new – you can have it for that.'

Mrs Smith was surprised and a little dismayed at the passion of Letty's sudden burst of tears. 'You are a good woman,' she said between her sobs, 'a good, good woman, though I thought hard things about you! I suppose it was because I was that miserable. You are a good woman!'

Letty always maintained that nobody knew the greatness of Mrs Smith's nature till there was occasion to test it. In proof of her greatness she adduced that Mrs Smith hated to be praised. When Letty married John Willett, Mrs Smith sat beside the minister at the wedding-feast. Beyond the circle of those three, there never crept a whisper of Letty's misdoing. It is the solitary secret the latter ever kept from her husband.

As to the piece of silk, it still lies in Letty's best-room bottom drawer, and when she wants to remind herself that well-meaning people may go far astray under sudden temptation or that human hearts are often kinder than the careless would believe, she takes out the piece of silk and looks at it.

A Rich Woman

Katharine Tynan

Katharine Tynan was born in 1861 and grew up on a farm in Clondalkin, County Dublin. Although her only formal education was obtained during a six-year stay at a Drogheda convent school, she was naturally bookish, read widely and began to write at an early age, despite eye troubles which left her with permanently impaired sight. A member of the Ladies' Land League as a young woman, Tynan presided over a well-known literary salon in the 1880's. With her friend W. B. Yeats, Tynan was an important member of the early circle of the Irish Literary Renaissance. Her inclusion in *Poems and Ballads of Young Ireland* and her collection *Louise de la Valliere* (London: Kegan Paul, Trench, 1885) combined to give her a reputation as the most promising of all the young Irish poets of the time.

Tynan's move to London on her marriage coincided with an ever-widening sphere of publications to which she contributed. Her voluminous correspondence, five volumes of memoirs and thousands of articles, interviews, reviews and sketches reflect a gradual distancing of close Irish ties and an increasing view of writing as a job rather than an art. She herself regarded her fiction as pot-boiling and her poetry as the true expression of her best work.

Of her 105 novels, there is not even one which could be considered especially good, though *The Playground* (London: Ward, Lock, 1932) is of interest because it, even more than her other novels, has distinct autobiographical elements. Tynan is remembered for her poetry: *The Wind in the Trees* (London: Grant Richards, 1898) is one of her best volumes. *The Poems of Katherine (sic) Tynan,* edited, with an introduction by Monk Gibbon (Dublin: Allen Figgis, 1963), is probably the most accessible book of her poems. Like most of Tynan's short stories, 'A Rich Woman' is better in general than her novels; with its blend of quiet humour and narrative control, it is, like all of her best stories, indicative of Tynan's very real skill as a story-teller, though she has never been seriously regarded as such.

Katharine Tynan died in 1931. Her work has not received much critical attention in proportion to her output. Ann Connerton Fallon's *Katharine Tynan* (Boston: Twayne, 1979) is the best general introduction to her life and work.

MARGRET LAFFAN was something of a mystery to the Island people. Long ago in comparative youth she had disappeared for a

half-dozen years. Then she had turned up one day in a coarse dress
of blue and white check, which looked suspiciously like workhouse
or asylum garb, and had greeted such of the neighbours as she
knew with a nod, for all the world as if she had seen them yesterday. It happened that the henwife at the Hall had been buried a day
or two earlier, and when Margret came asking a place from Mrs
Wilkinson, the lord's housekeeper, the position was yet unfilled
and Margret got it.

Not every one would have cared for the post. Only a misan-
thropic person indeed would have been satisfied with it. The henwife's cottage and the poultry settlement might have been many
miles from a human habitation, so lonely were they. They were in a
glen of red sandstone, and half the wood lay between them and the
Hall. The great red walls stood so high round the glen that you
could not even hear the sea calling. As for the village, it was a long
way below. You had to go down a steep path from the glen before
you came to an open space, where you could see the reek of the
chimneys under you. Every morning Margret brought the eggs
and the trussed chickens to the Hall. But no one disturbed her soli-
tude, except when the deer or the wild little red cattle came
gazing curiously through the netting at Margret and her charges.
There, for twenty-seven years, Margret lived with no company but
the fowl. On Sundays and holidays she went to mass to the Island
Chapel, but gave no encouragement to those who would have gone
a step of the road home with her. The Island women used to wonder how she could bear the loneliness. – 'Why, God be betune us
and harm!' they often said, 'Sure the crathur might be robbed and
murdhered any night of the year and no wan the wiser.' And so she
might, if the Island possessed robbers and murderers in its midst.
But it is a primitively innocent little community, which sleeps with
open doors as often as not, and there is nothing to tempt maraud-
ers or even beggars to migrate there.

By and by a feeling got about that Margret must be saving
money. Her wage as a henwife was no great thing, but then, as they
said, 'she looked as if she lived on the smell of an oil-rag,' and there
was plenty of food to be had in the Hall kitchen, where Margret
waited with her eggs and fowl every morning. Certainly her

clothes, though decent, were well-nigh threadbare. But the feelers that the neighbours sent out towards Margret met with no solid assurance. Grim and taciturn, Margret kept her own counsel, and was like enough to keep it till the day of her death.

Jack Laffan, Margret's brother, is the village carpenter, a sociable poor man, not the least bit in the world like his sister. Jack is rather fond of idling over a glass with his cronies in the public-house, but, as he is well under Mrs Jack's thumb, the habit is not likely to grow on him inconveniently. There are four daughters and a son, a lad of fifteen or thereabouts. Two of the daughters are domestic servants out in the big world, and are reported to wear streamers to their caps and fine lace aprons every day. Another is handmaiden to Miss Bell at the post office, and knows the contents of all the letters, except Father Tiernay's, before the people they belong to. Fanny is at home with her father and mother, and is supposed to be too fond of fal-lals, pinchbeck brooches and 'cheap ribbons, which come to her from her sisters out in the world. She often talks of emigration, and is not sought after by the young men of the Island, who regard her as a 'vain paycocky thing'.

Mrs Jack has the reputation of being a hard, managing woman. There was never much love lost between her and Margret, and when the latter came back from her six years' absence on the mainland, Mrs Jack's were perhaps the most ill-natured surmises as to the reasons for Margret's silence and the meaning of that queer checked garb.

For a quarter of a century Margret lived among her fowl, untroubled by her kin. Then the talk about the money grew from little beginnings like a snowball. It fired Mrs Jack with a curious excitement, for she was an ignorant woman and ready to believe any extravagant story. She amazed Jack by putting the blame of their long ignoring of Margret on his shoulders entirely, and when he stared at her, dumbfounded, she seized and shook him till his teeth rattled. 'You great stupid omadhaun!' she hissed between the shakes, 'that couldn't have the nature in you to see to your own sister, an' she a lone woman!'

That very day Jack went off stupidly to try to bridge over with Margret the gulf of nearly thirty years. He got very little help from his sister. She watched him with what seemed like grim enjoyment while he wriggled miserably on the edge of his chair and tried to talk naturally. At length he jerked out his wife's invitation to have a bit of dinner with them on the coming Sunday, which Margret accepted without showing any pleasure, and then he bolted.

Margret came to dinner on the Sunday, and was well entertained with a fat chicken and a bit of bacon, for the Laffans were well-to-do people. She thoroughly enjoyed her dinner, though she spoke little and that little monosyllabic; but Margret was taciturn even as a girl, and her solitary habit for years seemed to have made speech more difficult for her. Mrs Jack heaped her plate with great heartiness and made quite an honoured guest of her. But outside enjoying the dinner Margret did not seem to respond. Young Jack was brought forward to display his accomplishments, which he did in the most hang-dog fashion. The cleverness and good-looks and goodness of the girls were expatiated upon, but Margret gave no sign of interest. Once Fanny caught her looking at her with a queer saturnine glance, that made her feel all at once hot and uncomfortable, though she had felt pretty secure of her smartness before that. Margret's reception of Mrs Jack's overtures did not satisfy that enterprising lady. When she had departed Mrs Jack put her down as 'a flinty-hearted ould maid'. 'Her sort,' she declared, 'is ever an' always sour an' bitther to them the Lord blesses wid a family.' But all the same it became a regular thing for Margret to eat her Sunday dinner with the Laffans, and Mrs Jack discovered after a time that the good dinners were putting a skin and roundness on Margret that might give her a new lease of life – perhaps a not quite desirable result.

The neighbours looked on at Mrs Jack's 'antics' with something little short of scandal. They met by twos and threes to talk over it, and came to the conclusion that Mrs Jack had no shame at all, at all, in her pursuit of the old woman's money. Truth to tell, there was scarcely a woman in the Island but thought she had as good a right to Margret's money as her newly-attentive kinsfolk. Mrs Devine and Mrs Cahill might agree in the morning, with many shakings of the head, that 'Liza Laffan's avarice and greed were beyond measure loathsome. Yet neither seemed pleased to see the other a little later in the day, when Mrs Cahill climbing the hill with a full basket met Mrs Devine descending with an empty one.

For all of a sudden a pilgrimage to Margret's cottage in the Red Glen became the recognised thing. It was surprising how old childish friendships and the most distant ties of kindred were furbished up and brought into the light of day. The grass in the lane to the glen became trampled to a regular track. If the women themselves did not come panting up the hill they sent the little girsha, or wee Tommy or Larry, with a little fish, or a griddle cake, or a few fresh greens for Margret. The men of the Island were somewhat scornful of these proceedings on the part of their dames; but as a rule the Island wives hold their own and do pretty well as they will. All this friendship for Margret created curious divisions and many enmities.

Margret, indeed, throve on all the good things, but whether any one person was in her favour more than another it would be impossible to say. Margret got up a way of thanking all alike in a honeyed voice that had a queer sound of mockery in it, and after a time some of the more independent spirits dropped out of the chase, 'pitching,' as they expressed it, 'her ould money to the divil.' Mrs Jack was fairly confident all the time that if any one on the Island got Margret's nest-egg it would be herself, but she had a misgiving which she imparted to her husband that the whole might go to Father Tiernay for charities. Any attempt at getting inside the shell which hid Margret's heart from the world her sister-in-law had long given up. She had also given up trying to interest Margret in 'the childher', or bidding young Jack be on his best behaviour before the Sunday guest. The young folk didn't like the derision in Margret's pale eyes, and kept out of her way as much as possible, since they feared their mother too much to flout her openly, as they were often tempted to do.

Two or three years had passed before Margret showed signs of failing. Then at the end of one very cold winter people noticed that she grew feebler. She was away from mass one or two Sundays, and then one Sunday she reappeared walking with the aid of a stick and looking plainly ill and weak. After mass she had a private talk with Father Tiernay at the presbytery; and then went slowly down to

Jack's house for the usual dinner. Both Jack and Mrs Jack saw her home in the afternoon, and a hard task the plucky old woman found it, for all their assistance, to get back to her cottage up the steep hill. When they had reached the top she paused for a rest. Then she said quietly, 'I'm thinkin' I'll make no more journeys to the Chapel. Father Tiernay'll have to be coming to me instead.'

'Tut, tut, woman dear,' said Mrs Jack, with two hard red spots coming into her cheeks, 'we'll be seein' you about finely when the weather gets milder.' And then she insinuated in a wheedling voice something about Margret's affairs being settled.

Margret looked up at her with a queer mirthfulness in her glance. 'Sure what wud a poor ould woman like me have to settle? Sure that's what they say when a sthrong farmer takes to dyin'.'

Mrs Jack was too fearful of possible consequences to press the matter. She was anxious that Margret should have Fanny to look after the house and the fowl for her, but this Margret refused. 'I'll be able to do for myself a little longer,' she said, 'an' thank you kindly all the same.'

When it was known that Margret was failing, the attentions to her became more urgent. Neighbours passed each other now in the lane with a toss of the head and 'a wag of the tail'. As for Mrs Jack, who would fain have installed herself altogether in the henwife's cottage, she spent her days quivering with indignation at the meddlesomeness of the other women. She woke Jack up once in the night with a fiery declaration that she'd speak to Father Tiernay about the pursuit of her moneyed relative, but Jack threw cold water on that scheme. 'Sure his Riverince himself, small blame to him, 'ud be as glad as another to have the bit. 'Twould be buildin' him the new schoolhouse he's wantin' this many a day, so it would.' And this suggestion made Mrs Jack look askance at her pastor, as being also in the running for the money.

It was surprising how many queer presents found their way to Margret's larder in those days. They who had not the most suitable gift for an invalid brought what they had, and Margret received them all with the same inscrutability. She might have been provisioning for a siege. Mrs Jack's chickens were flanked by a coarse bit of American bacon; here was a piece of salt ling, there some

potatoes in a sack; a slice of salt butter was side by side with a
griddle cake. Many a good woman appreciated the waste of good
food even while she added to it, and sighed after that full larder for
the benefit of her man and the weans at home; but all the time
there was the dancing marsh-light of Margret's money luring the
good souls on. There had never been any organised robbery in the
Island since the cattle-lifting of the kernes long ago; but many a
good woman fell of a tremble now when she thought of Margret
and her 'stocking' alone through the silent night, and at the mercy
of midnight robbers.

There was not a day that several offerings were not laid at Margret's feet. But suddenly she changed her stereotyped form of
thanks to a mysterious utterance, 'You're maybe feeding more than
you know, kind neighbours,' was the dark saying that set the
women conjecturing about Margret's sanity.

Then the bolt fell. One day a big angular, shambling girl, with
Margret's suspicious eyes and cynical mouth, crossed by the ferry
to the Island. She had a trunk, which Barney Ryder, general carrier
to the Island, would have lifted to his asscart, but the new-comer
scornfully waved him away. 'Come here, you two gorsoons,' she
said, seizing upon young Jack Laffan and a comrade who were gazing at her grinning, 'take a hoult o' the thrunk an' lead the way to
Margret Laffan's in the Red Glen. I'll crack sixpence betune yez
when I get there.' The lads, full of curiousity, lifted up the trunk,
and preceded her up the mile or so of hill to Margret's. She stalked
after them into the sunny kitchen where Margret sat waiting,
handed them the sixpence when they had put down the trunk,
bundled them out and shut the door before she looked towards
Margret in her chimney-corner.

The explanation came first from his Reverence, who was walking in the evening glow, when Mrs Jack Laffan came flying
towards him with her cap-strings streaming.

'Little Jack has a quare story, yer Riverince,' she cried out panting, 'about a girl's come visitin' ould Margret in the glen, an' wid a
thrunk as big as a house. Him an' little Martin was kilt draggin' it
up the hill.'

His Reverence waved away her excitement gently.

'I know all about it,' he said. 'Indeed I've been the means in a way of restoring Margret's daughter to her. You never knew your sister-in-law was married, Mrs Laffan? An odd woman to drop her married name. We must call her by it in future. Mrs Conneely is the name.'

But Mrs Jack, with an emotion which even the presence of his Reverence could not quell, let what the neighbours described after-wards as a 'screech out of her fit to wake the dead', and fled into her house, where on her bed she had an attack which came as near being hysterical as the strong-minded woman could compass. She only recovered when Mrs Devine and Mrs Cahill and the widow Mulvany, running in, proposed to drench her with cold water, when her heels suddenly left off drumming and she stood up, very determinedly, and bade them be off about their own business. She always spoke afterwards of Margret as the robber of the widow and orphan, which was satisfying if not quite appropriate.

We all heard afterwards how Margret had married on the main-land, and after this girl was born had had an attack of mania, for which she was placed in the county asylum. In time she was declared cured, and it was arranged that her husband should come for her on a certain day and remove her; but Margret, having had enough of marriage and its responsibilities, left the asylum quietly before that day came and made her way to the Island. She had been well content to be regarded as a spinster till she felt her health fail-ing, and then she had entrusted to Father Tiernay her secret, and he had found her daughter for her.

Margret lived some months after that, and left at the time of her death thirty pounds to the fortunate heiress. The well-stocked lar-der had sufficed the two for quite a long time without any recourse to 'the stocking.' There was very little further friendship between the village and the Red Glen. Such of the neighbours as were led there at first by curiosity found the door shut in their faces, for Mary had Margret's suspiciousness many times intensified. After the Laffan family had recovered from the first shock of disappoint-ment Fanny made various approaches to her cousin when she met her at mass on the Sundays, and, unheeding rebuffs, sent her a brooch and an apron at Christmas. I wish I could have seen Mar-

gret's face and Mary's over that present. It was returned to poor
Fanny, with a curt intimation that Mary had no use for it, and there
the matter ended.

I once asked Mary, when I knew her well enough to take the
liberty, about that meeting between her and her mother, after the
door was shut on young Jack's and little Martin's departing
footsteps. 'Well,' said Mary, 'she looked hard at me, an' then she
said, "You've grown up yalla an' bad-lookin', but a strong girl for
the work. You favour meself, though I've a genteeler nose." And
then,' said Mary, 'I turned in an' boiled the kettle for the tay.'

The money did not even remain in the Island, for as soon as
Margret was laid in a grave in the Abbey – with a vacant space
beside her, for, said Mary, 'you couldn't tell but I'd be takin' a fancy
to be buried there myself some day,' – Mary fled in the early morning before the neighbours were about. Mary looked on the Island
where so many had coveted her money as a 'nest of robbers', and so
she fled, with 'the stocking' in the bosom of her gown, one morning
at low tide. She wouldn't trust the money to the post office in the
Island, because her cousin Lizzie was Miss Bell's servant. 'Divil a
letther but the priest's they don't open an' read,' she said, 'an' tells
the news afterwards to the man or woman that owns it. The news
gets to them before the letter. An' if I put the fortune in there I'm
doubtin' 'twould ever see London. I know an honest man in the
Whiterock post office I'd betther be trustin'.'

And that is how Margret's 'stocking' left the Island.

At The River's Edge

Violet Martin

Violet Florence Martin, better known as Martin Ross, the pseudonym under which she collaborated with her cousin Edith Somerville, was born into an old Anglo-Irish Ascendancy family at Ross House, County Galway, in 1862. On the death of her father and the closure of Ross House, Martin, aged ten, went with her mother and sisters to live in Dublin. The meeting with Somerville, in 1886, changed both their lives: Martin's writing acquired direction, and by the time that the family returned to live in Galway two years later, the cousins' literary partnership was well established.

After the success of *The Real Charlotte* (London: Ward and Downey, 1894), the cousins wrote several other novels and travel books, and began to plan another major novel. But Martin's serious injuries in a hunting accident in 1898, and her subsequent declining health, precluded such a work. Instead, the comic-story series *Some Experiences of an Irish R.M.* (London: Longmans and Green, 1899) emerged, bringing the pair international success and wide fame.

By the time that Martin died, in 1915, the collaboration had begun to be recognised as important for its depiction of a fast-disappearing way of life; Martin was posthumously honoured in a joint honorary D.Litt. which was conferred on the partners in 1932. The Somerville and Ross collaboration continues to attract critical attention, and *The Real Charlotte* is now considered to be one of the masterpieces of nineteenth-century fiction. Maurice Collis' *Somerville and Ross, A Biography* (London: Faber and Faber, 1968) is a joint literary biography of the cousins.

'At the River's Edge', a lyrical reflection of peasant life that is, at the same time, without romantic sentiment, is one of the few examples of Martin writing on her own. The communication between the story's two women, who are from such different worlds, demonstrates Martin's own experience of the two cultures and is a rare portrait of the way in which vastly dissimilar lives are brought together through the shared experience of womanhood.

IT HAPPENED to me to spend a winter night in the company of Anastasia.

It was in a village on the border of Connemara; we sat by the fire, and talked intermittently during our spell of watching. I did not wholly care for Anastasia, but she was companionable, and her interest in others was so abounding that it often overflowed as sympathy; that she was at all times a sympathetic talker went without saying. In the West of Ireland that is so ordinary a matter as not to be noticeable, until some withering experiences in other lands place it in its proper light. She was, of course, an Irish speaker by nature and by practice, but her English was fluent, and was set to the leisurely chant of West Galway; in time of need it could serve her purpose like slings and arrows. In all her sixty years she had never been beyond the town of Galway, and she was illiterate, two potent factors in her agreeability.

Everything about her was clumsy, except her large, watchful grey eyes; I have never seen a cow seat itself in an armchair, but I imagine that it would do so in the manner of Anastasia. She smoothed her clean blue apron over a skirt that was less clean than it, and continued to drop a few pebbles of talk into the dark pool of the midnight. Like pebbles they sank, and the midnight took them greedily into its deeps, because they were concerned with spiritual things.

'I wouldn't believe in fairies meself, but as for thim Connemara people, they'd believe anything.'

Nothing was more certain than that Anastasia did believe in fairies, but it would have been impolite on my part to traverse a statement made to suit the standard of an auditor who could read books, and had travelled beyond Galway town.

'Out where me mother's people live, there's a big rock near the sea, and they say the fairies has a house inside in it. They have some owld talk that ye'd hear the children crying when the fairies does be bringing them in it.'

Anastasia blew a sigh through her broad nostrils, vaguely religious, compassionate for the darkness of the Connemara people; to exhibit freely the devoutness which she indeed possessed was a gift bestowed upon her by nature. I asked her what she thought about the origin of the fairies.

'It's what they say, the fairies was the fallen angels, and when they were threw out of Heaven, they asked might they stay on the earth, and they got leave. 'Tis best for me go stir the grool.'

In the silence that followed, while the gruel was being stirred, the low yet eager voice of the river outside made itself heard. The hazy full moon stared upon the water, and the water answered with glitter and with swirl, as it fled through the trance of the January night. The Galway river races under its bridges like a pack of white hounds; this little river, its blood relation, runs like a troop of playing children.

'But there's quare things do happen,' resumed Anastasia, sitting down again with the caution that comes of perfect acquaintance with three-legged stools and four-legged stools on hilly mud floors. 'There was a woman near me own village, and she seen me one Sunday evening coming over the road, and a bag of turf on me back, and she said I stood up agin' a big white rock that's in it, as I'd be resting the bag on the rock. Sure not a bit of me was next or nigh the place. But not a bit in the world happened me afther it, thanks be to God.'

Anastasia sighed, in modest acceptance of her favoured position.

'It wasn't only two days afther that agin, there was a man from the same village seen me the same way. He thought to go over to a place he had his cattle, to look at them, and he said when he was starting out he seen meself coming over the road, and a bag of turf on me back, and he turned back; sure he knew I'd tell him how was the cattle.'

The man was confident in Anastasia, as he would have been in any other woman of his acquaintance: he knew that she would look at his cattle as she passed, and that she would also be able to tell him how they were; this was a matter of course in their lives.

'Sure, I wasn't in the place at all, but whatever was in it, the Lord save us, he seen the woman, and he knew well it was meself, and she coming to him, and she in a valley, and it was the fall of the evening in harvest-time.'

Her heavy face had not changed, and the rhythm of her quiet speech had neither hastened nor slackened, yet the reaped fields and the dusk must have been before her eyes, must have seemed inevitable to the story. Better than 'dusk' or twilight', or any other motionless word, was 'the fall of the evening' – the dew was in it, and the gentleness, and the folding of wings. There was that in the diction that summoned suddenly to mind the Shunamite, and the child who went out with his father to the reapers. Anastasia had never, I felt sure, heard of the Shunamitish woman, yet, had I read the story to her, she would instantly have understood that strong heart, and its pride and grief and rapture. Human nature was as clear to her as to the other illiterate people of her village and countryside, and, like them, she had the scriptural method of narrative, that curves on its way like running water, and sinks to its one and inevitable channel. I bethought me of the theory that the original Irish race, or some constituent of it, came from a southern shore of the Mediterranean; and all the while the boots of Anastasia confronted me, planted at the edge of the turf ashes on the hearth, like boulders on a foamy beach.

'But that woman that seen me the first time,' she resumed, 'she was a little strange that way in her mind, and when she came to live inside here in the town they said she drew a great many of Thim Things round the place. You'd hear them walking round the doors at night. Well, there's many a quare thing like that, and ye wouldn't know –'

The narrative faded out in murmurs that seemed to be both apologetic and religious, intended, I think, to present a proper diplomatic attitude towards all the powers of darkness. Anastasia lived by herself outside the village, in a crooked cabin with a broken door; she did well to recognise officially the existence of Thim Things. Her brother, over whose establishment she had once reigned, had married, and his wife was not favourable to Anastasia; that she herself had not married was not an unusual state of affairs, but it implied no slur upon her attractions, nor did it imply the blighted love affair. Marriage, not flirtation, is the concern of Anastasia's social circle; the creature that we indulgently and sympathetically term Passion is by them flogged to kennel under another name.

Looking at Anastasia, I remembered a summer evening when I went to a Mission Service in a white-washed chapel, and saw the burly mission priest standing before the altar in his soutane, with the biretta forming an uncompromising summit to a square and threatening countenance of the bulldog type. The seatless floor of the chapel was covered with kneeling women and girls, in dun-coloured shawls or fashionable hats; the men stood at the back and along the walls, where the reds and blues of the stations of the cross flared forth their story. Even in their crude presentment of anguish, they seemed to say, 'It is sown in weakness,' but the oratory of the missioner was a thunderstorm above them. Young men and women were not to walk together in wood, or lanes, or after nightfall; the matter was made very clear, and was illustrated with stories appropriate to it. The audience was eager in the up-take, pliant and sensitive to every grade of thunder.

'I knew a most respectable young man,' narrated the missioner; 'and his wife, a decent young girl; they had a nice young family.' The congregation laughed delightedly and sympathetically, and the missioner glowered upon them. This was not going to be a laughing matter. Soon there was drink in it, and a Protestant some-where, I think; worse things followed. 'The two of them are burn-ing together in the flames of purgatory,' concluded the missioner, with ferocity, and rumbled at them like an angry bull. The women swayed and groaned in horror, and ejaculated prayers.

I saw the congregation go home in the dusk, the women walking in parties by themselves, the men silently passing the public-house as if it had *Dhroch hool,* which means the evil eye.

'There was a priest that was a relation of me own,' continued Anastasia, rising to the surface of her thoughts again, in the manner that always suggested the rhythmic reappearance of a por-poise in a summer swell, 'and he was telling me of a woman out near his own place, and she had a daughter that married and lived with her in the house, herself and the husband, and she got great annnoyance with them, and they took the land from her. 'Well,' says she to the husband, 'when I die I'll rise out of the grave to punish you for what ye done;' and it wasn't long after till she died. I dare say they had too much whisky taken, and maybe they didn't bury her the right way: ye wouldn't know, indeed, but in any case the priest went taking a walk for himself shortly after, and he went around the graveyard, the way he'd have a quiet place to be reading his exercises. Whatever he seen in it he wouldn't all out say, but "I

seen plenty," says he, and sure the coffin was there, and it above
the ground and no doubt at all but he seen plenty besides that. The
man then that married the daughter went out, and he buried the
coffin, and he got a pain in his finger, and he burying it, and the
pain didn't leave him till he died in the course of a few weeks. The
daughter was in a bad way too, after he dying; sure she got fits, and
she had them always till she went to a suspinded priest that lived
behind Galway, and he cured her. Sure thim has the power of God,
whether they're suspinded or no.'

I asked her presently if she had heard of a priest, renowned for
his preaching, who had lived in the village forty years before.

'I did, to be sure, though I wasn't only a young little girl at the
same time. He was a great priest, and after he died, it's what the
people said, he went through purgatory like a flash o' lightning;
there wasn't a singe on him. Often me mother told me about a sermon he preached, and I'd remember of a piece of it, and the way
you'd say it in English was "Oh, black seas of Eternity, without top
nor bottom, beginning nor end, bay, brink, nor shore, how can any
one look into your depths and neglect the salvation of his soul?"'

The translation came forth easily, with the lilt of metre and the
cadence of melancholy. Anastasia looked into the fire and said,
after a pause, ''Twas thrue for him.'

I asked what she thought of the Irish that was being taught now.

'Musha, I wouldn't hardly know what they'd be saying; and
there's an old man that has great Irish – a wayfaring man that does
be going the roads – and he says to me, "Till yestherday comes
again," says he, "the Irish that they're teaching now will never be
like the old Irish." The Irish were deep-spoken people long ago,'
continued Anastasia, yawning lamentably; 'it was all love-songs
they had. The people used to be in love then. Sure, there's no talk
of love now.'

She said it comfortably, and presently dozed, and I wondered
what talk of love she had heard. With the large eyelids closed, her
face gained in tranquillity, because the grey eyes were not truly
tranquil, they were only slow, with side-glances that revealed a dis-
position both ruminative and quick. It was not easy to imagine that
such glances had ever fallen, abashed, before a fond or daring gaze,

or been fused into oneness with it, yet Anastasia would have understood to its nethermost such a gaze; she could have translated it with Irish phrases and endearments that had the pang of devotion in them – phrases that flash as softly as a grey sea that the sun gazes upon suddenly through slow clouds. What she would not have understood is the physical love, frosted cunningly with spiritual, that is the romance of today; if any downfall of virtue shook her community (and rarely was it so shaken), she said, in chorus with her fellows, 'Why wouldn't she mind herself?'

When Anastasia tended the sick, as she did at intervals through the night, she was clumsy in movement yet swift, perceptive yet unmoved, patient, but from philosophy rather than from that tenderness that has its heart within the need for its tended one.

The night had clouded over, and when the dawn came it was a long and gentle growth of greyness, without a sunrise in it. The song of the robin trickled through the stillness, like a string of little silver beads across a sad embroidery; at the other side of the river a bell in the whitewashed convent intoned in a clear treble, and christened the day to its faith and purpose. The quiet hopelessness of the sickroom ceased to be the central thing in life; others were travelling on the same road and would reach the same gate.

Anastasia had gone out to the kitchen, where activities of an intermittent sort had sprung up. A girl was rattling tin cans, and humming a song that I had heard before:

> Oh, I bought my love a dandy cap,
> Oh yes, indeed, a dandy cap;
> I bought my love a dandy cap,
> With eight and thirty borders.

> *Oh, beela shula geelahoo,*
> *Oh, gra machree, for ever you,*
> *Oh, beela shula geelahoo,*
> *Indeed you are my darling.*

> Oh, I wish I was in Galway Town,
> Oh yes, indeed, in Galway Town;
> I wish I was in Galway Town,
> It's there I'd meet my darling.

It was a minor air, that swayed in low and persistent dejection. There was a pause, while the tin cans clanked again in time to a jovial footstep, and I saw the songster at the edge of the river. She slapped her cans on to the water, and the stream plunged into them and pulled them under, and she pulled them forth from it easily, though she was slight, with small, fine hands. She sat down at the brink and began to scour a wooden bowl with river sand and a wisp of straw, lilting 'Lanigan's Ball', and scouring in time to its elastic rhythm. A young man in a creamy flannel bauneen and a soft black hat came riding down the opposite bank on a bare-backed, yellow Connemara pony, and splashed out into mid-stream (and, incidentally, into the spawning-bed that there resided). The yellow pony stretched forth her neck and laid her black lip on the sliding current. 'Lanigan's Ball' did not cease.

'Mary Ellen,' said the young man, leaning back with his hand on the mare's quarter while she drew the water up her long throat, 'I'm goin' to be married this Shraft, and I'll give you the preference.'

Mary Ellen glanced up at him with ethereal grey eyes, from under wisps of auburn hair.

'Thank ye, Johnny, I'd sooner stay as I am,' she replied, as if she were declining the loan of an umbrella, and instantly and blithely resumed the interrupted phrase of 'Lanigan's Ball,' with its whirling sand and straw obligato.

The yellow pony splashed and stumbled through the spawning-bed, and returned to the further shore.

'Maybe it's looking for me on Shrove Tuesday you'll be,' said her rider, over his shoulder, as he ascended the opposite bank.

Mary Ellen lilted and scoured, and in due season returned to the house.

After her return, conversation arose in the kitchen, and immediately throve; there was long-drawn laughter, with Anastasia as humorist; it was comfortable to hear it.

In the grass between the window and the river the young spikes of the daffodils were grouped like companies of spearmen, resolute in the cold opposition of January. A thorn-tree leaned stiffly over the hastening water, and the robin that had been drifting near its roots shot up, as if tossed from the ground, accomplished a lofty curve, and sank again, in exquisite transitory yielding to the earth-force that would some day defeat it for ever. The low wind gathered purpose, and a mist began to thicken the sky. It went and came, as though it must return to press the house to its bosom, and tell those within of its love and its despondency.

By God's Mercy

Dorothy Macardle

Dorothy Macardle, who sometimes wrote under the name of Margaret Callan, was a member of the Dundalk brewing family. She was born in 1899 of titled Anglo-Irish parents, graduated from the National University of Ireland with honours and began to teach. Despite her family background, Macardle became a stauch Republican and was arrested by the British Army in her classroom during the Troubles.

Macardle chose the republican side during the ensuing Civil War and later wrote a massive historical study of politics during the revolutionary period, *The Irish Republic* (London: Gollancz, 1937). Between the First and Second World Wars, Macardle worked as a journalist with the League of Nations and after 1945, she worked on behalf of displaced and refugee children.

'By God's Mercy' shows Macardle's concern with the effects of revolutionary struggle on the women involved. It was written, like the rest of the stories in her only volume of short fiction, during her imprisonment in Kilmainham and Mountjoy for republican activities. For many years she was a drama critic for the *Irish Press* and the founder of the Irish Women Writers' Club. Macardle also wrote plays and several novels, the best known of which is probably *Fantastic Summer* (London: Peter Davies, 1946).

She died in 1958, and her work has been all but forgotten.

MAEVE HAD brought with her from Ireland, in the capacity of maid, a girl from the wilderness of Clare. I saw her one day at Maeve's hotel and could not afterwards forget the sweet, sallow little face and great suffering eyes; I had never seen, in a young face, such resignation mingled with such pain. Her name, Maeve told me, was Nannie Maher. 'A dear, splendid girl,' she said. 'We talk and lecture and write, but it is people like Nannie who are winning Ireland's war.' She brought her to the studio one Sunday night.

At first Nannie was a little shy, but very soon with talk of folk and places that they both knew, Una and she made friends; her shyness gave way to a soft garrulity and she began to talk about her brother, Brian, and 'the boys'.

'I would like you to tell my friends about Brian,' Maeve said to her then: 'I think it should be remembered; I think it should all be written down – Would you mind?'

'I'd like well,' Nannie answered simply, and with the frank, gracious candour of the West, she began telling us one of those tragic little stories of Ireland's war that are forgotten only because so many are told.

"Twas four months ago it happened,' she said. 'That time my mother and I were mostly alone. A hard winter it was for us, too, for we'd no near neighbours and Brian was away.'

'With a flying column?' Frank asked, and Nannie answered, 'He was with the Chief. The murder-gang were after the Chief that time and they'd got word he was in the West; the boys were terrible anxious and careful of him; Brian knew the country well and, young and all as he was, they'd appointed him guard. My poor mother didn't know where he was or when she'd see him at all, and there were times she would sit by the fire crying to herself for the loneliness and the dread. The best times would be when the lads from the column would come to us for a night's rest; a good rest we were able to give them too, for we were never raided, God be praised; the military took no notice of us at all.

'Well that day, early in the morning, when I was wetting the tea for breakfast, didn't Brian walk in. I near dropped the pot with the wonder and delight and when mother came in with eggs didn't she drop them in earnest to see him standing there laughing on the floor! Grand he was looking too, – a proud, shining look on him, the way I knew he had great news.

'Guess who is coming to you the night? says he, and I said, joking him, 'From the importance of the air you have it should be the Chief!' 'And the Chief it is,' says he.

'He sat down to his breakfast then and told us about it. I'll never forget the meal he ate! The poor lad was ravenous; 'twas a week since he got a meal under a roof. He told us the Chief was ill – not too bad, but needing a couple of days' rest and a quiet place where he could meet some of the staff, and he was coming to us after dark.'

'You were pleased?' Una asked.

'Pleased isn't the word for it,' she answered, 'but didn't mother begin shaking with the fright. 'God help us, Brian,' says she, 'I'd sooner see yourself slaughtered before my eyes! If the Chief's lost, Ireland's lost!' she says.

'Is it that you'll refuse to take him, Mother?' says Brian, very quiet-like, and with that she set to work. He was not to be in the house at all, Brian said, for fear of anyone looking in; so we readied up the loft of the barn. Fine and comfortable we made it, working like three fire-engines till the set of sun. We had it fixed up with a bed and table for his writing and a stove and all, and when everything was done we brought in the Sacred Heart picture and made up an altar and said a prayer that he'd be saved and guarded from all harm. Brian was delighted, his blue eyes were dancing in his head and he planning and fixing the place as if for a year. He was pleased you know, that they'd put that much trust in us, to let us mind the Chief. A happy day we had, thanks be to God!

'Well, by the time we had our tea over and I'd done baking and cleaning the house and put a tray ready for his supper when he'd come, it was very late, but mother wouldn't hear of going to bed, so the three of us sat talking round the fire. The plan was that about midnight Brian'd go down to the bridge at the bottom of the bohereen and wait, and about one o'clock the Chief would come that way with a couple of guards and they'd turn back and Brian'd bring him up and they'd go straight into the barn. And the others that were coming to see him in the morning would be disguised as tinkers and labouring men.

'I couldn't make out what ailed mother; she used generally be easy-minded about the house; 'twas so quiet and safe; Brian got downright vexed with her fears. 'If the Chief comes to harm and he in my charge,' he said, 'I'll get you to cut my throat! Don't you think I have my plans made? Or am I a babbler or a fool or a traitor that I'd lead him into a trap? The rest'll do their part,' says he, 'and I'll do mine, with the help of God, and the Chief's safe.'

'With the help of God,' mother said then, and she got very patient and quiet. Then to make all happy again Brian began chatting to her and remembering old times. 'Do you mind, Mother,' says he, laughing, 'when I was a gorsoon and I used to be playing tricks on you and my Da, and mitching school? And you used to be saying, 'Mind what you're at now, for God's looking at you, if I'm not!' Well, that's the way I do feel sometimes about the Chief, and he not in it at all – you couldn't do a mean or a dirty thing. Whatever misfortunes we get, while he's living we'll get no disgrace.'

'He got up then and took his cap, though 'twas only half eleven and 'twas a wet night. 'I'll scout round a bit,' he said, 'and see are the others at their posts before I go to the bridge.'

A queer feeling came over me when I saw him taking down his cap, 'Whist,' I said, and he looked at me, wondering, and I said, more for an excuse than anything – 'I thought I heard a lorry below on the road.' So we stopped, listening, and I thought I heard it again, but he heard nothing at all. It upset mother though and her face was white. 'Ah, Mother darling!' says he, in the sudden, loving way he had, like a child, 'You'll be the proud woman tomorrow, though 'tis a silly old worriter you are tonight,' and he gave her a hug and a kiss and went off. But two minutes later I heard him tapping at the window and there he was with the lamplight on his face and his black hair wet with the rain. 'Pull the curtain and put out the lamp,' he said, 'for fear anyone'd wonder at the light, and whatever happens,' says he, 'don't look out. Don't be worrying now, but pray for us,' he said.

'He went off then and I did what he told me and we sat by the fire, quiet, a long time.

'The quiet preyed on me and the waiting and I could see mother was terrible anxious, so the two of us knelt down and said the whole rosary for the safety of the Chief. When we were at the last mystery, the clock struck one and we stopped to listen, but there was not a sound. Then we finished the rosary and stood up. I began making up the fire, but mother said suddenly, in a kind of whisper, 'Listen, now listen!' She was standing stiff in the middle of the floor. I don't know what she had heard, but I know what I heard then – two shots close to us, sharp and clear, and then two more.

'Mother cried out and fell down on her knees by the chair. I didn't hear another sound. The thoughts were racing one another through my mind – mother was gasping and moaning to herself: 'God have mercy on us, the boy is destroyed and broken!' she said, 'Ireland is lost forever, and we'll be cursed and shamed in the grave!'

'What are you saying, Mother?' I whispered to her, and I shaking at her talk.

'The Chief is murdered under his protection,' she went on moaning, 'Brian'll die of shame.'

'I tell you the world went black before my eyes and she saying it. I clutched hold of the curtains; I nearly fell. Then I heard the tapping at the window the same as before, and it put the heart across me till I heard Brian's voice, whispering and gasping, full of dread, 'The bridge, quick, quick!' it said, 'For God's sake, quick, quick, to the bridge!'

'Brian's outside, wounded, Mother,' I said, but I ran out myself on to the road, not stopping to look for him, left or right. I had one thought only in my mind – the Chief lying in his blood – I ran down into the bohereen.

'A black night it was, under those twisted trees and neither moon nor stars in the sky. I was running on, the heart threshing within me like a machine, till I came in sight of the bottom of the bohereen and the turn of the road that goes on to the bridge. I was certain sure he was lying there dead. Then something startled me and I stopped – stopped dead, I did, and crouched down in the ditch, and then I saw what it was. I saw men moving, quick and quiet, not a whisper out of them, behind the trees; one after another they lay down, flat on their faces, their rifles levelled on the road and when the last was down there was not a sight nor sign of them – you'd think the road was safe and clear.

'The terror that fell on me was awful. I knew those'd shoot at a shadow; those'd kill a woman as easy as they'd kill a dog. . . I thought I'd never move hand or foot again till the world's end. Then all of a sudden the understanding rushed on me – what it meant, like Heaven opening over a lost soul. I knew they hadn't killed the Chief; they were waiting for him; he hadn't come. 'Quick,

quick, quick,' I heard it then, Brian whispering in my heart, and the thought came to me what to do. Out into the middle of the bohereen I went, staggering and singing and talking like a drunk woman to myself. Quite slowly I went past them, reeling from one side to another of the road; just as I turned the corner I heard one of them smothering a laugh. I near laughed myself with the lightness and triumph in my heart. But when I turned the corner, out of sight, I ran. . . O God, the way I ran to the bridge! When I got to it I was dizzy. I'd have fallen, but a man caught me by the arm.

'Steady,' he said in a whisper, holding me, and another came up from the far side of the road.

'Who are you?' said the first, and the other said, "Tis Brian's sister. Where's Brian?' he said.

'I could hardly speak, I said just, 'He sent me to the bridge. . . the bohereen's swarming. . . military' . . . but he understood. 'Twas Mick Brady: I knew him well. The other said in a sharp voice, 'Turn back,' and they left me without a word. I ran after Mick and caught him and said, 'Is the Chief safe?' 'He is,' said Mick and the other said, 'Tell Brian he did his work well.'

'I went home by the back way over the fields, slowly. I was tired – so tired I forgot about Brian being wounded up at the house; too happy I was, altogether. . .

'When I got back the men were raging all over the house, plain clothes men and Black and Tans. Mother was standing in the kitchen, her face terrible white, but she was trying not to let them see she was upset.

'They were shouting to one another with voices that'd sicken you, and using awful words. They let me in and stood round me, bullying, showing their revolvers, asking where were the men. I told them, 'You'll get no men here.' They were smashing open cupboards and ripping up mattresses, flinging things about, tearing up the boards – Mother watched them, not saying a word; she was brave.

'Is he safe?' she whispered to me when she got a chance. 'He is, thank God,' I said. 'God be praised!' says she: 'What matter now if they burn the house.' 'And where's Brian?' I asked her and she told me she didn't know; he wasn't outside.

'Then the men found the room in the barn and started shouting and got petrol and set fire to it and come throwing petrol about the house.

'Come on!' says Mother to me, gathering up some clothes only, and I put on my shawl.

'Will you not leave out the bits of furniture?' I said to one of the men.

'He swore. He swore the way you wouldn't swear at a brute beast and said it was more than we deserved if he let us out ourselves.

'Go out of that door now!' he shouted, 'and go to Hell, you. . .' Ah, I wouldn't soil my tongue with the words he used.

'You're welcome to the house,' my Mother answered back to him. 'You haven't got Ireland yet.

'That maddened him and he came down the bohereen yelling after us. 'If you want your son, I'll tell you where to look for him!' he shouted, and we stopped at that.

'Where is he?' Mother said to him, so quiet that he got ashamed.

'Try under the bridge,' he said, and went back to the house.

'A great blaze the house made by that time and in the light of it we got quick enough down the bohereen. There wasn't a soul on the road or at the bridge itself. We went down the slippery bank into the dark under it, calling, but there was no answer at all.

'We got his body half in and half out of the water. He had four bullets in the chest.'

She paused a little; none of us spoke; then she looked up at me.

'The people of the next farm came looking for us with a cart,' she said, 'and they took up the body and took us home. They were very good.'

'Your Mother. . . your Mother?' Una asked in a stifled voice.

'She didn't seem to fret too much,' Nannie answered: 'You see, she'd been prepared for worse. She would keep on saying, 'He did his work well, by God's mercy; he did his work well.' But she died on me before the month was out.'

Bridget Kiernan

Norah Hoult

Norah Hoult was born in Dublin in 1889. Her Anglo-Irish parents died in her early childhood and Hoult was educated in England though she returned to Ireland, first to collect material for her writing and then to live in County Wicklow, where she resided until her death in 1984.

Hoult is primarily a novelist, though it was her first book of short stories which established her as a writer and earned her a critical reputation. *Holy Ireland* (London: Heinemann, 1935) and *Coming from the Fair* (London: Heinemann, 1937) are her novels which deal specifically with Ireland, and are two of her best.

'Bridget Kiernan,' Hoult says, is, like all of her work, a story 'created from life' based on an experience in a middle-class household in which Hoult was staying. Although Hoult herself feels that she weighs more heavily on the Anglo, rather than on the Irish side, her depiction of 'young, careless Bridget' shows that she understands the psychology, not only of a woman of Bridget's type, but of the particular experience of the Irish exile in Britain. The controlled probing of Bridget's thoughts and feelings make this one of her finest stories. There has been no critical study of Norah Hoult's writings.

'BRIDGET! Bridget!'

Bridget Kiernan answered before she was fully awake, some automatic impulse propelling her.

'Yes, ma'am.'

'Are you getting up?'

'Yes, ma'am. I'll be down in a minute.'

'Well, be quick. It's twenty past seven. You ought to have been ready long ago.'

Bridget raised herself reluctantly, and, sitting on the side of the bed, reached for her stockings. Listening, she heard Mrs Fitzroy's door close. Isn't that the devil's own luck now, she thought. That one would be as cross as two sticks all day because she had had to shout to her to get up. It was queer she hadn't heard the alarum:

she must have been sleeping very heavy. . .

Merciful Jesus! For the moment she had forgotten. . .

Bridget stood still, holding her vest in her hand. Full consciousness gripped her with a cold squeeze. Jim! Jim had gone. And what was worse, she was beginning to be afraid she might be going to have a child. Nothing had happened yet. And she had been awake half the night with the worry of it.

Well, there was no time to think about it now. Pull on her clothes quick to keep out the creeping November cold. She'd have to hurry or there'd be no breakfast for the master. But all the same it was nearly dead she was for want of sleep.

'Bridget! I thought you said you were nearly ready.'

The mistress again!

'Yes, ma'am. I won't be a moment, ma'am. I'm coming now.'

'Why *don't* you come then? Half-past seven, and not a sign of you. It's disgraceful.'

With fingers made fumbling with haste, Bridget twisted up her hair into a knot, and stuck in two hairpins. There was certainly no time to wash; anyway it was too cold. There wouldn't be time either for her to kneel down and say a mite of a prayer. But she remembered to cross herself hastily and murmur, 'Jesus, Mary and Joseph, I give you my heart and soul,' before she opened her door. SHE was waiting with her bedroom door open. SHE'D be shouting at her again in another minute. It was terrible the way that hard thin voice made her lose her poor head altogether.

As she came out of her attic bedroom, she felt a little dizzy with cold, excitement and haste. But there was no time to stop and collect herself. Just keep on walking down the narrow stairs, holding the balustrade for support. As she passed the front bedroom Mrs Fitzroy poked her head out. 'That's right, Bridget,' she said with bitter sarcasm. 'Take your time. It's only getting on for eight.'

Bridget quickened her steps without replying. She was in the kitchen now, and the first thing to do was to rake out the fire. If only she'd done it the night before. But she had felt too tired and bothered, small blame to her.

How cold it was! She felt her body trembling with cold. And her hands hadn't any feeling in them at all. The air being full of dust and ashes made it all the colder. Cold and dirty. Just shove the cinders into the grate and leave them. No time to take them away now.

She eased herself and rubbed her hands together for warmth. Now she had to go down to the cellar to bring up coal and sticks. It was colder than ever in the cellar, and dark and ghostly. Wasn't that a rat she heard scurrying in the corner? Perhaps only a mouse. Never pay any heed. Shovel the coal into the bucket and bring it up. It would be better when she had got the fire set and lit.

The sound of the sticks crackling and the look of the flames as they tried to push their way up comforted her. Nothing was so bad after the fire had been lit, and you were sure it was going. And it was going well to-day. Who knew but that that mightn't be a good sign for herself. She mightn't be going to have a baby after all. Sure, it was only a few days yet over the time. No need to fret herself.

She went into the scullery to get the breakfast things. She ought, she knew, by rights sweep out the kitchen and the kitchen passage first. But it would be just like Mrs Fitzroy, the old devil – 'God forgive me,' murmured Bridget under her breath as she heard the bad word come – it would be just like herself to hurry up with her dressing and come running down post-haste to have the satisfaction of saying, 'And the table not laid yet, Bridget!'

Well, she wouldn't give her that pleasure anyway.

The dining-room was very mournful-looking with the yellow blinds still down. It hadn't woken up yet, and it didn't want to be woken yet. But the Fitzroys got up so early! Much earlier than the Gallaghers in Dublin, where her sister was. You wouldn't think the gentry would want to get up so early. But you wouldn't call the Fitzroys gentry. No style about them at all, there wasn't.

Those white cups and saucers and plates on the white tablecloth were terrible chilly-looking. Why wouldn't she have a few flowers on her cups, something a little bright? Bridget let her mind survey disapprovingly all Mrs Fitzroy's crockery. So little there was of it, too! Why wouldn't she have a fire in the dining-room this bitter cold? It wasn't much comfort for the master setting off on a morning the like of this. Not that she minded. It would make much more work for her, and that was the truth. Carrying up coals. And before breakfast. But it was hard on the master never to have a proper warm before he went off. And it just showed the meaness of her.

She ran down to see to the fire, and then reloaded her tray, thinking of Mr Fitzroy. A nice quiet man, he was. One who'd always pass the time of the day with her when the mistress wasn't by to hear. A little stiff, perhaps, but that was the way Englishmen were.

If he heard she was going to have a baby how would he behave? Pass her by with eyes turned down, most likely. Pretend not to have seen her at all. That was what another man would do, if he had proper feelings, and wasn't the kind that would be encouraged immediately to think he could do the same with her.

Stop thinking, now, about that! Herself would be down and in the devil's own tantrums at finding no kettle on. She ran downstairs again, and her quick arrival in the kitchen gave her the impression that she was getting on rapidly with her work: she took the bread out of the bin, and banged the lid down, pleasantly conscious of the bustle she was making. What about making some toast? Wouldn't that be a way of getting the mistress into a good temper? Ah, but the fire was not good for toast yet. And it was ten past eight, a bit after. She'd better be cutting the rind off the bacon for frying.

Bridget jabbed at the white fat with an over-blunt kitchen knife, and once again questioned her mistress's ideas. What was in her head, now, that she made her cut the rind off before frying it in the pan? Because wouldn't anyone know that it was much easier to cut it when it was cooked: that is if you were so particular, and couldn't cut it off when it was on your plate.

That was Mr Fitzroy in the bathroom. SHE'D be down any moment now fussing round and chattering about how late it was. For God's sake! Wasn't that her step?

No! It was all right. There was no one. But she'd better be quick and get the rinds shoved into the dustbin in the yard, or else she'd be complaining that she'd cut off too much of the rasher with them.

She returned from the back door with a relieved feeling. Three eggs, for himself, herself, and Miss Paula. They wouldn't spare one for her, of course. Only bacon! Did anyone ever hear the like? Eggs regarded as though they might be a great luxury, and held away from the servant!

There! SHE was calling out to Miss Paula. Now she was on the stairs.

Bridget rushed for the frying-pan, and was laying the rashers in with an intent face when Mrs Fitzroy came in. She was interrupted by a cry of horror from her mistress.

'Bridget! For Heaven's sake!'

Bridget was confounded. What was it she was doing wrongly?

'Your filthy black hands, all over coal dust, Bridget. Touching the food we are going to eat. How *can* you?'

Bridget was still perplexed. What was it that she was meant to do then? She looked at her hands, and then at the pieces of bacon.

'Use a fork, girl, can't you? And look at the fire! Nothing but smoke. How can you expect to fry anything on that? And there's no good leaving the kettle on.' She removed it with a firm hand. 'It would take an hour to boil like that. Can't you see?'

Bridget couldn't. She was conscious that she knew nothing, and that since the appearance of Mrs Fitzroy the cooking of the breakfast had become surrounded by immense difficulties.

'Don't stand there doing nothing. Get a newspaper; there's one in the sitting-room, under the armchair cushion; and hold it in front of the fire.'

For twenty minutes the atmosphere was heavily charged with vexation and turmoil. Bridget no longer thought. She became merely what she appeared to Mrs Fitzroy to be – an evil-doer, who made breakfast late, and was far too stupid to be capable of atoning for her transgressions. She had done so many things wrongly that now Mrs Fitzroy was standing in front of the fire cooking the bacon herself, and only occasionally uttering a command, or asking in a carefully restrained voice that denoted the pitch of fury at which she had arrived, some question which revealed all the things Bridget had left undone. There were one or two terrible moments when Bridget was left standing with idle hands. She dare not remain still, yet there was nothing, she felt, she dare do. Her guilt, symbolised in the figure of Mrs Fitzroy cooking her own breakfast, seemed then too heavy to be bourne.

To avert disgraceful tears, she went over to the kitchen table, and began to lay her own cloth. Anything was better than standing like a fool. But Mrs Fitzroy, watching her out of the corner of an eye, reflected bitterly: 'That's all she's thinking about. Her own breakfast. I've got a good mind to throw her piece of bacon into the fire.'

But she did not go so far. She only disassociated it from the rest by thrusting it viciously into the side of the pan, where only a minor degree of heat could reach it. Then triumphantly she noticed an omission.

'If you can spare a minute, Bridget' – Bridget, startled, turned apprehensively – 'get me the bacon dish cover. You have only got the plates and dish warming here.'

Bridget went hastily to the pantry. She wasn't supposed to be setting her own breakfast, then. What she ought to have done, perhaps, was to go upstairs and give the sitting-room a dust? But it was too late now. Would she ever do anything right for that one, with her face like a thunderstorm?

Paula came running into the kitchen. She was a pale child of seven, with fair bobbed hair, heavy cheeks, and hard staring light-grey eyes. 'Mummy, I'm ready. So's Daddy. He wants his breakfast.'

Mrs Fitzroy turned from the fire, and spoke with the terrible calm of the martyr. 'Tell Daddy, breakfast is just coming. I'm cooking it myself.'

At last it was over. The tea had been mashed and taken up, and Bridget was free to get her own breakfast. She gave another turn to her rasher. There wasn't any dip left. Well, thanks to the mistress being in such a temper, she had lost all her appetite. A cup of good strong tea was what she wanted, and she wasn't going to spare the tea either.

As she was washing up her own cup and plate in the scullery, she heard the front door bang. That was the master gone. A minute later Mrs Fitzroy bore down like an avenging angel.

'You can clear, Bridget. Your master hasn't been able to have a proper breakfast because it was so late. Do you see now all the trouble you cause by not getting up in time?'

'Yes, ma'am.'

The two women stood facing each other. Bridget saw through downcast lids a tall thin woman wearing an old skirt and yellow-brown cardigan. Mrs Fitzroy never dressed properly till after breakfast; and her brown hair, badly shingled, had a greasy matted appearance. Her rather large nose was reddened at the tip by the hot tea she had been drinking, and she wore a fretted expression. She was a woman who always gave the impression that she was only in her present place for a few moments, and that it was not worth while to unbend and settle herself comfortably. But to Bridget at the moment her appearance resolved itself into a matter of cold blue accusing eyes, and an ugly red nose; while she listened to the precise English accent which made her feel she was dealing with someone she could never approach as an ordinary human being; one who must be an inhabitant of a quite different world from herself.

And Mrs Fitzroy viewed Bridget with an equal distaste. She saw an exceedingly slatternly servant girl with a dirty pale face and un-tidy dark hair that was always falling over her face. It was true, she had previously admitted, that the young woman mightn't be so bad-looking if she would only keep herself clean and tidy. She had large clear eyes, and thick black lashes – if she only had not had such a disconcerting habit of dropping them, which gave her a deceitful air. But then her mouth was always a little open, a thing which always irritated Mrs Fitzroy in anybody. 'Makes the girl look half-witted,' she decided. But it wasn't so much her appearance as her way of dragging herself about as if there was no such thing as time in the world which annoyed Mrs Fitzroy. 'And she looks,' re-flected Mrs Fitzroy again, 'as if she has been crying. That seems her usual occupation. Though I'm sure she gives me far more to cry about than ever I do her.'

Leaving instructions, Mrs Fitzroy went away to get dressed in a spirit of acute dissatisfaction. It was a reflection on the house, she thought, to have such an untidy depressed-looking girl about as Bridget. And Irish people were supposed to be bright and witty!

Sooner or later she'd have to give her notice, and start the search all over again. Or move into a flat with a gas stove, and manage herself with a day girl. This servant problem was really driving responsible women like herself mad.

Bridget cleared the upstairs table, and washed up. Then she laid a fire in the study, where Paula had her morning lessons from a visiting governess. As she dusted the room, Paula sat on a chair, looking at a book. She kept calling Bridget to show her pictures and to tell her about the story they illustrated. Bridget went on saying, 'Is that so?' and 'Yes, Miss Paula,' with mechanical regularity. It was hard to keep her attention alert that morning, but alert it had to be while Mrs Fitzroy was still in the house. For you never knew when SHE'D be coming in with some question or other, just an excuse, of course, to see what you were after doing. And if you were taken by surprise, as well you might with her flopping softly round in bedroom slippers, and started, then she'd say, 'Dreaming again, Bridget,' or look very suspicious as if she thought you had just stolen something.

So Bridget kept listening all the while she was turning out the dining-room. The dirt rose from the carpet and settled in her hair and all about her. Her hands were swollen and purple, and she felt stifled for want of a breath of clean fresh air. She wished she was back home, back where the air was soft and people moved slowly.

At last Mrs Fitzroy went out to do her shopping, and Bridget came thankfully back to the kitchen fire for a comfortable warm before going up to do the bedrooms. She disliked doing the big room, because she always felt the mistress didn't really care for her being in there at all. It was the most unfriendly room in the whole house to her, and her eyelids were downcast when she entered it. Yet all the same you couldn't help being impressed by it in a way. All those silver things on the dressing-table, and the lovely blue eiderdown that was so rich-looking. And the big real mahogany wardrobe must have cost something, that must have. Then there was that picture of a lady in evening dress, real evening dress, that showed a bit of her bosom like grand ladies did when they were off to a ball of an evening. A bit like the mistress this lady was, only lashings better-looking. A sister, it might be, who had married a richer man than the master, and had a motor-car, and lived in the real London you read about in stories, the London where there was a real gay life, not like this Ealing place! Sure, Dublin itself was a hundred times as lively.

Now there were the potatoes to peel in the scullery. It was work that gave her a few minutes to think of herself before Mrs Fitzroy came back, and there was the usual set-to about getting the bite she called lunch.

Well, here she was, Bridget Mary Kiernan, aged twenty-five, in a pretty plight, and she might as well face it here and now. She had committed a mortal sin, fornication, and unless she had a piece of luck she might be going to have a baby. All because of that good-for-nothing fellow, Jim – Jim, with his lovely blue suit, and smart figure, and wavy fair hair, and laughing blue eyes. And his warm lips that held yours till they seemed to draw you out of yourself into a great fire and confusion. Stop now! That was no way to be thinking. Where was her pride? A likely-looking lad enough, maybe, but he had gone now and left her for ever. Deserted her! Deserted – that was the word they called it.

And there was no way of speaking to him, a boy that she'd met in the pictures three months gone, and had never got to know anything about, though he had met her regular every Thursday evening up to four weeks ago. No, three weeks. It was a month now that *that* had happened between them, God forgive her!. . . She ought to have known the sort of fellow his lordship was when he had started hinting. But there it was. It was her own fault in a way, because she hadn't chosen to take heed of his free style of talking. She had liked the feel of his arms about her in the pictures too much to frighten him off with being prim and proper. And there was an ache in her all the time till he was with her again, and she felt him touch her. Sure, no one with a heart in them could blame her too much. Wasn't he the only friend she had in London? And everybody wanted a bit of fun now and again.

She hadn't really known, before God she hadn't, what he meant when he suggested going to a restaurant instead of to the pictures that Thursday. And she had felt shy even in her best clothes, and glad to know that it was in what was called a private room they were going to have dinner, where there'd only be the two of them.

It was true she had felt there was something wrong when he was muttering so long with the waiter. And it was such an odd dirty place, not like a proper restaurant at all. She had felt all queer when she saw the big sofa. But all the same she was dying to know what he was going to do. And he must have spent some money to get that room all to themselves. Half a bottle of expensive wine, too. She had laughed a lot. Wine always made her laugh a lot. But afterwards, in his arms. . . it just didn't seem to matter at all. Give him his way. . . She couldn't really see now that it was such a terrible thing as the way in which people talked about it. But, of course, it was badness, and she'd been bad; she had so.

All the same it was difficult to understand anything one way or another, and all that a poor ignorant girl the like of herself could do was to be good and leave the matters to the priests and learned people to settle. She had done wrong, and there was no use her trying to get out of it. Her mother would be terrible upset when she heard about it – that was if she had to hear – and there was no one at all to help her.

She ought to go and make her confession. Whom would she go to? She had never been to confession the whole long year she had been in England, not the five months she had been in the Isle of Man, nor the six months, as it nearly was, that she had been with Mrs Fitzroy. It was so different here, where no one seemed to have any religion at all. Even Mass sounded different, and had different things in it. And she had never been very particular about religion. Perhaps it was a pity she hadn't.

Jim had no religion, any more than that fellow she had gone out with in the Isle of Man – Frank – had. Perhaps if Jim had had religion, been a Catholic, he'd have behaved different. He had thought light enough of what they had done. Just laughed when she said they had been wicked, and then got cross when she wouldn't let him kiss her. Walking away like that in the street when she had told him what she thought of him. She was an Irish girl, and wasn't going to put up with being treated any way. Walking away and leaving her like that in the street! She'd never forgive him for that, never. Ah, well, no good exciting herself with thinking of that all over again. But she had her pride, and even if he wanted to marry her she wouldn't. No one might believe it, but she wouldn't not if he went down on his bended knees.

The potatoes were finished now. She carried them into the kitchen, and at the same moment she heard the latch of the front door turn. Her High and Mightyship was back. There'd be no peace now for a while.

Mrs Fitzroy brought down the parcels she had been carrying. 'Here, Bridget, is the chop I got for your dinner. And the potatoes are in the basket. Those are tomatoes that I've got for tomorrow to fry with the bacon. We've got eggs, haven't we? Miss Rowbotham and Miss Paula and I are having scrambled eggs. And coffee. Can you do the eggs?'

'Yes, ma'am.'

'You ought to, considering the number of times I've had to stand over you to show you.'

'Have you laid the table?'

'No, ma'am.'

'Well, go and do it now. It's twenty to one. And I don't want lunch later than one because of Miss Rowbotham.'

Miss Rowbotham came out of the nursery as Bridget passed on her way to the dining-room. She had curly brown hair, a small round face and bright brown eyes that peered over her plump little body with an air of being willing to meet everybody half way.

'Good morning, Bridget,' she said with an air of cheerful bene-volence. You-always-have-to-be-so-careful-with-the-servants was one of Miss Rowbotham's maxims.

'Good morning, Miss.'

The girl seems respectful enough, thought Miss Rowbotham, and, by way of rewarding her, she gave a little shiver and said, 'Isn't it cold?' in a little upward rush of words.

'Indeed it is, Miss.'

They parted, and Bridget, laying the cloth, thought: 'The Eng-lish are always saying, 'Good morning,' or 'Good afternoon,' or something like that. And that teacher will be washing her hands again before her dinner. Is it to please Mrs F. or to suit herself that she's so particular? I wouldn't be surprised but that she's scared stiff of her, like the master, and every blessed one in this house.'

Paula came silently in, thrusting her under-lip forward as was her habit when she was in a bad temper, and stood watching Bridget arranging the knives and forks. 'You do look dirty and horrid, Bridget,' she remarked after a thoughtful pause.

Bridget made no reply. 'Mother says you are the dirtiest girl she has ever had, but that all Irish people are dirty. Is that true?'

Bridget thought it politic to refrain from uttering a direct denial. She'd only be making trouble with her mother, the little brat, she thought.

'The dirty Irish, the dirty Irish!' cried Paula in sudden excitement, dancing up and down, and then pulling Bridget's apron-strings loose before springing away.

'Ah, go away now, Miss Paula, and leave me alone,' said Bridget, the blood mounting to her cheeks.

'Shan't, shan't. The dirty Irish!'

Bridget felt an angry despair surging up. They were all against her, shouting at her and mocking at her. Very well, she'd stick up for herself. She had some spirit left in her, thank God. She turned round smartly on Paula.

'Do you hear what I say? Go out from here. This minute.'

'Don't speak to me like that. Or I'll tell my mother of you.'

For a moment the two stood confronting each other: Paula, pouting and lowering, Bridget with flashing eyes, and a look on her face new to the child. After a moment Paula, discomfited, ran out of the room, turning at the door to make a last thrust: 'I hate you, you horrid girl.'

Bridget stood still for a moment with a hand pressed to her rapidly beating heart, and then went on setting the table. But when she went back to the kitchen, Mrs Fitzroy observed on her face what she described as her mulish look, and deemed it better to postpone a complaint that too many potatoes had been peeled till later.

'You go on making the toast, Bridget. I've beaten up the eggs.'

The task of getting lunch proceeded silently, the two women ignoring each other's presence as far as possible. At last it was done, and taken up, and Bridget was left to fry her own chop.

She ate absent-mindedly, occupied with the new feelings which Paula's attack had aroused in her. Now they'd got her blood up she wouldn't care what she did, and she wouldn't be asking help from nobody either. If she was going to have a baby, what need was there for any great to-do? They'd have to take her in at the work-house anyway, and then she'd go on the streets. . . steal. Get put in prison? What matter? . . .

There was Margaret Callaghan of Carrickmore, that the priest had sent away out of the parish because she wouldn't tell him the name of the fellow that was after giving her a child. And she had just sailed off as cool as you please to Dublin, and, so they said, was seen walking down Grafton Street, dressed up to kill, with not a feather off her. Well, those girls might be bad, she wouldn't say they weren't, but didn't they have a better time than sticking on toiling and moiling day after day with no thanks from any-body? . . .

The great thing was not to get in a stew or to be put on by any-body. If there wasn't anyone to help her, there wasn't anyone, and there was an end of that. And hadn't many another girl had her trouble, and got through it, and nobody the wiser?

She washed the dishes, with her thoughts repeating themselves in gestures of defiance, and she became almost happy in her new boldness. Now she could think of Jim with indifference and even contempt. A poor ordinary skulking fellow he was, doing an ordin-ary mean sort of thing, and then afraid to face the band. In love with him? Not a bit of it! A bit of a fancy perhaps, but she was well out of it and over it now, thanks be to God.

It was as if she had suddenly grown a year older, having come to read things aright that an hour or two ago had been confused and dark. She went about the house, finishing her work with a deter-mination that perplexed Mrs Fitzroy, and made her suspicious. 'It's not her afternoon and evening off,' she pondered. 'What's she up to now, I wonder?'

It was almost strange to Bridget, so conscious was she of this change in her outlook, to find that the streets outside looked just the same when she went out to take Paula for her walk.

She went up the long stretch of Pitshanger Road, staring with

unwonted curiosity about her. It was, she thought to herself, as if in
the usual way you went along never looking up to take more than a
pennyworth of notice of anything about you, and thinking your
own thoughts about the things that had happened to you, and the
things that might happen to you, and then one day you got a shove
when you weren't expecting it, and you were startled into taking
heed of things that had been there all the while only you hadn't
bothered your head about them.

Those houses now, big and dark and silent, frowning away there
they were, as if the devil himself had taken possession of them.
Sure, no one would know who and what lived in a house the like of
that one there unless you went up and knocked and were shown in.
And the cracks in the pavement stones, streaks of black amid grey,
hadn't they the queer way of shooting up into your eyes, so that
having noticed them you had to go on noticing them. And in front
the wide hard road stretching on and on with an errand boy bicy-
cling down. There was the red 150 bus just turning the corner; and,
coming towards them, a white dog rooting along with its nose to
the pavement. A nice garden that one was, with its yellow
chrysanths; and there was a woman in blue with dark hair sitting by
the window. More cheerful-looking than the other houses it was,
and she did right to be proud of her garden as surely she would be.
Then, if you looked up, there was the still grey wintry-looking sky
over everything. . . no change in it as far as your eyes could stretch.

Bridget puckered her brows, feeling suddenly tired.

What did these things stand for? What sense was there, after all,
in them? They were things that went on, and would always go on
whatever misfortune happened to a girl like herself; but what
meaning was to be got out of them it would take a wiser girl than
she was to find out.

Paula, who had been walking on a little in front to make Bridget
think that she didn't choose to own her, or have anything to do
with her, got tired of her own company, and decided to talk.
'Bridget, did you see that lady with the red face and the fur coat
who went by on the opposite side? Mother knows her. She's Lady,
Lady. . . something, I forget what. That's a very important thing to
be, you know,' she added condescendingly.

'Yes, Miss,' said Bridget dreamily.

'Do you have ladies in Ireland? Like Lady Jane Grey, and Lady Duff Gordon? And Lady Astor? You don't, do you?'

'Ah, sure every country has them. You read about them in the papers.'

'Not every country. You are ignorant, Bridget. You couldn't have them in France, because in France they talk a different language. They talk French. I learn French with Miss Rowbotham. But you're too stupid to understand things like that.'

'Haven't I told you not to speak that way to me, Miss Paula?'

'Mother does.'

'Aren't you brought up the way you know how to speak nicely?'

'Yes, if I want to.'

There was a silence. Bridget thought without resentment that it was a pity Paula wanted so much pleasing, and was so unfriendly. But there was no use taking to heart what a child would be saying. A spoilt little madam she was, and no mistake. But then she was an only child, which was an unnatural thing for a child to be.

As she turned home the melancholy of gathering dusk took possession of her. Paula, who had chattered more than usual, disturbing Bridget with her questions and comments, and achieving a triumph in being the one to remember they had forgotten to buy more eggs, was now quiet; and Bridget realised that in her growing weariness something had escaped from her. This was the time when she was most put in mind of her own country with its creeping mists that counselled resignation. She heard the doleful cries of the grey birds that would be wheeling in from the mountains, and saw the tree in the middle of the field at the back of her mother's cottage. It would be bare-looking now standing lonely against the sky. Inside, there would be a warm fire, making the red patchwork rug look gay and snug. And the little statue of Our Lady smiling down from her niche on the wall. Her mother would be chatting as likely as not to Mrs Connolly over a cup of tea, bragging, for all that she knew to the contrary, about one of her children or another. Bridget herself, maybe, it would be, who had a grand post as a help in London, where everyone was rich and there were more people than anywhere else in the whole wide world. Except New York, in

America, where Kevin was. Ah, well, her mother was an old
woman now, and she ought to be allowed her bit of romancing.

It was queer and lonesome when you got thinking of home. It
was a pity in one way that she had crossed the water, though two
fortune-tellers had told her that that would be her fate, and that she
would marry a handsome fair man, and keep her own servant.
Well, there was a laugh to be got out of that bit. She had certainly
thought Jim might be her fate when she met him. She had never
been very partial to the one in the Isle of Man, and he was dark and
small, but Jim had really been the spit of the fortune-teller's description. Well, she had had her wish to travel, and now she was
landed with one of the crossest women you could ever meet, a bold
forward child, and nothing but cross words, however much she
killed herself dead with trying to do work in new ways that no one
had ever heard of before.

She sighed gently, and raising her eyes murmured under her
breath, 'Blessed Virgin, help me. Sacred Heart of Jesus, have pity
on me!' It was no use her getting worked up. There was nothing
she could do. That was a certainty. She hadn't the price of her fare
home till the end of the month. And home was no place to go to
anyway if it was a child of badness she was bringing with her.
Bringing scandal into the parish and disgrace on her poor mother.
Ah, well, what did they say? That there was no use crossing a river
before you came to it.

That policeman was taking a good look at her. The cheek of
him! Now he was turning his head to stare after her. She knew it
without looking round. Would there by any harm in her glancing
back casual-like and giving him a bit of a smile? Better not. Paula
might notice and then come out with it. She was cute enough to
watch her even when she seemed to be seeing nothing at all. But,
all the same, the knowledge of the policeman's interest pleased her,
as if a sore place had received balm, and as they turned in at the
house, she said cheerfully, to Paula, 'Here we are. Now you'll get
your tea that you've been wanting.'

There was a light in the kitchen! That meant the mistress was
down there. It would be just like her if she had been prying into the
drawer where she kept her paper-backed Smart Novels. Three of

them, Bridget remembered, there were. She might even have thrown them out as rubbish. And she hadn't finished 'When Love Flies in at the Window.'

Mrs Fitzroy said nothing to her maid, but welcomed Paula expansively, 'Well, darling. Had a nice walk?'

'No,' said Paula. 'Just ordinary. Up to the shops. And Bridget forgot to get the eggs till I reminded her. So we had to turn back when we got to the Underground.'

'That was my clever little girl to remember for mother.'

Bridget carefully deposited the parcels on the table. She didn't like to say anything to the mistress unless she was spoken to. Mrs Fitzroy was so different from Mrs Reynolds, who had kept the Isle of Man boarding-house, and who was always ready for a chat. She might as well go upstairs and take off her things. But when she was half through the door, Mrs Fitzroy called her back: 'Oh, Bridget! Put on the kettle before you go up. And when you come down make some buttered toast. Three rounds. I've laid the table.'

Bridget put on the kettle ungraciously. 'Why, I wonder, couldn't she have done a little thing like that without calling me?' she asked herself. But when she came downstairs again she found the kitchen empty, and kneeling in front of the fire she looked round and took pleasure from the warmth and familiarity of the scene. She liked the room best in the evening, when Mrs Fitzroy only came in for a few moments just to see if her dinner was going all right. Then each item became definitely hers. The light shining on the plates on the dresser, and the firelight warming the blue and red tiles; the clean-scrubbed yellow deal table. Oh, it was a pleasant enough room when the little red curtains were drawn across the window. Quite friendly like. She liked looking, too, at the shiny red bread-bin with its big black-painted letters; and the tin tea-caddy that stood by its side with its picture of an Irish girl and an English girl and a Scotch girl all joining hands. And there was the old basket chair that she would be able to give herself a rest in later.

The day was getting through, thank God for it; and the furniture and crockery and tins that had been pushed and banged about were now given a moment of peace, so that they took on a quiet and solid look that was never theirs in the morning but which was the one natural to them.

Look at that now! She'd been and burnt the toast. Smoking away in blackness. No good doing anything with it. SHE would turn her nose up at it, however much it was scraped. She'd best hide it behind the clock on the mantlepiece, and do another piece. Perhaps she'd have it for her own tea. Or else throw it in the dustbin when the mistress was off out of the way.

Mrs Fitzroy was already in the dining-room when Bridget took up the tray. 'You've been a long time, Bridget. I suppose you burnt the toast or something. I thought there was a smell.'

'No, I did not, ma'am.'

'Why have you been so long then?'

'Was I long, ma'am?'

Mrs Fitzroy made an impatient movement, and then lifted the teapot towards her.

'Is there anything else you're wanting, ma'am?'

'No. Oh, yes. Bring up the biscuits I bought, please. They're in the pantry. And put them in the biscuit jar first.'

Bridget enjoyed her tea. She made herself more toast, and buttered it generously. It wasn't as if she had had much to eat that day, she thought to herself, noticing her appetite approvingly. And she wouldn't be having anything for her supper beyond a cupful of cocoa. Mrs F. was very close with food for the kitchen, and the meat didn't taste like good Irish meat at all, it didn't. She'd probably be taking a good look at that loaf, the old skinflint. It couldn't be helped. Didn't she have to keep up her strength some way? And she wasn't going to be treated worse than a dog all of the time, even if that one expected her to find nourishment out of the smell of what was cooking for herself and the master.

That put her in mind. She pulled out the drawer in the table. No, the three of them were there safe. If they hadn't been, she'd have asked her staight to her face, so she would: 'I see you've borrowed a book of mine, Mrs Fitzroy.' Or, 'Might I trouble you to give me my book back, ma'am?' 'I think you have interfered with my property, ma'am. Might I ask why?' Quite easy and polite, but enough to show that she wasn't intimidated by HER. That she knew her legal rights, which she did. There was the bell! Ah, she could wait.

She wasn't going up till she had finished her tea comfortably. Wasn't she ever to be allowed a bite of food quietly?

When she was washing up the tea things, she heard Mrs Fitzroy go into the kitchen, and she also heard the bread-bin being ransacked. A moment later her mistress came into the scullery wearing her gravest face.

'Bridget, I'm not sure that there'll be enough bread to last us till the baker comes tomorrow. When you have finished you'd better run out to Paley's and get another loaf.'

'Yes, ma'am.'

'There ought to have been sufficient, but it seems to have gone very fast today.' There was a note of interrogation and disapproval in her voice, which Bridget ignored.

Mrs Fitzroy sighed. 'When you've got your things on, tell me, and I'll give you the money.'

Bridget hurried up. It was a pleasure to go out by herself in the evening, even if only to post a letter, and ponder over the recipient. Now she shut the door behind her with alacrity, and it seemed to her that the lamps to her right and left threw a friendly regard her way. There were two young men standing at the corner as she passed, and one raised his hat, and said 'Good evening.'

Of course she didn't reply, but hurried on, her heart beating faster. The nerve of that one! But it was very gentlemanlike the way he raised his hat. Better-class than when they just coughed. Not that she cared that much for any of them! Weren't all the men the same? A few soft words to wheedle you. 'What wonderful eyes you've got!' and that sort of light chat, and then away, chasing after someone fresh. Oh, she knew them, the sort they were.

Still it cheered her up being out of the house on her own, and feeling the keen air against her face. And the little lighted shops looked gay. Would you believe it – the Christmas cards were out already! When she had got the bread she was loth to leave them, and sauntered slowly, looking in the windows.

How pretty the red apples and yellow oranges looked all piled up together in that tasty way! Those writing-pads at threepence each were very cheap. A real bargain! Then the array of magazines and papers with their bright red and blue and yellow covers adorned with pictures of smiling girls and illustrations of frocks and cami-knickers (some with patterns to be given away) held her eyes. That was a notion! She'd treat herself to *Home Notes* that evening. Sure, the way things were, didn't she need something to take her mind out of herself?

The woman inside was friendly, and said it was a lovely evening, very seasonable. 'Indeed it is,' replied Bridget heartily, and went out feeling really light-hearted.

As she had come so far she might as well slip along and have a look to see what was on the cinema. It was only a minute away; no one at all would be the wiser.

She walked fast now, feeling a little guilty; but when she got to the entrance she lingered fascinated. 'The Sins Ye Do,' the big film was called; and there was a huge picture at the side of a beautiful girl standing outside a great palace of a house with a baby in her arms. She wouldn't be married, because she was poorly dressed, and looked desparately miserable. That would be where her mother and father were living, and they wouldn't have anything to do with her any more. Staring big blue eyes the girl had.

It would be a tragic film. Wasn't it a pity now she couldn't see it, for how did she know but that she wasn't going to be the same way as that young lady. And she might have got a hint or two from the film what to do. But, of course, that girl was extra beautiful, so that she'd be sure to meet someone after a bit who'd fall really in love with her, and forgive her everything. There'd be a fade-out with a man in evening-dress kissing her over a cradle with the baby in it, and saying that he'd never hold it against her.

Or if it were a really tragic film the girl would die a beautiful death with everyone sorry and weeping that they'd been so unkind, and hadn't known that she was more sinned against than sinning. Or something. Anyway, it would be lovely to see it. It was after six and people were just starting to go in. She watched a young man clink money down while his girl stood waiting. They'd have a grand time inside with the orchestra playing, sitting so comfortable on the red velvet seats, with the warm darkness wrapping them round. And after a while she'd put her head on his shoulder. . . Well, no use standing there.

She found she had lost her light-heartedness as she walked quickly back. The picture had come as a sharp reminder of something she had almost forgotten. But she felt a little important, too, because the picture's subject had brought her the assurance that many people would regard her as a sad victim of man's wickedness. 'She gave her all and he left her to pay the price.' The sentence came into her head, and she muttered it to herself with a sort of satisfaction. She, Bridget Kiernan, was one of that sort of women, more shame to the man.

She was so deep in her thoughts that she was taken aback when she heard the sharp edge of Mrs Fitzroy's voice: 'Here you are at last. You've been long enough to buy out the whole shop.'

'They were sold out at Paley's, so I had to go along to Bowen's,' said Bridget glibly, and admired herself for the way she had found on the spur of the moment a feasible explanation. She'll hardly take the trouble to go out to Paley's and see, she assured herself.

Mrs Fitzroy looked disbelieving. 'That's queer. I've hardly ever known Paley's sold out before. They always keep a few loaves for the next day. Some of their customers only like it when it's a day old. And in any case I wouldn't have thought it took half an hour even to go to Bowen's.'

Bridget was silent. She had said her say, and if Mrs F. didn't like it she could lump it. She noticed that her mistress had changed into her brown crepe de Chine frock and powdered her face. You could well see where the powder ended on her nose. If she only knew she needn't think it improved her, because it didn't. She was a plain-looking woman, and a cross woman, and she, Bridget, wasn't going to demean herself by answering her for all her disagreeableness and innuendoes.

Mrs Fitzroy turned angry. 'Understand this, Bridget, when I send you out for bread, I don't mean you to go for a walk. This isn't your evening off, you know. Be quick now, please. I want some coals taken up to the study.'

Bridget went upstairs to her room without a word, and banged the door behind her. She sat down on the bed and thought murderously of Mrs Fitzroy. She imagined her in hell, and the flames scorching her that she screeched out for mercy. But there wasn't

one would have mercy on her. Wasn't it true that they said all Pro-
testants had to go to hell? And it might be so. Certainly it would be
true for a woman with a temper the like of hers. And meaness! And
ugliness! And her thin, pinched voice!

She mimicked it to herself. 'Understand, please, I don't want you
to go for a walk. It's not your evening off.'

'I'll walk out of here, anyway, Mrs Fitzroy. *And* I'll have my
wages *if* you please!' That would have been a great thing to have
answered her with. And she'd say it, too, if there was much more of
her impudence. Sure a black or a slave would get more decently
spoke to. They would so.

She pulled off her hat and coat, and went down with a feeling of
going into mortal combat. No one in the kitchen. SHE'D be up in
the study with Paula. What was the time? Twenty after six. A bit
more, for the clock was slow. Into the dirty cellar again, and yet was
expected to keep as clean as a shining angel in Paradise!

She clattered about, and after a while her rage wore down. The
joint was cold; that was a mercy. Potatoes on to boil. SHE'D
brought in a cauliflower. When Mrs Fitzroy came down to make
what she described as a sweet, Bridget went upstairs to lay the
table. Mr Fitzroy had returned, and was in the dining-room,
measuring out a whisky and soda.

'Good evening, Bridget.'

'Good evening, sir.'

That was a nice smile he had given her! But it made her feel shy
like, being there all alone with him.

Mr Fitzroy observed Bridget without appearing to do so. She
seemed a bit down in the mouth, he thought. Not bad-looking.
Pretty hair, and good eyes. Irish, she was. Cheer her up a bit. No
harm in a friendly word.

'Well, Bridget, how do you like London?'

Bridget knew she didn't know. She'd only been up to London
proper twice. Once with Jim, for THAT! And then when she had
had tea in a Lyons, near Oxford Cicus, and been terrified of getting
lost. Still he wouldn't expect her to hand out all that piece.

'I like it well enough, sir.'

'I suppose it strikes you as very big and noisy after the country.

So much traffic, and all that.'

'Oh, indeed, you're right, sir. Very big. . . And very smelly,' she added thoughtfully, remembering her first impression on arriving at Euston.

Mr Fitzroy was a little puzzled by the last word. But at the same time he thought he heard a sound on the stairs. 'You'll soon get used to it,' he said rather hastily; and went thoughtfully out of the room. It wouldn't do for Dorothy to hear him talking to the maid. She was always so suspicious. And he didn't want her to know he was having an appetiser. Women always called it, 'Drinking again!'

Bridget knew why the master had gone out so suddenly. She could have told him the mistress was safely away for a few minutes. Ah, well, the poor man had a good heart, and you could only pity him, seeing the sort of woman he was married to.

Sadness came upon her as she smoothed the table-cloth. The room looked pretty now with the pink shade over the electric light. And the rose-coloured chrysanths on the white tablecloth, and the glittering silver on the mahogany sideboard. But it didn't belong to her. It wasn't intended for her. There didn't seem anything that belonged to her in the whole wide world.

She went to the window to draw the curtains. The sitting-room of the house opposite was lit up, and a piano was tinkling out a tune. It was meant to be gay; yes, 'Where's my sweetie hiding?' That was it. They played it at the pictures. But it was mournful-sounding all the same, coming across the dark quiet road. The more the person playing banged it out, the more it caught at your heart-strings, because of the lonesome way the notes flowed into the silence.

There she was, playing the fool again! Standing dreaming! Bridget pulled the curtains to with a determined hand, and went back to the kitchen.

Mrs Fitzroy looked up from the table at which she was standing.

'Don't you think, Bridget,' she said in a voice that sounded strained in her effort to speak pleasantly when she was moved by a spasm of sharp irritation, 'that you might give your face a wash? There's a clean towel on the roller in the scullery.'

Bridget did not trust herself to speak. She would have burst into tears if she had. And she couldn't disobey the old beast without saying one word. She put the tray down, and, glad to get her back turned, went down into the scullery.

'Oh, God, can't she die? Kill her! Kill her! Kill her!' she prayed violently as she splashed a little water on her face down which tears of anger and mortification came rolling fast. 'Bad luck to her in her life and in her dying and in her death. Oh, kill her, kill her, kill her, and may she suffer the tortures of the damned, the eternally damned!'

She choked a sob in the towel. To be humiliated that way! To be spoken to like that! Told to wash! She, Bridget Kiernan! An Irish girl! She'd get her own back somehow, she would so.

She stood for a moment getting her breath under control. Paula came running downstairs and into the kitchen. Bridget turned back to the basin, and washed her hands noisily. Anything to give herself a few seconds out of the sight of the mistress. She wouldn't give the old bitch – she didn't care; that was the right name for her – she wouldn't give the old bitch the chance to see she'd been crying.

She went back with the water-jug filled. The mistress didn't turn round from the fire, but Paula stared at her, and said in her shrill voice: 'You have got a red face, Bridget. You look as if you'd been crying.'

'Run upstairs, Paula, till you're called to have your cocoa,' said Mrs Fitzroy firmly; and Paula, running after Bridget, pushed past her so that Bridget nearly stumbled. 'Will you look where you're going, and don't push,' said the girl so sharply that Paula was surprised into saying, 'Sorry.'

Ah, but the dining-room had a blessed coolness with no one in it. If she could only lock the door, and stand there for ever by herself.

The piano across the road was still playing. She listened to it awhile, her lips apart and a dreamy look in her eyes. She and the pain inside her, and the little song in the night, and the silence that surrounded them were all part of one another, or seemed so in some queer fashion that brought its soothing message. After a while she stirred herself, and gave a little thoughtful nod. That was the way things were, God pity us all.

When dinner had been taken upstairs there was Paula to be seen to, and the cocoa made for them both. When they were drinking it the bell rang, and Bridget took up the pudding and clean plates on a tray. As soon as she got in the room she knew they had been talking about her because of the sudden conscious silence into which they were immediately plunged. She held her head high as she went out of the room.

Then Paula was sent for to say good-night; and Bridget had to prepare her bath. She felt a sudden impulse to be determined and hasten things along.

'Will you come now, Miss Paula?' she called irritably from the bathroom.

Paula came running in with just her little vest on. 'Didn't your mother say you were to wear your slippers and put on your dressing-gown?' Bridget demanded mechanically.

Paula disdained reply. She put her fingers in the water. 'It's too cold, turn some more hot on.'

Bridget obeyed, testing the water with her hand meanwhile. Paula decided to be naughty. 'I don't like you putting your dirty red hands into my bath water,' she said, wrinkling her nose with disgust.

Bridget turned off the tap with a jerk. Then she brought her face close to Paula.

'You don't speak to me like that. Do you hear me now? You don't speak to me like that.'

There was so much passion behind her words that Paula, abashed, got into the bath without replying. She meditated bursting into tears, for she knew that in the ordinary way it was just because Bridget, like the previous maids, was afraid of her crying and bringing up her mother that she got her own way. But Bridget was different tonight. Perhaps it wasn't worth it.

Going back to get Paula's nightgown and slippers Bridget looked at herself in the wardrobe glass. She had a vague impression of a queer-faced girl with a lot of dark hair, eyes that seemed all black pupils, and a white apron over a black dress. It was strange and queer that that should be herself, Bridget Kiernan!

Paula was put into bed and left with her picture book till her mother should come and put out the light. Bridget went down, and cleared away the dinner things. her brain had stopped registering anything; she felt very tired, and her back ached; only a dull hate burned within her.

As she cleaned the knives she heard voices in the hall. Were they after going out? Please God, they were! She stopped and listened attentively.

Someone had gone upstairs. She'd take the silver up to the dining-room; that would give her a chance to see what was going on. Returning, she saw Mrs Fitzroy come down the stairs with her hat and coat on. 'Oh, Bridget, I'm going out. Have you washed up?'

'I have, ma'am.'

'Wait a minute then.'

She went into the study and lifted the coal-box lid. 'You'd better bring up some more coals.' When Bridget came back, she found Mrs Fitzroy still in the room. Mr Fitzroy was sitting reading the evening paper. So he wasn't going out.

'If anyone calls, Bridget, tell them I'm out, but that Mr Fitzroy is in.'

'Yes, I will, ma'am.'

No one had ever called since Bridget had been there, except the mistress's brother. And once the master had brought home a friend. But SHE always told her to say that. SHE had told her to bring up more coal when it wasn't wanted, because she didn't want her to come in the room with the master there by himself. Oh, she saw through her well enough.

Bridget returned to the kitchen, and stood waiting till she heard the front door slam. There it was! She relaxed. The old devil was out of the house for a while. Thanks be to God for it!

'Isn't it a pity she hasn't taken herself off for good?' she muttered to herself. 'Begob, she's the worst vixen in the world; and it wouldn't hurt me at all to know that she'd fallen down where she stood and died. Not at all it wouldn't.'

She shook her head, the sense of all her wrongs coming uppermost to her mind. Then she sat down in the easy chair, and buried her head in her arms. Soon she found herself shaken by sobs, the sobs that had been pent up within her for the last hour or two.

They grew more and more unrestrained till she recollected herself in a fright, and, with her hand pressed to her mouth, got up and closed the kitchen door. The master mustn't be let hear.

Now for a good cry. It would relieve her feelings. She sniffed and whimpered and gasped, while her nose became swollen, and her eyes grew small as they disappeared under her puffy eyelids. Sometimes her grief would slacken in its expression for a moment; but then the remembrance of one or another of her troubles and resentments would surge up again, and she would renew her sobs. It was a shame for her! A shame! And no one cared a tither.

At last she cried herself out. At first she was conscious of nothing but that her skin seemed pressed tightly over the top of her head, and that her body was giving little uncontrollable shivers. She poked up the fire and turned her chair round to it. For some while she sat thus, smoothing out the pain at the back of her forehead with her fingers.

Slowly odd fragments of thoughts began to drift to and fro in her mind. The delf was still in the scullery, she'd have to put it away. Wasn't it very still? You couldn't hear a sound. . . it was twenty to nine. . . the big picture would be about be on at the cinema; what would happen to the girl in it? Anyway there'd likely be a happy ending. . . There was her *Home Notes,* and she didn't feel like reading it at all. . . she'd have all her pleasure spoilt. . . would those two fellows have picked up two girls? . . . were they having a good time? . . . It was a shame the way she was put on by the mistress. . .

'Bridget!'

My God! Was that someone calling? Bridget went quickly to the door and opened it. It was Mr Fitzroy. He was standing at the top of the kitchen stairs.

'Yes, sir.'

'Are you there, Bridget? I thought you might like to look at the evening paper?'

Bridget went quickly upstairs, feeling the perplexity suggested by her temperament. Did he mean her to take the paper or not? He might be depriving himself.

'Ah, sure, it's all right, sir,' she said hesitatingly.

'I've finished with it.'

'Thank you very much, sir.'

She took the newspaper and turned her back as quickly as possible, leaving Mr Fitzroy to return to his chair disturbed. The girl had been crying. There was no doubt about it. Poor little soul! It seemed a bit thick for her to be crying down in the kitchen while he sat there. Was she homesick? Her home was a long way away, and the Irish, of course, were very patriotic. Or Dorothy might have been sharp with her? She had been complaining at dinner about her being stupid and dirty.

He went into the dining-room, and poured himself out a whisky. It was a pity he couldn't go down to the kitchen and comfort the girl. But too dangerous. He'd never forget Dorothy catching him out kissing that girl – what was her name? Alice – they had had a couple of years ago. Never gave him a chance to forget it, she didn't. Ah, well!

He returned to the fire. Dorothy would be back soon. He'd speak to her about it. Or better not. Women were the devil to one another. The girl wasn't bad-looking either. Something soft and appealing about her. The way she spoke perhaps.

No good letting his mind run on women.

Bridget had carefully spread the paper out on the table. She stood for a moment, looking at it unseeingly, and feeling warmed by the kindness shown her. 'That's a decent one,' she thought to herself. 'He deserved a better one for his marriage bed. Wouldn't it be grand now if I could get a place with a man by himself, as his housekeeper. Someone who'd know how to treat a girl polite.'

She moved into the scullery and restored the crockery to its right place. Then she sat down again.

Well, she felt better now that she'd had her cry out. She wouldn't have minded a bit of a read. Nothing like a good story to take your mind off things. Only she ought to think of her position really seriously like. Suppose, strange and impossible as it sounded, she really was going to have a baby? She'd give herself another week, and then, God help her, if she didn't come on, she'd be sure she was in the way.

The terrible part of it all was that there wasn't a creature she

could talk it over with. Now these London girls would be sure to be
up to all sorts of tricks for stopping things. There was the girl next
door that she'd passed the time of day with. But could she go and
say to her. . . ah, of course she couldn't. It wouldn't be decent.

There was her mother. 'My dear mother, I take my pen in my
hand to tell you I have bad news for you. There was a fellow I met,
and I am sorry to say he has got me into trouble. . .'

Oh, Holy Mary! What would her mother say, and she reading a
letter with news the like of that. Oh, didn't it sound terrible when
you came to put it into words. A disgrace to her poor mother she
was, and a disgrace to herself. . .

Tears were unloosened again, but her mind was no longer still.
It seemed to her she was weeping for remorse at her wickedness,
and the thought vaguely comforted her. The first thing she must
do was to repent. Wasn't there the Blessed Mary Magdalene? She'd
pray for her intercession. And she'd say an Act of Contrition as if it
were to the priest himself. First she'd confess.

Bridget knelt down on the floor and with folded hands repeated
the Confiteor. When she came to the words, 'I have sinned exceedingly in thought and word and deed, through my fault, through my
fault, through my most grievous fault,' she had to pause for sobbing. The magnitude of her sin overwhelmed her, and it seemed to
her that she had been hard and unashamed up to now.

Then she repeated the Act of Contrition. That was better. Sure,
God would forgive her if she truly repented and offended Him no
more. And she did truly repent. Perhaps He'd let her off having a
baby. Now a Hail Mary. 'Hail Mary, full of grace, the Lord is with
thee: blessed art thou among women, and blessed is the fruit of thy
womb, Jesus. Holy Mary, Mother of God, pray for us sinners, now
and at the hour of our death.'

The familiar words soothed Bridget. There's nothing so com-
forting as a Hail Mary when deep troubles come upon you, she reflected, and repeated the invocation several times. Then she said
the 'Hail Holy Queen,' and then an Our Father. And then she
turned back once more to the words which gave her the most heal-
ing, 'Holy Mary, Mother of God, pray for us sinners, now and at
the hour of our death.'

Hadn't Father Reilly once preached a sermon – she remembered the time well, because she had been wondering if it would be right to pray for a bit of money so that she could get herself the new cute hat in Murphy's – hadn't he said then that the Blessed Virgin never denied Her intercession to those who approached Her in sorrow and contrition?

That was true. There were the words, 'A contrite and a humble heart, O God, Thou wilt not despise.'

She blessed herself and rose. She felt tired, but there was a sort of happiness with her all the same. There was a great help in saying a few prayers, and no one could say else. She had been brought up badly, and that was the truth. It was her father's blame. For ever cursing and swearing at the priests and saying they were the bane of the country. God forgive him! Well, he was dead and knew better now. God spare him and deliver him from distress and torments.

'Deliver him, O Lord, from eternal death.'

In a fashion it was due to him and the way he'd never set an example that she'd lost her beads which Father Reilly had blessed. In the Isle of Man she'd never given a hoot. Well, indeed and indeed, it would be different from this time on. She'd be chaste and pure; she'd put away all thought of badness, kissing and such-like. She'd buy a new Rosary as soon as she got her money; she'd go to Mass every Sunday; she'd go to confession. . .

But that last wasn't too pleasant to think about. What would the priest be after saying at all? Would he tell her to confide in her mistress? She wouldn't do that. Never. After all, the mistress was a Protestant. Would he let her off if she told him that? He might.

You could never tell what an English priest would do. He might be poking his nose in her affairs all the time. Hadn't her father always said they were the meddlesome fellows, making trouble and bringing ill-luck wherever they went.

What was she thinking? Ah, nothing! Nothing at all. (She crossed herself quickly.) She wasn't meaning any harm. But it was difficult. The more you thought the more troublesome everything was.

A red bank of cinders broke and fell to the bottom of the grate.

Bridget roused herself, and gave the fire a poke. Watching the flames dart swiftly upwards, she meditated whether she would put some more coal on. Better not. SHE'D march in, stare hard at the fire, as if she'd never seen such a thing in all her life before, and say something about wasting coals at night-time. What was the time? Half-past nine. She must not forget she had the shoes to clean. Would SHE want hot milk when she got in? Another saucepan to clean. Never cared what trouble she gave.

Her evening off tomorrow. Nobody to meet. It might be a good thing to go up to the church, and see if she could find anything out about a priest. Somebody might be giving her a tip about getting hold of the decentest one; someone with a bit of sympathy in him. Ay, there was no call yet. There mightn't be anything in it after all. And she worrying herself to flitters with no need. It was the thinking and worrying that had you driven distracted.

A wind blew up, murmured, complained, and sank down. Bridget heard and shivered. You never knew your luck, of course, and it was a queer world to be in. Anything might happen to anyone at any time. God help us all!

It wouldn't hurt her at all to die at this moment.

It would be a way out of all the confusion. No more getting dog's abuse from morning to night. No more cleaning out the grates. Eternal rest. She couldn't kill herself, or else she'd go to hell maybe. 'The horrid darkness, the hissing flames, and the excruciating tortures.' Ah, no! But to die quietly as she was sitting there. Heart failure. And then people would be sorry. Mrs Fitz. would be shown up for what she was. Her mother and the neighbours would be weeping and crying when they heard the news. 'Is it Bridget?' they would say. 'Is it Bridget Kiernan?' 'She that went to the Isle of Man and London?' 'Poor Bridget's gone.' 'Is she now?' 'That's bad.'

Was that the front door? Bridget sat up alertly. Yes, a key was turning in the lock. It was the mistress back. If she came down, she'd better look as if she'd been reading the paper. Oh, she'd gone in the room to the master. Better go and get the shoes done.

As she was knocking off the dry dirt into the coal-bucket, she heard Mrs Fitzroy call:

'Bring me up a cup of hot milk, please.'

'Yes, ma'am.'

She filled the saucepan and brought it to the fire. There was only a little fire left. What she'd best do was to hold a paper in front. The paper on the table would do well enough. The master had said he'd done with it. Unthinkingly she held the newspaper to the fire, her heart heavy again with apprehension. There was no happiness possible when that one was about.

A flame singed the edge of the sheet, and Bridget was only just in time to prevent it catching fire. The fire would do now. But the milk wasn't near boiling. She tested it with her finger. Only tepid. Had she better go up and tell the mistress that the fire was nearly out? But it was like taking poison to go near her. And she didn't like speaking in front of the master.

Her predicament was decided by the study bell going.

That was terrible. Mrs Fitz. didn't often ring the bell, at least not so late in the evening. It meant she must be in one of her tantrums again: would it be that she'd get herself scolded in front of the master for being so slow with the milk?

When she opened the door of the room, Mrs Fitzroy was sitting on the couch, looking very solemn, while Mr Fitzroy appeared to be reading some book intently. 'Oh, Bridget, I should like to see the evening paper if you've finished with it. And isn't the milk ready?'

'Yes, ma'am. I'll bring it up, ma'am, but the fire isn't very grand.'

'I suppose you mean there's no fire at all. Why didn't you say so before? Well, bring up the saucepan here, and I'll see to it on this fire. And a cup and saucer. On a tray. *On a tray,* remember.'

'I will, ma'am.'

Bridget went downstairs with her cheeks burning. She hated it when Mrs Fitzroy put on that thin voice with no sort of expression in it at all. As if she were speaking to a piece of furniture, and as if she, Bridget, wasn't really flesh and blood, and couldn't be expected to understand things like other people. Those English airs!

She fetched the tray and pondered for a moment on the question of putting the saucepan on it as well as the cup and saucer. Perhaps not, because it would make a dirty mark. But if she didn't it would sure to be wrong. . . And then the paper that was burnt! Arrange it so as not to show the singed place. Sure, she'd probably never look at it. Only wanted it out of spite. She went upstairs again.

Mrs Fitzroy nodded. 'All right, I'll see to it. Give me the saucepan, and leave the tray on the desk. That's right. You'd better get off to bed now. It's after ten. Is your alarum clock working correctly?'

'It is, ma'am.'

'And you've cleaned the shoes?'

'Yes ma'am.'

Mrs Fitzroy dismissed her with a nod. Mr Fitzroy turned over another page.

She went back to the kitchen feeling guilty and yet triumphant. She had got out of that all right, so long as the mistress didn't take it into her head to walk into the kitchen and see the shoes only half done. Ah, well, it wouldn't take her long to polish them off. It was no use telling *her* that she hadn't finished them, and give her a chance to be disagreeable in front of the master.

Upstairs, Mrs Fitzroy poured out the milk, and then started to read the paper. As she turned it over, she noticed the burnt place. 'With all respect, Harry,' she said suddenly, 'I don't think Bridget does much newspaper reading. I am quite sure she had never looked at this the whole evening – just used it to get the fire going. Look! Newspapers are not in Bridget's line. She keeps incredibly dirty-looking paper novelettes for her reading purposes.'

'Sorry, my dear. I won't give it her again.'

Dorothy Fitzroy was unable to control a grimace of irritation. Men were so stupid; answering you as if you had said things you never had.

'It isn't that. I'm sure I should be only too glad if she showed an intelligent interest in anything. I don't want her not to get every consideration. But she's an absolute fool. And a liar. That's what I object to most.'

Her voice grew shriller, and her husband didn't reply. Usually he was more sympathetic than this.

'You think I'm hard on her? Well, just take today. At twenty past seven there was not a sign of her, and I had to get out of my bed, and go and call her. That meant that I had to cook the breakfast myself so as to get you off in time. You ought to have seen her

standing gaping at me, incapable of doing a thing. Just the same
with luncheon; she's always wriggling out of doing things, so that
it's simpler to get them done myself. And it makes me feel ill,
positively ill, in any case, to see her dirty hands – she never washes
unless she's told, and I did tell her this evening; unless, of course
she's going out for the evening, and then she'd dressed up and
powdered to kill – well, it makes me sick to see her hands poking
into the food we're going to eat.'

Mr Fitzroy murmured agreement.

'It's the same with errands. She forgot to get the eggs this afternoon when she was out with Paula, until the child reminded her.
And after tea, when I sent her to get some more bread – there's nothing wrong with her appetite, I'm always having to get extra bread
and tea and potatoes in, and butter – she took over half an hour
over it. And then pretended they were sold out at Paley's and she
had had to go just a few doors further on to Bowen's. What do you
think of that for a story? A child could see through her. Walking
up, and down, staring at the shops, as cool as a cucumber, of
course.

'And the way she throws food away! After all, we're not
millionaires. When she was out I found in the dust-bin a huge
piece of toast she had thrown away. Burnt it, you see, and then
sneaked it away, thinking I should never see. She's always burning
bread. And she throws away half the potatoes with the peel.'

'If she was only willing to learn I'd never say a word. But she's
not. She lets you do anything rather than do it herself. Just stands
by and stares at you, without raising a finger. And if you speak a
word to her, then she goes away and cries. Or else looks like a
thunderstorm. I really sometimes think she can't be all there the
way she goes on.'

She paused, and Mr Fitzroy saw a reply was expected. He
moved uneasily, remembering Bridget's swollen tear-stained face.
'Perhaps she's homesick?'

'If she hasn't got over that by now, she ought to. She came to me
of her own free will, didn't she? And she'd been in the Isle of Man
before that. Though she's obviously never been properly trained.
You don't seem to bother about me, but I can tell you it's not very

pleasant having a girl going about the house all day looking like a sick cow. As if she might burst into tears at any moment.

'And she hasn't gone up to bed now. I told her to go off, because I was determined she shouldn't have any excuse for not getting up tomorrow. But she calmly disobeys me. It's waste of time saying anything to her. But I believe I know what she's doing.'

Dorothy got up suddenly and went to the door, opening it very quietly. She went a few steps along the passage, and then listened. Presently she returned and closed the door.

'As I thought,' she said triumphantly. 'She's cleaning the shoes. You heard her say, didn't you, that she had done them?'

Mr Fitzroy pursed his lips gloomily, and nodded.

'Another lie! Then she was afraid I'd find her out. So she sneaks down, and does them on the quiet. That's the sort of thing I'm always having to put up with. You see for yourself now?'

'Why don't you dismiss her then if you're not satisfied?'

'I expect it'll come to that. But it's no joke getting girls in these days. They're nearly all as bad. Or unkind to Paula.'

Mr Fitzroy let his eyes return to his book. He wished Dorothy would go to bed so that he could have another whiskey.

Mrs Fitzroy observed him with resentment. He was not really sympathetic. You worked from morning to night to see that the house was run properly, and got no thanks for it. People seemed to think you liked being disagreeable. As if it wouldn't be far easier to let the maids do as they liked and not give a button, like some women. The house would be dirty, and bills run up, but it wouldn't matter to them. Or apparently it wouldn't. Just give Harry the chance to see how uncomfortable he would be if she didn't look after things. It would make him sing a different tune then. . .

But she was tired to death of it all. You wore yourself out coping with dirty ignorant lying sluts, and no one cared. . . no one cared.

Bridget passed the door, and though she was going softly Mrs Fitzroy, who had been waiting for the sound, heard her. There the girl was, she thought, creeping up to bed like a thief. Well, if she had any more trouble getting her up in the morning she'd give her notice. She'd made up her mind to that.

She turned her attention to the leading article headed 'More

Efficiency', and read it with approval. It comforted her, for it secured to her the feeling that she was in the right. Cleanliness, speaking the truth, punctuality, capability, were things that mattered. The whole country would be in the workhouse otherwise. And she and Henry would be in the workhouse, if she took her hands off the household helm (something like that the paper said, and very rightly). It was the individual's contribution that mattered. Well, she would go on doing her share, whether she got any sympathy or not!

Upstairs, Bridget was lying in bed wrapped round in a blissful feeling of security. She had made a discovery. She was safe after all. No baby on the way! Wasn't that the great mercy? God had answered her prayers. The Blessed Virgin had not interceded in vain. After this you couldn't say but that there was a great deal in religion. Oh, she'd keep her word to Our Blessed Lord, and be a good girl for keeps. Wait till marriage after this scare! It was she was the happy girl, with the relief of it. The mistress didn't matter, not at all she didn't. She'd give her notice one day soon, see if she didn't. It wouldn't be difficult to get another job. There was a great shortage of domestic servants, so the papers were always setting forth. A job now where she'd see a bit more life would suit her grand. She must mind and remember to get the beads all the same. Sure, God was good, and it wasn't a bad world, if a queer up-and-down one at that.

For Richer, For Poorer

Edith Somerville

Edith Œone Somerville was born at Corfu, where her father's regiment was stationed, in 1858; her Ascendancy Anglo-Irish family returned to Drishane, their home at Castletownshend, Cork, when she was less than a year old. Educated at home, Somerville early developed an interest in drawing and painting, which she pursued throughout her life. By 1884 she had managed to study art in London, Dusseldorf, and Paris and seemed set on a genteel career as a painter and illustrator, but two years later she met her cousin Violet Martin.

The first book on which they collaborated, *An Irish Cousin* (London: Richard Bentley, 1889) was followed by many others. But when Martin died in 1915, Somerville, deeply bereaved, thought that she would never write again. For some time before Martin's death, the cousins had been interested in spiritualism, and in 1916, Somerville became convinced that she had made contact with her cousin's spirit and returned to writing. All of her subsequent books were signed with both names. Somerville never doubted that the collaboration was being actively continued.

Somerville's twin passions for art and hunting figure strongly in the Somerville and Ross books; in 1903 she became the first female M.F.H. in Ireland, and in her old age she began to exhibit and sell her paintings. *The Big House at Inver* (London: Heinemann, 1925) is the most noteworthy book produced after Martin's death, but Somerville published their final book in the year of her own death, 1949. In 1932 she was invited to become a member of the Irish Academy of Letters, and in the same year she was awarded, jointly, an honorary D.Litt.; the Irish Academy's award of the Gregory Medal consolidated the position of Somerville and Ross in Anglo-Irish Letters.

Irish Memories (London: Longmans, Green, 1917), *Stray-Aways* (London: Longmans, Green, 1920) and *Wheel-Tracks* (London: Longmans, Green, 1923) are of interest because these collections of essays, sketches and memories reveal a great deal about the nature of the cousins' experiences and collaboration.

'For Richer, For Poorer', a loose collection of sketches linked thematically, is of importance not only because it can be contrasted interestingly with Violet Martin's somewhat similar sketches but also because it is, like all of the Somerville and Ross writing, not very far removed from the reality of their experiences.

After Hilary Robinson's *Somerville and Ross: A Critical Appreciation* (Dublin: Gill and Macmillan, 1980) and Geraldine Cummin's Somerville biography, there are several books which deal with the literary partnership: Violet Powell's

The Irish Cousins (London: Heinemann, 1970) provides interesting reading about them and their collaboration, for which there is no sign of diminishing public appetite.

'HASTE TO the Wedding' is a light-hearted and cheerful tune that suggests cutting capers and dancing jigs, and holds no hint of Romance, or of the gravity of the Holy Estate of Matrimony. Still less does one associate its laughing gaiety with the austerity of Finance. Yet there are not many marriages among the country-people of Southern Ireland that are not based on sound business principles, and on the traditional assertion that there isn't the value of a cow between any two women – which may, from one point of view, be true, but is a rather crude and one-sided way of putting it.

It is one of Ireland's many inconsistencies that in affairs of the heart she is strictly practical, while in the practical affair of Politics she is inveterately romantic. But, so thorough is her inconsistency, these State alliances, founded though they may be on the common-place of financial security, have a way of making for happiness that love matches do not invariably achieve, and one begins dispassionately to wonder if the Romantics and the Poets haven't been wrong all the time, and the stern, business-like parents right.

As Martin Ross has said in an article on this same subject:

> Writers of novels, and readers of novels, had better shut their eyes to the fact, the inexorable fact, that such marriages are rushed into every day – loveless, sordid marriages, such as we are taught to hold in abhorrence, and that from them springs, like a flower from a dust heap, the unsullied, uneventful home-life of Western Ireland. It is romance that holds the two-edged sword, the sharp ecstasy and the severing scythe stroke, the expectancy and the disillusioning, the trance and the clearer vision.
>
> It is even more than passive domestic toleration that blossoms in the cramped and dirty cabin life, affection grows with years, and where personal attraction never counted for much, the loss of it hurts nobody.

So it is that a Mother could say approvingly of an elderly suitor, advanced by a match-maker, 'He's a warm man and he have a nate house. Sure he's not all out so old atall! If it were to be Mary was marri'd in the counthry near me, I'd stand still in my mind, and I'd stand in peace in my mind.'

And the Father could add that he had the land walked and it would carry a good share of cattle, and there was no doubt that the proposed husband was a nice respectable quiet man, and he had turf stacked for years. That is to say abundant firing. What more could be asked?

It cannot, however, be denied that the high contracting parties sometimes take risks. There was a marriage that happened so long ago that it is now ancient history (and therefore possibly apocryphal), when all the eyes concerned were wide open, but the risk was faced. The scene was a small provincial town, in – or so I have heard – the County Clare: one of those neighbourly little towns where everyone knows a good deal more about everyone else than they know themselves. So it was no secret that the Bridegroom, a very well-to-do young man, 'took a drop'. In fact, when it was known that he had chosen as his Best Man a friend of like passions with himself, the Bride's Mother insisted on an understudy, 'for,' she said, 'no doubt Tom' – the Bridegroom – 'would have a drop taken, and maybe between himself and Dick' – (the Best Man) – 'who might also, it was likely, take a drop for himself, the ring itself might go astray on them.'

So what was genially spoken of as a Second-best Man was nominated. On the wedding morning the Best Men agreed that their charge would be the better for 'something to put blood in his eye' before the ceremony, and three bottles of champagne were procured for the purpose. The regrettable result of this precaution was that when the priest tendered the Bridegroom the book with the ring on it, the Bridegroom, taking the priest by force and surprise, crammed the ring on his thumb. A violent struggle ensued, in the course of which the ring, having, with considerable difficulty, been removed from his thumb by the priest, undoubtedly went astray on them, for it fell down a hot-air grating and was lost for ever in the bowels of the church.

A hurried consultation ensued, during which it is said that the waiting Bridegroom fell asleep. The Bride's Mother, being anxious to avoid postponement, since the breakfast was prepared, laid all blame on the Best Men. The Bridegroom's Mother, saying it was a shame for them two fellas to hoodwink the poor boy that way, giving him drink and him nervous enough already, sent forth an emissary to buy another ring. And the Bride, who had been well taught to remember that those whom her mother was accustomed to speak of compassionately as 'the min, God help us!' were by reason of their sex and the fraility of their natures to be excused, was undaunted by a bad start.

So the service was concluded.

After this it was found advisable to withdraw the Bridegroom and the Best Men from the festivities, and to put them temporarily to bed at a neighbouring hotel. It is said that the subsequent married life thus, rather unfortunately, begun, was entirely happy and satisfactory, and was no exception to the rule that marriages based on sound commercial principles do credit to the judgment of those who have arranged them.

Happily for story-tellers the rule is not without exceptions. There is, for example, the case of Slow Jerry. Jerry determined to soothe the latter days of his pilgrimage by taking to himself a wife, who should not only serve as nurse and general slave in his household, but should also bring a dowry that would contribute to its maintenance. He was then near sixty years old, a mature age that was in keeping with his general habit of deliberation, and it was unlucky that when delay and careful consideration were advisable, he should have shown a rare and, as the event proved, inopportune impetuosity. It was his sister who told the story of his marriage, and, unexpectedly, it was his mercenariness and not his sloth that she denounced.

'Jerry had a right not to be so covetous,' said the sister, a stout, foxy countrywoman, very unlike her brother, who with his red beard and thin saintly face, looked like a starved apostle. 'But he was all for the money! Sure when he had his mind made to get marri'd, I told him of one that'd suit him to fortune, an' I said I'd make the match for him – a nice decent quiet widda woman; ye'd couldn't but like her, she was so blushy and respectable.'

The question as to whether her charms, in addition to complexion and social standing, included a balance at the Bank, was
received by Jerry's sister with a sarcastic laugh.

'Ye've hit it now, faith!' she said, approvingly. 'The husband
died on her, and she hadn't what'd keep herself but as little. This
woman he's after marrin' is as cross as briars, but when Jerry heard
she had forty pound, six shillin', and two pince in the post office,
nothing would content him only to marry her. Three days before
the marriage I went to her and I seduced her to get out the forty
pound, and herself and meself took down the pass-book to the
post-masther's to try could we get the money. But the post-
masther said we could not for three days, and I said to Jerry "Take
my advice and wait the three days!" And that was the end of it. It
was for the sake o' the forty pound he had marri'd her, and she was
that crabbed all she'd give him was the book! And what good was
that to him? She had her mind changed to leave the forty pound in
the post office. She wouldn't give him a ha'-penny! If he were to die
dead she wouldn't give him an egg itself!'

She paused for a moment, not so much to draw breath as to give
me time to offer a suitable comment, while she put back a straying
lock of red hair that the denunciations of her sister-in-law had
loosened from under the black shawl that covered her head.

'And cross!' she continued. 'Sure she's dancin' before him
always, tearing the face off him! God knows I melted her there to
the divil under me teeth on Sunday after chapel!'

I could wish to have viewed that scene, from a safe distance –
behind the chapel gate perhaps (but within earshot) – I question if
any theatre in Europe could have staged its equal.

'He was ill there three days, above in the room, and all she done
was turn the kay in the door and go out! If it was a young hen that'd
be worth a sixpence she'd let him die for the want of it! And look!'
She shot a lean hand from under the black shawl, her green eyes
sparkling. 'Didn't That One think he hadn't but a few months o'
life in him, and look at him now! He's not sixty years at all! If he's
fifty-five it's the heighth of him! He's one that'll last during dura-
tion! Ah-ha! The two o' them was took in – the one as good as
th'other!'

But not always is Romance mocked and made subservient to
Money, or Love thwarted by Expediency. There was a time, long
ago, when a comely young coachman, made beautiful by the dash-
ing livery of his now nearly obsolete office, loved an under-house-
maid, a pretty pale girl, with the dark eyes and raven hair that had
probably come down to her from some Spanish ancestor, who had
been flung into West Carbery by the tempest that wrecked the
Armada. (Have we not a long stretch of rocky coast that is
called Spain in memory of those involuntary invaders?)

To these two Love came in the traditional fashion, free of the
fetters of family and finance. They plighted their mutual troth, and
settled down to wait.

Michael-John was his name, and hers was Mary-Ellen. In our
country, if one possesses a second name, one makes it work for its
living, and thus it is spared the degradation of shrivelling into an
initial.

The orderly changeless years moved on. Michael-John's master
was High Sheriff for the County one year, and Michael-John, looking more beautiful than ever in new livery, cocked hat and top-
boots, drove his master and the Judge to the court-house, and
wrote to Mary-Ellen saying 'Me and my horses is admired by all.'
Which was no more than the truth, and was repeated reverentially
by Mary-Ellen to all her friends. They 'walked-out' together every
Sunday afternoon, pacing decorously side by side, speaking little, a
space ever between them that was never crossed by a stealing hand
seeking the peace and sense of completion that a touch can give.
Carriage-horses, in the old days when such things were, had, undoubtedly, some power of silently communicating with one
another. Barney, on the off side of the pole, would telepathically
advise Larry, on the near, that there was a stone or a donkey worth
shying at; and Larry would swing and curtsey with as appropriate
panic as if he had seen either the one or the other.

Thus, one can only suppose, the souls of Michael-John and
Mary-Ellen conversed, as, speechlessly, they moved side by side
along the road consecrated by custom to walking-out. And thus the
years passed, as is their relentless way, and still the souls of these

faithful lovers had for consolation but the decorous Sunday walk. Michael-John had a father and a sister, the one very old, the other crippled, both very cross, both entirely reliant on him, and both firmly assured that Michael-John was theirs, to have and to hold till death them did part, quite regardless of Michael-John's possible views on the matter.

The carriage and its horses faded away; Michael-John became a chauffeur and ran to flesh. Mary-Ellen went to England, and worked hard, and grew thin. And thus for seventeen years the course of true love ran through dry and arid places. Tragic to think that it was over two graves that at last their hands were joined. One wonders if the father and the sister, looking on from the other side of death, felt any compunction for what had been their part in the affair. And yet why should they be penitent? 'They went' – as a philosophical neighbour said – 'when the time came for them, the cratures! Sure people can't be stopping alive for ever at all! They must go – worse luck!'

And so, in the latter end, Michael-John and Mary-Ellen were happy. When, after some two-score years, the time came for Michael-John, and he fell on the steering-wheel of the motor one day, and died, as a fellow-servant reported, as quietly as a little fish, Mary-Ellen could say, 'What'll the children and me do without him? We were so happy we were like four angels together.'

It may be said, and truly, that the success of this love-match was paid for by long and weary waiting, and that marriages made by authority have at least the merit of getting under way at once, and with a fair wind. Moreover, they contrive a double bet to pay, because they are often based upon a system of compensation. It is a very general custom that the dowry brought by a daughter-in-law is devoted to continuing its career as a dowry, by becoming the marriage-portion of the bridegroom's sister, a convenient arrangement which may, to some extent, explain the attempt to wreck the fortunes of two true lovers by certain youths whose sympathies should have been with them.

This is the story.

A match had been made for a young girl with a prosperous

farmer who was something older than her father. That she had given her heart to a schoolfellow, a lad of her own age, was known to the negotiating family, but was ignored as a youthful fancy, not worthy of discussion. The Family, father, mother, brother, aunts and uncles, demanded to know, oratorically, and of no one in particular – what call had Nora to go agin her parents' arrangements? Surely themselves should know what was best for her!

Nora acquiesced. She viewed docilely the preparations for her wedding, the whisky, the tea, the cakes, and old Mickel-Paudeen the Piper, bespoke. She helped her mother to 'clean down' the house, and when all was ready, and she and the rest of the tired family had gone to bed, she slipped out of her bedroom window, and stole away to the cottage of a distant neighbour, a widow who had a feeling heart, and – what was equally valuable – an old-standing quarrel with Mr William Horrigan, the prospective bridegroom. Also, the young lover was her nephew.

For two days the secret of the refuge was kept. The lover lost no time in making ready for the lass. At the second midnight after the flight, Nora and the widow, waiting by the fireside for news, heard a tapping on the window-pane and knew who was there. All was ready, the ring was in his pocket, the priest was warned, and they would be married, quietly and early, the next morning.

The young man was a personable fellow, the girl was sweet and twenty. They sat side by side on two low stools by the fire, facing the Woman of the House, who was the boy's aunt. I expect she felt she was doing good work in admitting no impediment to the marriage of true minds, especially when the impediment took the form of her enemy, William Horrigan.

The turf fire had burned away to red and grey ashes before the talk had ended, and the Woman of the House felt that a move must be made.

'Run away home now, Johnny,' she said, ''tis late! 'Twill shortly be making day itself, and you have your work set for the morning!'

And Johnny was preparing to run away, when there came a thundering on the door of the cottage, and loud voices demanding admittance, shouting threats, swearing dead or alive they would have what they came for.

'The back-door, Johnny!' hissed the Woman of the House, advancing to the fray, screaming defiances to the foe, hearing them without – as she afterwards narrated – 'leppin' and rarin' an' ravin',' holding them there by sheer force of abuse until she judged that Johnny had got well away. For two or three minutes only her blighting tongue held them, then they would be held no longer, and they kicked in the door, smashing the timber and wrenching the hinges, and burst into the house.

There were four of them, tall young men, all dressed alike – with, presumably, the idea of concealing their identity – in the white flannel jackets that are called 'bauneens,' and grey homespun trousers, their faces half-covered by black masks, all full of 'taspy' (which is a local word that denotes impudence and exuberance) and of what they felt to be the noble resolve to uphold parental authority.

The Woman of the House thrust the girl into that inner chamber that is known as Back-in-the-room, and planted herself in the doorway, daring the invaders to lay a finger on her or on her visitor, while the latter, having, in spite of the masks, recognised her brother and three of her cousins, denounced them by name over the protecting shoulder of her hostess. One gathers that there then ensued an exchange of opinions of considerable violence, in the conduct of which the four young men were quite outclassed by the Woman of the House. Assuring them that she was prepared to swear to every one of them before any magistrate in any court in the Globe of Ireland, she proceeded to offer, in the tones of a trombone, able and scandalous biographies of them, their parents, and their grandparents to the third and fourth generation. She threatened them with the penalties for housebreaking, pointing to the door that was hanging crookedly on a single hinge, and then, with a dramatic change of manner to a sinister politeness, she waved a skinny arm towards the gaping hole into the night that had been their work, and said:

'There's nothin' stopping ye! Walk out, me gintlemin!'

The gentlemen, feeling that their mission had not turned out as they had expected, began to shuffle indeterminately towards the doorway. The Woman of the House snatched up her broom and took but one step forward, and her uninvited guests stayed not upon the order of their going, but went at once.

It may be added that the wedding of Nora and Johnny took place without interruption the following morning, and the 'summonses' to four young housebreakers were averted by the arrival of a carpenter with a new door.

It was during the last days of Shraft, before Ash Wednesday had forbidden all such worldly affairs as Matrimony, that I was paying a visit to a young country-woman, a widow, and the subject of marriage, as was appropriate to the time, came under discussion. I remember that she told me of the recent grand wedding of a rich elderly cattle-buyer and when I asked how he had made all the money, she replied, with a laugh:

"Tis what the people say he does be jobbing in widows! This now is the third one he's got for himself!'

We were standing on the verge of the western cliffs, looking away across a rough grey sea to Cape Clear. The clouds were low, but not implacably low, there was a pale light over the horizon, and through a high rift in the cloudy roof a thin screen of silver reached from sky to sea, ending in a long dazzling streak. Seventy feet below us the sea was growling in the heart of a long cave, conquered in its onslaught by the iron rocks of that fierce coast. Every now and then a sullen boom, like a blast in a mine, followed by a puff of white spray, told where an imprisoned wave had burst its way out of a cleft in the cliff that faced where we were standing. My widow owned a small farm that went back from the cliff to the hills. A lonely place; the small house and farm-sheds were down in a hollow below a high bank, on which some alder bushes and a few miserable wind-thrashed ash-trees tried to give protection from the south-westerly storms. She had a half-dozen of hungry little cattle and a handful of 'mountainy' sheep; she lived a life as solitary as Robinson Crusoe's, save that the parts of Man Friday and the parrots were played by an old father and three little children.

She was a hardy, handsome creature, fair and weather-beaten, big and bony. She stood beside me in the sea wind, on the heathery ground over the cliff, firm as a tower, with a pair of men's big boots on her feet. It was easy to think of her tramping about her narrow fields, working like a man, the thought of the three children and the old man, all dependent on her, always in her mind. Perhaps she guessed at what I was thinking, for she said the times were hard enough, and it wasn't easy for one that'd be alone.

So I asked her whether she thought a married life or a single one was the happier.

She considered a moment, her sea-blue eyes remote and thoughtful. Then she said:

'Well indeed it is what I think, once ye'd got over the disgrace of it, a single life'd be the more airy. But faith!' she added with a laugh, 'if ye get marri'd, or if ye stay single, it's aiqual which way it is, ye'll be sorry!'

Unwelcome Idea

Elizabeth Bowen

Elizabeth Bowen, one of the great names in Anglo-Irish literature, was born in Dublin in 1899. Though Bowen was educated in England and spent most of her life there, she was acutely aware of her Anglo-Irish family background, of the Ascendancy in decay, and of her own position as its representative, caught between the two cultures.

Bowen's first book of short stories appeared in 1923, and, throughout her career, she continued to write short fiction as well as novels. *The House in Paris* (London: Gollancz, 1936) and *The Death of the Heart* (London: Gallancz, 1938) are generally considered to be her finest works. *Seven Winters: Memories of a Dublin Childhood* (Dublin: Cuala, 1942) portrays Bowen's early years; it, and *Bowen's Court* (London: Longmans, 1942), tell a great deal about Bowen and the tradition which she recognised as her inheritance. *Collected Impressions* (London: Longmans, 1950) and *Afterthoughts: Pieces About Writing* (London: Longmans, Green, 1962) are important in providing insights into Bowen's views on, and approaches to, literature.

'Unwelcome Idea' is a cruelly accurate story, exposing the inanities of female suburban life in Dublin during the Emergency – the Second World War in the rest of the world. It is one of Bowen's few 'Irish' stories, and it is significant not merely because it deals with neutral Ireland at a time when Bowen herself was acting as an air raid warden in London, but because of its attention to the petty concerns of rarely recorded lives.

Elizabeth Bowen was awarded an honorary D.Litt. from Trinity College, Dublin, in 1949, and a second, from Oxford, in 1957. She died in 1973. Victoria Glendinning's biography, *Elizabeth Bowen: Portrait of a Writer* (London: Weidenfeld and Nicolson, 1977), chronicles her intensely full life as artist, critic and personality. The novels and stories of Elizabeth Bowen are constantly being re-issued and critical attention to her work remains at a high level. *Elizabeth Bowen* by Allan E. Austin (New York: Twayne, 1971) is a good introduction. *Elizabeth Bowen: An Estimation* by Hermione Lee (London: Vision, 1981) is a perceptive critique.

ALONG DUBLIN Bay, on a sunny July morning, the public gardens along the Dalkey tramline look bright as a series of parasols. Chalkblue sea appears at the ends of the roads of villas turning downhill – but these are still the suburbs, not the seaside. In the distance, floating across the bay, buildings glitter out of the heat-haze on the neck to Howth, and Howth Head looks higher veiled. After inland Ballsbridge, the tram from Dublin speeds up; it zooms through the residential reaches with the gathering steadiness of a launched ship. Its red velvet seating accommodation is seldom crowded – its rival, the quicker bus, lurches ahead of it down the same road.

After Ballsbridge, the ozone smell of the bay sifts more and more through the smell of chimneys and pollen and the July-darkened garden trees as the bay and line converge. Then at a point you see the whole bay open – there are nothing but flats of grass and the sunk railway between the running tram and the still sea. An immense glaring reflection floods through the tram. When high terraces, backs to the tramline, shut out the view again, even their backs have a salted, marine air: their cotton window-blinds are pulled half down, crooked; here and there an inner door left open lets you see a flash of sea through a house. The weathered lions on gate posts ought to be dolphins. Red, low-lying villas have been fitted between earlier terraces, ornate, shabby, glassy hotels, bow-fronted mansions all built in the first place to stand up over spaces of grass. Looks from trams and voices from public gardens invade the old walled lawns with their grottos and weeping willows. Spit-and-polish alternates with decay. But stucco, slate and slate-fronts, blotched Italian pink-wash, dusty windows, lace curtains and dolphin-lions seem to be the eternity of this tram route. Quite soon the modern will sag, chip, fade. Change leaves everything at the same level. Nothing stays bright but mornings.

The tram slides to stops for its not many passengers. The Blackrock bottleneck checks it, then the Dun Laoghaire. These are the shopping centres strung on the line: their animation congests them. Housewives with burnt bare arms out of their cotton dresses mass blinking and talking among the halted traffic, knocking their shopping-bags on each others's thighs. Forgotten Protestant ladies from 'rooms' near the esplanade stand squeezed between the kerb and the shops. A file of booted children threads its way through the crush, a nun at the head like a needle. Children by themselves curl

their toes in their plimsolls and suck sweets and disregard everything. The goods stacked in the shops look very static and hot. Out
from the tops of the shops on brackets stand a number of clocks.
As though wrought up by the clocks the tram-driver smites his bell
again and again, till the checked tram noses its way through.

By half-past eleven this morning one tram to Dalkey is not far
on its way. All the time it approaches the Ballsbridge stop Mrs
Kearney looks undecided, but when it does pull up she steps
aboard because she has seen no bus. In a slither of rather ungirt
parcels, including a dress-box, with a magazine held firmly
between her teeth, she clutches her way up the stairs to the top. She
settles herself on a velvet seat: she is hot. But the doors at each end
and the windows are half-open, and as the tram moves air rushes
smoothly through. There are only four people and no man smokes
a pipe. Mrs Kearney has finished wedging her parcels between her
hip and the side of the tram and is intending to look at her
magazine when she stares hard ahead and shows interest in someone's back. She moves herself and everything three seats up, leans
forward and gives a poke at the back. 'Isn't that you?' she says.

Miss Kevin jumps round so wholeheartedly that the brims of the
two hats almost clash. 'Why, for goodness sake! . . . Are you on the
tram?' She settled round in her seat with her elbow hooked over the
back – it is bare and sharp, with a rubbed joint: she and Mrs Kearney are of an age, and the age is about thirty-five. They both wear
printed dresses that in this weather stick close to their backs; they
are enthusiastic, not close friends but as close as they are ever likely
to be. They both have high, fresh, pink colouring: Mrs Kearney
could do with a little less weight and Miss Kevin could do with a
little more.

They agree they are out early. Miss Kevin has been in town for
the July sales but is now due home to let her mother go out. She has
parcels with her but they are compact and shiny, having been made
up at the counters of shops. 'They all say, buy now. You never
know.' She cannot help looking at Mrs Kearney's parcels, bursting
out from their string. 'And aren't you very laden, also,' she says.

'I tell you what I've been doing,' says Mrs Kearney. 'I've been
saying goodbye to my sister Maureen in Ballsbridge, and who

knows how long it's to be for! My sister's off to County Cavan this morning with the whole of her family and the maid.'

'For goodness' sake,' says Miss Kevin. 'Has she relatives there?'

'She has, but it's not that. She's evacuating. For the holidays they always go to Tramore, but this year she says she should evacuate.' This brings Mrs Kearney's parcels into the picture. 'So she asked me to keep a few of her things for her.' She does not add that Maureen has given her these old things, including the month-old magazine.

'Isn't it well for her,' says Miss Kevin politely. 'But won't she find it terribly slow down there?'

'She will, I tell you,' says Mrs Kearney. 'However, they're all driving down in the car. She's full of it. She says we should all go somewhere where we don't live. It's nothing to her to shift when she has the motor. But the latest thing I hear they say now in the paper is that we'll be shot if we don't stay where we are. They say now we're all to keep off the roads – and there's my sister this morning with her car at the door. Do you think they'll halt her, Miss Kevin?'

'They might,' says Miss Kevin. 'I hear they're very suspicious. I declare, with the instructions changing so quickly it's better to take no notice. You'd be upside down if you tried to follow them all. It's of the first importance to keep calm, they say, and however would we keep calm doing this, then that? Still, we don't get half the instructions they get in England. I should think they'd really pity themselves. . . Have you earth in your house, Mrs Kearney? We have, we have three buckets. The warden's delighted with us: he says we're models. We haven't a refuge, though. Have you one?'

'We have a kind of pump, but I don't know it is much good. And nothing would satisfy Fergus till he turned out the cellar.'

'Well, you're very fashionable!'

'The contents are on the lawn, and the lawn's ruined. He's crazy,' she says glumly, 'with A.R.P.'

'Aren't men very thorough,' says Miss Kevin with a virgin detachment that is rather annoying. She has kept thumbing her sales parcels, and now she cannot resist undoing one. 'Listen,' she says, 'isn't this a pretty delaine?' She runs the end of a fold between her finger and thumb. 'It drapes sweetly. I've enough for a dress and a bolero. It's French: they say we won't get any more now.'

'And that Coty scent – isn't that French?'

Their faces flood with the glare struck from the sea as the tram zooms smoothly along the open reach – wall and trees on its inland side, grass and bay on the other. The tips of their shingles and the thoughts in their heads are for the minute blown about and re-freshed. Mrs Kearney flutters in the holiday breeze, but Miss Kevin is looking inside her purse. Mrs Kearney thinks she will take the kids to the strand. 'Are you a great swimmer, Miss Kevin?'

'I don't care for it: I've a bad circulation. It's a fright to see me go blue. They say now the sea's full of mines,' she says,with a look at the great, innocent bay.

'Ah, they're tethered; they'd never bump you.'

'I'm not nervous at any time, but I take a terrible chill!'

'My sister Maureeen's nervous. At Tramore she'll never ap-proach the water: it's the plage she enjoys. I wonder what will she do if they stop the car – she has all her plate with her in the back with the maid. And her kiddies are very nervous: they'd never stand it. I wish now I'd asked her to send me a telegram. Or should I telegraph her to know did she arrive? . . . Wasn't it you said we had to keep off the roads?'

'That's in the event of invasion, Mrs Kearney. In the event of not it's correct to evacuate.'

'She's correct all right, then,' says Mrs Kearney, with a momen-tary return to gloom. 'And if nothing's up by the finish she'll say she went for the holiday, and I shouldn't wonder if she still went to Tramore. Still, I'm sure I'm greatly relieved to hear what you say. . . Is that your father's opinion?'

Miss Kevin becomes rather pettish. 'Him?' she says, 'oh gra-cious, I'd never ask him. He has a great comtempt for the whole war. My mother and I daren't refer to it – isn't it very mean of him? He does nothing but read the papers and roar away to himself. And will he let my mother or me near him when he has the news on? You'd think,' Miss Kevin says with a clear laugh, 'that the two of us originated the war to spite him: he doesn't seem to blame Hitler at all. He's really very unreasonable when he's not well. We'd a great fight to get in the buckets of earth, and now he makes out they're only there for the cat. And to hear the warden praising us makes him sour. Isn't it very mean to want us out of it all, when they say the whole of the country is drawn together? He doesn't take any pleasure in A.R.P.'

'To tell you the truth I don't either,' says Mrs Kearney. 'Isn't it that stopped Horse Show? Wouldn't that take the heart out of you – isn't that a great blow to national life? I never yet missed a Horse Show – Sheila was nearly born there. And isn't that a terrible blow to trade? I haven't the heart to look for a new hat. To my mind this war's getting very monotonous: all the interest of it is confined to a few . . . Did you go to the Red Cross Fête?'

The tram grinds to a halt in Dun Laoghaire Street. Simultaneously Miss Kevin and Mrs Kearney move up to the window ends of their seats and look closely down on the shop windows and shoppers. Town heat comes off the street in a quiver and begins to pervade the immobile tram. 'I declare to goodness,' exclaims Miss Kevin, 'there's my same delaine! French, indeed! And watch the figure it's on – it would sicken you.'

But with parallel indignation Mrs Kearney has just noticed a clock. 'Will you look at the time!' she says, plaintively. 'Isn't this an awfully slow tram! There's my morning gone, and not a thing touched at home, from attending evacuations. It's well for her! She expected me on her step by ten – 'It's a terrible parting,' she says on the p.c. But all she does at the last is to chuck the parcels at me, then keep me running to see had they the luncheon basket and what had they done with her fur coat. . . I'll be off at the next stop, Miss Kevin dear. Will you tell your father and mother I was inquiring for them?' Crimson again at the very notion of moving, she begins to scrape her parcels under her wing. 'Well,' she says, 'I'm off with the *objets d'art*.' The heels of a pair of evening slippers protrude from a gap at the end of the dress box. The tram-driver, by smiting his bell, drowns any remark Miss Kevin could put out: the tram clears the crowd and moves down Dun Laoghaire Street, between high flights of steps, lace curtains, gardens with round beds. 'Bye-bye, now,' says Mrs Kearney, rising and swaying.

'Bye-bye to you,' said Miss Kevin. 'Happy days to us all.'

Mrs Kearney, near the top of the stairs, is preparing to bite on the magazine. 'Go on!' she says. 'I'll be seeing you before then.'

The Apple

Elizabeth Connor

Elizabeth Connor was a *nom-de-plume* of Una Walsh, who was born in Clonmel, County Tipperary. Walsh dropped the name in 1955; since then, her novels have appeared under her maiden name, Una Troy. A short-story writer, an Abbey playwright in the 1940s with works such as *Swan and Geese* and *The Dark Road,* and a novelist, Walsh has not attracted critical attention. She lives in County Waterford.

The predicament of the protagonist of 'The Apple' is, rather surprisingly, almost entirely unexplored in Anglo-Irish literature. Quietly powerful, rather than overtly dogmatic, Walsh's deft handling of deliberate sin and subsequent revelation suggests that a closer study of her writing, particularly her drama, would repay attention.

SHE HAD never used her mind for thinking, only for recording the thoughts of others. She was happy. She had always been happy. Walking now in the convent garden, her fingers staying automatically at the big, smooth beads of the Rosary that hung from her waist, her habit brushing on the bright June grass hedging the flower beds, she thanked God, with a simple, unsearching happiness, because the sky was blue, because the sun shone; she thanked Him, most fervently, for making this day, of all days, so fine and lovely, with no shadow of a cloud.

She was not afraid of being happy; she was used to it. Reverend Mother was coming down the path towards her. She was smiling as she came.

'Are you very excited, child?'

Mother Mary Aloysius blushed.

'A little Reverend Mother,'

Reverend Mother laughed.

'You're not the only one! They're like a pack of babies inside. I declare I've almost forgotten myself what the sea looks like.'

Forgotten the sea! Oh, but you couldn't! Even if you only saw it once in your life, you could never forget the sea. Today, it was blue – pale, pale blue, with no horizon but a misty curve far off where it sloped up to meet the sloping sky. I can see it, flowing over the roses there by the wall and the gulls' crying is loud above the blackbird's song. . .

'It's fifty years since I've seen it,' said Reverend Mother, and there was a gleam in her old eyes.

Mother Mary Aloysius saw the gleam and she kept her face tight and hard so that it wouldn't smile. Because Reverend Mother hadn't wanted to go at all – and now she was as bad as any of them. When the Bishop had altered the strict rule that forbade any member of the Order to set foot outside the Convent grounds, Reverend Mother had been very angry. 'What was good enough for me when I entered,' she said, 'is good enough for me now,' and she didn't speak at all kindly of the Bishop, who was only doing his best, poor man. 'I won't budge,' she said, and she didn't. She sent her nuns off on visits to the Convents at Michelstown, at Fermoy, at Kilkenny, and received them back with a sympathetic conscious-ness of her own firm virtue. But this year the Bishop himself had come and tackled her, like a brave man. She wasn't looking well, he said; the doctor prescribed a change; she needed the sea air. She was to take herself and four of her nuns off to the new house the order had bought at Youghal and she was to stay there for a month too. So, of course, Reverend Mother had to say 'yes' because Obedience was one of the Vows, but Mother Mary Aloysius was sure that she hadn't said it very meekly.

Mother Mary Aloysius had prayed for weeks that she would be one of the chosen. Oh, not because she wanted to be in Youghal – but because, if she went, they would travel the road by her own sea, her own rocks and cliffs, her own shining strand, her own home. 'Oh, please God,' she prayed, hoping hard it wasn't wrong to pray such a worldly prayer and telling Him if it was, not to grant it, 'please God, let Reverend Mother take me,' and God let her be taken, so everything was all right.

'It's thirty years since I saw the sea,' said Mother Mary Aloysius and kept on watching it flow beside her feet.

'Is it now, child? Well, well how times does go, to be sure! Who'd think it was that length since you came to us! It makes me feel an old woman,' said Reverend Mother, indignantly, glaring at her seventy odd years. 'Sure, you must be near fifty now?'

'Forty-nine,' said Mother Mary Aloysius.

Reverend Mother opened her mouth to speak and snapped it shut again with a click of her teeth. It was a disconcerting habit. But Mother Mary Aloysius knew it. She waited.

'I was thinking –,' said Reverend Mother.

'Yes?' said Mother Mary Aloysius.

'We'll pass by your old home this evening, won't we?'

'Yes Reverend Mother.'

'Hm! I heard you talking about it in the Refectory. I was thinking – Would you like, now, if we stopped and you went and had a look at it? You know we still can't go inside any house, or even any other convent but our own Order's, but you could,' said Reverend Mother, 'you could walk around outside and you could,' said Reverend Mother, suddenly, 'you *could* look in through the windows.'

Mother Mary Aloysius gaped at her.

'Oh, Reverend Mother!' she said at last.

'Yes, child, yes,' said Reverend Mother.

'Oh, Reverend *Mother*! said Mother Mary Aloysius.

'Yes. Well – we'll be leaving in half-an-hour,' said Reverend Mother, briskly, and was gone.

Mother Mary Aloysius hardly spoke at all in the car. She sat very straight and stiff between Sister Peter and Mother Mary Assumpta. She said yes, it would be very nice to see her home again after thirty years, and she said yes, that was a pretty view by those trees, and she said yes, that must be Waterford in the distance. And once Reverend Mother turned around from the front seat and smiled at her and Mother Mary Aloysius smiled back, but she smiled right through Reverend Mother.

She rode home from the hayfield on Susie, holding tightly on to Susie's mane, because her legs were very short and Susie was very very fat. Her father walked beside her; his hat was pushed on the

back of his head and he carried a sprong over his shoulder. She dipped her fingers in the milk and held them out to teach the sucky-
calves how to drink; she felt their rough, unaccustomed tongues
drag at her hand. She scattered meal to the chickens and they came
running. Chuck-chuck-chuck-chuck! She turned the wheel and
blew the fire until it shone red in all their faces. She watched her
mother put the cake in the pot-oven; it was special soda bread, with
currants because it was her birthday. Tom and Mollie and Joe and
she played hide-and-seek; the haggard was 'home'.

'Be a good girl and say your prayers and you'll be happy,' her
mother said. 'Early to bed and early to rise,' said her father. 'That's
my own girl,' said her mother, proudly, when she brought back the
'Extract from Literature' that she won at school. 'I declare to God,
she's nearly as big as yourself, ma'am,' said Father O'Shea.

'It's a grand thing to be a nun,' her mother said. 'Such a happy
life – and a person hasn't a care or trouble in the world. I'd be easy
in my mind – of course, 'tisn't everyone that God gives the call to.'

All the same, her mother cried when she was leaving and the
first weeks at the Convent were lonely ones. But they weren't unhappy – and the weeks after that, and all the weeks since, were
happy as her mother had said they would be. Every hour was
mapped our for you and you could see right on to the end, where
God would take you to Himself and you'd meet Father and Mother
again – and Moll that got a cold on the lungs – and the others that
might be there before you – and you'd be there waiting to welcome
the ones that were yet to come. They'd be all home together, loving
one another like they used to be, and it would be home for ever and
ever then. . .

She saw a familiar curving line of mountainy distance. With a
jerk of the heart, she came back from yesterday and tomorrow to
the living moment. She was looking out eagerly now, with wide
hungry eyes. All at once, the road twisted to the left and beyond a
field of young wheat was the sea.

'We're not so far now,' said Reverend Mother.

'Five miles,' she said. 'I know every inch of the way from here
on. I used to come as far as this in the horse and trap to see my

cousins!'

'Do they know at home you're passing?' Sister Peter asked and the look she gave at Mother Mary Aloysius had a lot of envy in it.

'No. There's only Paddy left at the farm. There used to be – ten of us it is that was in it long ago.'

There was an ache in her eyes, that were looking and looking at so much; there was an ache in her heart, too, there was loving and grasping at all that she saw.

'Here's the village!' she said, and now she began to chatter because it helped to dull that odd feeling in her breast. 'That's Biddy Casey's – oh! of course she must be dead long ago – and there's a new name over the Post Office – Paddy didn't tell me – and that's old Mrs Graney's where I used to spend my penny on sweets. Pink ones I always bought. Isn't it queer how you remember things?'

Reverend Mother said gently: 'Maybe it is.'

She saw it. The car stopped. They were there. Her heart wasn't big enough to hold it all – Paddy standing by the car, and the thatch and pink walls, and the chip off the left pier of the gate. Everything the same – perhaps not so trim as it used to be but still just the same. It was crowding out her heart and hurting it. She must have a very small heart.

'Go around now, child, and have a look at things,' Reverend Mother said. She looked in through the front window. Everything was the same; Paddy had altered nothing. If he had had a wife, she would have made changes. She was glad, until she stopped herself, that he hadn't a wife. She was at the back of the house now, and alone. She couldn't even hear the voices at the gate. She laid her hand on the walls; she stroked them. She looked through the windows. The same – all the same. The back door was open; she looked through into the kitchen. The blue plates were on the dresser; the clock ticked on the wall; the fire was a smoulder of turf on the hearth. She looked up and, under the strawy eaves, saw the tiny window of her own room. So often she would kneel at that window and see, out beyond the fields, the sea under the sun or under the moon. The beams curved up oddly in the ceiling of that room; her bed was in the corner; on a shelf by the door were her books. Maybe they were still there. . .

'I wish –' she said softly. 'If I had a ladder –' and then laughed to imagine Mother Mary Aloysius climbing a ladder with her black skirts flapping around her, Mother Mary Aloysius perched on top, peering in through a little window at a little room.

The back door was open. There was one green pane of glass in the four cramped panes of that crooked window. When you looked through it, you looked into a new world where the sea had come in and covered everything and you were living safely, a mermaid on the sea-floor. There was a picture of a dog and a child hanging over your bed. The back door was open. A board was loose by the window; it squeaked when you stood on it; you could press it up and down with your foot and frighten yourself by pretending there was a mouse in the room. You weren't really frightened of that mouse. It was a pet one; its name was Florrie. The back door was open. There were three nails where clothes hung. . . The back door was open.

'If I go in,' said Mother Mary Aloysius, 'it will be a mortal sin.' She stood there rigidly.

'A mortal sin,' said Mother Mary Aloysius firmly, and went in. She went through every room in the house. Last of all, and longest of all, she knelt by the window of her own little bedroom and gazed across the pasture land and the gold cliff-tops at her own sea. The sun shone on it, and the moon; the frosty stars hung low over it; the sea-mist and the night hid it from all eyes but hers. When she came climbing down the narrow attic stairs, her habit clutched high in one hand, she carried the little room and all that was to be seen from it, safely in her heart. Her heart was so small that was all it could hold; and that fitted exactly into it as the egg to its shell. 'And now,' Mother Mary Aloysius said as she stepped out into the sunshine, 'I am in mortal sin.'

The delicate blades of grass growing through the crevice of the stones by the door were silver with lights; two shadows crossed the sun; a gull went calling towards the tide.

'My soul is black,' she said.

A poppy swayed at her from the hedge over the bohereen; a soft wind blew about her; her treasure, loveliest of all the loveliness of the day, was warm in her breast.

'Black. . ,' she said.

But the poppy nodded; the breeze went rustling along; the grass and the birds flew into the sun.

And suddenly a dreadful thing happened to her. She could not understand it; she fought against it. 'But they told me so,' she said. 'They told me thus – and thus. They are right – they are always right.' She gripped at the beads of her Rosary; they slid from her blind fingers.

The world fell away from her, the world that others had fashioned for her with loving minds; and now she must strive for ever to refashion out of chaos the world of her own mind.

'It was no sin,' she said.

Her mind worked quicker and yet more quickly, as she hurried back to the car. As she ran she held her hand to her breast as if to keep her treasure secure but she did not yet realise how precious and how terrible was the price she had paid for it.

The Proud Woman

Maura Laverty

Maura Laverty was born in 1907 in Rathangan, County Kildare, and spent her childhood and adolescence there. In 1925 she went to Madrid to work as a governess and, while in Spain, became in turn a secretary, foreign correspondent and journalist. When she returned to live in Ireland in 1928 she went to Dublin as a journalist and broadcaster. *Never No More (London: Longmans, 1942) and No More Than Human* (London: Longmans, 1944) are her two autobiographical novels. *Lift Up Your Gates* (London: Longmans, Green, 1946), a novel of life in the Dublin slums, is the work for which she is best known.

'The Proud Woman' is a sensitive story which conveys Laverty's grasp of the special poignancy in an old countrywoman's abdication of her position. The difficulties between mother-in-law and daughter-in-law shape a theme that is persistent – and understandably so – in writings by Irish women about rural life.

THE OLD woman cleared the breakfast-table sullenly, hugging to herself the memory of last night's quarrel when bitter words had passed between herself and her daughter-in-law. There was resentment in every movement of her meagre body as she piled the dishes in the tin basin and poured water on them from the heavy ash-coated kettle. She had the kitchen to herself, for her son had gone out to yoke the jennet, and his wife was in the bedroom getting herself ready for the road. The couple were going to Newbridge for the day to buy a churn.

Presently the young wife came out of the bedroom. She was a neat-figured girl and she looked very smart in her costume of navy serge. Her round face was bright and eager below the red beret, and her brown eyes were dancing. She was delighted with the prospect of the jaunt to Newbridge, and her mother-in-law's bad humour did not upset her.

'Won't you boil yourself an egg for your dinner, mother?' she said kindly. 'There's cold potatoes and a few rashers in the press if you like to fry them.'

'A cup of tea will do me, thanks,' the old woman said, and self-pity made her voice tremble. The young woman went to the kitchen door. She stood there pulling on her fabric gloves, and looked up at the sky over which were scattered dingy-looking white clouds like untidy bundles of washing.

'It looks changeable,' she said in a worried voice back over her shoulder. 'I wouldn't be surprised but it would rain tonight.'

Just then her husband came round the side of the house leading the jennet. He was a tall young man, spare but healthy-looking, with small merry blue eyes and a brown long-jawed face. He, too, was delighted to be having this day's respite from work. He had stuck a dog-rose in the lapel of his grey coat and it gave him a gay holiday air. Annie continued to look at the sky.

'I'm put out about the turf, Patrick,' she said. 'There's a good half-day heaping to be done on it yet. By right, I should be on my way to the bog this minute. It's a mortal sin to leave the footings on the ground to get drenched.'

'Don't be worrying yourself, girl,' her husband said indulgently. 'Up in the cart with you and think of nothing but the day that's before you.'

'Goodbye, mother,' he called gaily. 'Don't run away with a soldier before we come back.'

'God be with you,' came the old woman's voice from the kitchen. The blessing came mechanically, like a Christmas wish from a shopkeeper.

When the dishes had been washed and put back on the dresser, the fire mended and the floor swept, the old woman took her beads from the pocket of her skirt, and twining them about her swollen fingers sat down at the fire. But she did not pray. She was still thinking of what her daughter-in-law had said to her yesterday when she came home to find the fire out under the pig's food.

'Aren't you the useless old woman?' she had cried, flying into a temper. She shook her gray head slowly and the easy tears of old age came to her eyes and dribbled down her cheeks.

'It'd serve her right if I walk out of the house on her and went into the Union,' she muttered vindictively. A little smile of satisfaction came from her mouth as she thought of the humiliation that would bring on Annie.

'She threw her mother-in-law out of the house and the creature had to go into the Union,' the neighbours would say. 'Mary Byrne, a decent, respectable woman like her, to end her days in the Union.' A useless old woman, indheadh! Well, well! So it wasn't enough to knit and clean and bake? Maybe she ought to go out and snag turnips as well! Or maybe Annie would like her to go out and work on the bog. She stopped rocking and sat still as stone, her eyes narrowed, and her mouth tightening. . .

She slipped her beads in her pocket and got up from her chair as quickly as the rheumatism would let her.

It was after twelve when she reached the bog. She felt fresh enough, for she had only had to walk a half-mile or so of the road. Mylie Keogh had caught up with her and had given her a lift the rest of the way. He helped her down when they reached the turf-bank. Shading her eyes with her hand, she stood on the roadside for a minute and looked at their turf. In spite of her bitterness to-wards Annie, she had to nod in admiration of the girl's work. The circular heapings had been beautifully done; each sod placed at the precise angle to support another; the whole a miracle of loosely-balanced buildings calculated to snare both sun and wind. In hip-high symmetrical pyramids the heapings stretched away up the turf-bank. They ended about thirty feet from the top. Here began the little low footings that still remained to be heaped.

The old woman stepped carefully across the bridge of scraws that spanned the narrow brown stream dividing the bog from the road. She turned, threaded a zig-zag between the heapings with the heavy uneven steps of the old. To her right a woman and a young boy were working. The woman wore a man's check-cap on her head. The child wore an old felt hat with a hole in the crown through which a tuft of his fair hair sprouted like a wisp of hay. When they saw the old woman they stopped working. The child took off his battered hat and examined it seriously. The woman called out a genial greeting, grateful for an excuse to straighten her back even for a moment.

'Did you come out to see how the turf is getting on, Mrs Byrne?'

she called.

'Faith, I didn't, Polly,' the old woman answered, trying to sound jocular and light-hearted. It wouldn't do to give Polly Daly anything to talk about. 'I got tired of sitting with me heels in the ashes, so I thought I'd come out and see if I could keep me hand in.'

'More power to you! There's nothing like a bit of hard work for keeping you young.'

She bent again to the sods and the old woman continued up the bank. Arrived at the spot where the heapings ended, she laid her bottle of milk and her paper-wrapped bread-and-butter in a tuft of heather. She took a safety-pin from the bosom of her jacket and, lifting the hem of her heavy black skirt, she lapped it around her waist, pinned it at the back, and bent to work.

It was well over ten years since she had worked on the bog and she had forgotten the knack of it. The rheumatism had made her stiff and awkward. However, after a few heapings her movements acquired a certain rhythm, though the lifting of the sods came hard on her wrists. She was glad that it was heaping she had to do and not footing. Had the sods been any heavier with damp she would not have been able to lift them at all.

She took six footings to a heap. There were many who said you should take ten. Lazy heapers, she called them. The six were better. They made a smaller heap that gave the sods a better chance to dry out. Annie always took six too. And a warm feeling came over her at the thought of Annie's face when she would tell her, and her mind jumped forward, planning the scene. . .

She carefully laid the top sod in place on her eleventh heaping. While she had been working and dreaming, twin pains had been born in her back, one just over her kidneys and the other between her shoulder-blades. They were insignificant at first, but with every sod she lifted they gathered malevolence, and when she bent to start work on the twelfth heaping they leaped and struck suddenly and viciously. She gasped in a long-drawn sigh that fluttered out to a mere breath as the pains, content with this first test of their power, withdrew, leaving her shaken and a little frightened. She worked on doggedly. Maybe she would not tell them at all. She would let them come out to the bog after supper and find it out for themselves. She saw herself sitting on the settle-bed knitting when they returned.

'Mother, the queerest thing – it beats out! I left a good half-day's heaping to be done but there's not a footing left – every sod of it is heaped. Who could have done it for us?' She would just give a quiet little smile then and look down at her knitting.

'Oh, mother, you don't mean to tell me –!'

A breeze sprang up in the bog – a mischievous breeze that fluttered the old woman's skirts around her thin legs, puffed wisps of hair in her eyes and tried to pull her straw hat from her head. It sent a sighing shiver over the whole bog, tearing the bog-cotton and reedy grass this way and that and making the tufts of heather strain and dance in a frenzy of rage. The breeze pushed impudently at the bog-willows, flicking over their leaves with a susurrus that said: 'Have a look at these for a sham! Lovely green on the outside! Sickly grey underneath!' The willows shook furious branches, but the breeze rushed away uncaring.

'It looks like rain, Mrs Byrne.'

The old woman started. She had forgotten there was anyone else on the bog. Slowly and painfully, she straightened herself and turned herself around. The Dalys had finished the heaping of their turf. The woman was putting on her coat. The little boy was down at the roadside, fastening the ass's harness.

'We're going home. Come on and we'll give you a lift. God knows you've done enough for today.'

Every bone in the old woman's body clamoured for rest.

'I won't go yet awhile,' she said.

Polly Daly shrugged. 'Goodbye, then,' she said. 'We're off, for we're mad with the hunger.' She swung down the bank on her strong red legs and got into the cart with the child. The old woman watched them go. Then she collected her bottle of milk and her bread, and lowered herself on to a tussock of heather to eat her lunch. Too fatigued to enjoy the food, she ate and drank mechanically. When she had finished, she sat listlessly for a few minutes, but when she saw the postman ride past on his bicycle she rose stiffly and slowly to her feet. Already half-past three?

The sods seemed to have doubled their weight since noon. The pains in her back were so bad that she faltered many times and wondered if she should not give in. The afternoon dragged itself suddenly away to make room for the evening. The pain multiplied. The six o'clock Angelus rang out but its chiming conveyed nothing to her. The white-blotched sky of the morning had now become a leaden threatening grey. The breeze redoubled, its playfulness gone and roamed now with a steady menacing gustiness over the bog. One by one, the other workers left their banks and went home.

When the last sod had been placed on the last heaping she felt no exultation; no relief, nothing but a great desire to drop down on the turf-bank and sleep. But a few drops of heavy rain fell on her and she felt the wind and the leaden sky and the loneliness of the deserted bog, and suddenly frightened, she longed for the kitchen and the fire and the company of her son and daughter-in-law. She thought of the three long miles before as she tottered towards the road, all her limbs trembling from strain, her back bent double as if she were still working.

She did not see them pull up the jennet, jump down from the cart and come running up the turf-bank to meet her. They were within a few feet of her when she saw them, dressed as they had been when setting out that morning. Her tired mind seized on that one fact.

'You're wearing your good clothes on the bog,' she said dully. She swayed a little. 'Your Sunday clothes on the bog?' she repeated stupidly.

'Mother!' her son's voice was full of concern. 'Why in God's name did you do it?'

The old woman's mind cleared and she remembered everything. Now was her moment of victory. Scorning the fierce soreness of her back she drew herself up proudly, raised her eyes to her daughter-in-law's face and opened her lips to speak the scathing words. But then she saw Annie's eyes and the great tender compassion that was in them and she faltered and hung her head.

'The heaping's finished, Annie,' she whispered humbly.

Frail Vessel

Mary Lavin

Mary Lavin was born of Irish parents in Massachusetts in 1912, but came to live in Ireland at the age of eleven. Lavin's academic career – an honours degree in English from University College, Dublin, and an honours M.A. from the same institution – ended when she began to write her first short story on the back of one of the pages of her in-progress doctoral dissertation. Her first short-story publication was in 1938; since then, she has received such literary prizes as the James Tait Black Memorial Prize, the Katherine Mansfield Award and Guggenheim fellowships. Although Lavin has written two novels, she prefers to write short fiction. Internationally recognised as one of the great Irish short-story writers, Lavin divides her time between her County Meath farm and a Dublin residence.

There have been various editions of individual volumes as well as collected editions of Mary Lavin's short fiction. For some years now, much of her new writing has appeared in *The New Yorker*. The recent spate of interest in Lavin's work has included a special issue of *The Irish University Review* devoted to her (Autumn 1979) and several critical studies, among which are Richard Peterson's *Mary Lavin* (New York: Twayne, 1978) and A. A. Kelly's *Mary Lavin: Quiet Rebel. A Study of Her Short Stories* (Dublin: Wolfhound Press, 1980).

Of her many stories – the bulk of which deal with the experiences of women in Ireland, whether as young girls, wives, mothers or widows – 'Frail Vessel' is one of her most archetypal. Its subtlety, even ambiguity, the way in which it is explicit on the surface yet charged with meaning and emotion, mark it as a typically Mary Lavin story.

Lavin was awarded an honorary D.Lit. in 1968 and is a member of the Irish Academy of Letters. There is every indication that critical interest in her work will continue and that her work will go on being collected and reprinted.

WHO WOULD have thought, as they stood at their mother's graveside, that they would both be married within the year? Why Liddy was only sixteen then! Wasn't it partly for her sake that she and Daniel had gone on with the arrangements for their own marriage?

She was glad to be able to give her little sister a home; a real family life again. It might prevent a repetition of what happened with Alice. People knew that was partly the reason for her haste. They appreciated the fact that she wasn't really in a position to postpone her marriage. And anyway, taking into consideration the precarious position of the business, and the fact that it would have collapsed years ago only for Daniel's good management, everyone sympathised with the necessity for an immediate formal settlement. There was certainly no disrespect intended towards the dead!

But Liddy! She was absolutely shocked to find that Liddy had so little regard for the fact that their mother was less than a year in the grave!

Naturally she – Bedelia – was opposed to it. She made every effort to persuade them to wait a while. But she soon saw her efforts were useless.

Whatever came over Liddy she could get no good of her at all. She was like a person that was light in the head.

And as for Alphonsus O'Brien, she could make nothing out of him from the start. To begin with she never could stand solicitors, anyway. You could never feel at ease with them. They were always too clever for you, no matter what you did. And then, she never could think of Alphonsus O'Brien as anything but a stranger. And what else was he?

He was only a few months in the town; a total stranger, with no connections – and no office you might say, except the use of a room at the Central Hotel. He was a kind of laughing-stock right from the start, sitting inside the hotel window and not a soul ever darkening the door. He made no effort to get to know the people either. Their Liddy was the only one he ever saluted!

Daniel used to laugh at her.

'He must expect to get a lot of business out of you, Liddy,' he said.

That was the whole trouble: they treated the thing as a joke, both she and Daniel. And indeed, Liddy took it all as a joke, too, in the start.

No one in their senses would have believed that it could turn into anything serious. No one on earth could have foreseen that a young girl would have lost her head to an old fellow like that.

Not that Alphonsus was so old: it was more that he was odd than anything else: but he was certainly a bit old for a man who was said to have just qualified.

'Just qualified!' she cried. 'But he's grey!'

Daniel, however, was able to explain things. He said probably O'Brien had been a law clerk.

'They have a hard time – it's harder that way. So he mightn't be as old as he looked.'

As a matter of fact Daniel was right, Alphonsus was a lot younger than he looked, but all the same it never occurred to her that there could be anything romantic about him. And the day that Liddy got so red, when they were passing the Central Hotel, she simply could not account for it.

They had been out for a walk together, she and Liddy, and they were coming home. They were talking about her own wedding, as a matter of fact, when she noticed suddenly that Liddy wasn't paying attention. And when she looked at her she saw that she was blushing.

Whatever for? That was her first thought, and she looked around the street. It could only be some boy, she supposed, and she couldn't help feeling annoyed because Liddy seemed too much of a child for that kind of thing. But although she scanned the street up and down there wasn't a soul in sight except Alphonsus O'Brien standing at the hotel door. It simply did not occur to her to attribute those blushes to him; she contented herself by thinking that they were due to embarrassment at the way the child was teased about him.

How differently she would have acted if there was a boy in the street that day, a young man that is to say. If there was anyone presentable at all in sight it would have been a warning to her. And although she was nearly distracted those days, with plans for her own wedding, she would have kept a better eye on Liddy.

As things were, however, she did not give the incident another thought.

She did notice, however, that Mr O'Brien had taken to standing a lot at the door of the hotel, because when she paused to look out the window occasionally she saw him there.

'He's coming out of his shell,' she said to Daniel.

Daniel was dressing the window in the gable-end at the time, and she was looking out over his shoulder into the street.

Daniel shook his head. 'You'd feel sorry for him,' he said. 'He can't be doing much practice.'

She felt a bit sorry for him herself, but as Liddy came into the shop just then she thought she'd make her laugh.

'We're looking out at your friend Mr O'Brien,' she said. 'He's always standing in the doorway of the hotel. Maybe he's got a job as hotel porter.'

'That must be it,' said Liddy. And she laughed.

Yes: Liddy laughed at him too. That deceived them completely.

If she had shown the slightest annoyance or taken his part in any way they might have been suspicious. But she deceived them completely. Either that, or she really and truly still regarded the whole thing as a joke at that time. She certainly didn't take his first proposal seriously. And no wonder!

As it happened, Bedelia herself was at the window, that day, and she saw him lean out as Liddy was passing and catch her by the plait.

She little knew what he had said to her!

'Well, Liddy?' she said, when the girl came running into the shop. 'I saw you!' She was partly disapproving; partly amused.

'But you didn't hear what he said to me!' cried Liddy. 'He told me to go home and ask you when you'd let me marry him!'

'Well, the cheek of him!' she cried. 'I didn't think he had it in him to make a joke.' Because, of course, they took it all as a joke, both of them.

But when it became a regular thing for him to pull Liddy's plait every time she went up or down the street, Bedelia felt obliged to speak to her.

Liddy didn't take it well either. She noticed that at once, and for the first time she felt uneasy.

'After all, Liddy, you must remember that I stand in your mother's place. And I think this thing is going beyond a joke.'

But her words were truer than she knew: it was already beyond a joke.

And when Liddy paid no heed to her, but continued to hang about the hotel door laughing and talking to the fellow, Bedelia had to resort to threats. They were upstairs at the time, in the big parlour over the shop. Bedelia jerked her head in the direction of the Central Hotel.

'If this thing doesn't stop, Liddy, I'll have to speak to Mr O'Brien!'

That was all she said, and indeed she hadn't any intention of carrying out such a threat. But to her surprise Liddy said nothing. Something odd about the silence made her look sharply at her.

Liddy's face was covered with blushes.

'I think he wants to speak to you too, Bedelia,' she said. Bedelia saw that her hands were trembling.

'To speak to me?' She was astonished.

Liddy's head was bent, but with a great effort she forced herself to look her in the face.

'I think he's coming to see you' – she said – 'today!'

Today?

But suddenly Liddy could control herself no longer.

'Oh, Bedelia!' she cried. And Bedelia honestly could not tell whether she was crying or laughing. 'Oh, Bedelia – you know the way he was always going on – about asking you if you'd let him marry me – you remember we thought he was joking – didn't we? Well – he wasn't!'

Bedelia could only gasp. And then, before she had time to get over the shock there was a loud rap on the hall door.

Never in her life was she thrown into such flurry. She stared at Liddy.

Liddy's blushes had died away.

'I expect that's him now,' she said, coolly, calmly, as if it were the most natural thing in the world.

In the few minutes before she went down to the little front parlour to see her prospective brother-in-law, Bedelia tried to gather her thoughts together.

She was absolutely bewildered. What was she to say to this strange man – this absolute stranger?

Her first impulse was to run down the back stairs and call Daniel in from the shop. Daniel would know how to deal with the situation. But as she decided to do so, some impulse made her turn back to the main stairs. It didn't seem fair to drag Daniel into it. Anyway, she doubted if he would be much use in this kind of situation. Daniel's talent was for figures; for keeping books and attending to the financial side of things. Of course, there was a financial side to this situation too, she realised. How was this fellow going to support a wife? Where was he going to bring his wife to live? And how soon did he propose to bring about the happy event?

All these questions ran through her head as she stood where Liddy had left her, but it was only her mind that was working: her practical common-sense mind, but what she felt about the matter she did not know: as to feeling, she was absolutely numb.

But as she stood there in the middle of her room, her eyes fell on the plain serge suit which was intended for her own wedding, it had just that day come from the dressmaker, and she was suddenly shot through and through with irritation. Why did this business about Liddy have to blow up on the verge of her own wedding?

Goodness knows, she hadn't expected much fuss to be made about her marriage, what with not being out of mourning, and Daniel having always lived in the house anyway; but it did seem a bit unfair to have all this excitement blow up aound Liddy.

Two rare, very rare, and angry tears squeezed out of Bedelia's pale eyes, and fell down her plain round cheeks. Because, of course, mourning or no mourning, a young girl like Liddy wasn't likely to get married in serge!

Bedelia felt just like as if a mean trick had been played on her! After all I've done for her! she thought. After being a mother to her! But this last thought made her feel more bitter than ever because it seemed to her suddenly that it was a measure of the difference between them as brides.

Already she could imagine the fuss there would be over Liddy – the exclamations and the sighs of pity and admiration. Such a lovely bride!

Whereas when she – oh, but it was so unfair because never at any time did she regard her own marriage as anything but a practical expedient. It was only that she hadn't counted on being up against this comparison. It was that she minded.

But here Bedelia called herself to order. Of course a lot depended upon when the others intended to bring their affairs to a head.

After all Alphonsus O'Brien couldn't have much money. Perhaps he only wanted her sanction to his suit? It might be years before they could get married.

Yes, of course. Of course. She was letting her imagination run away with her: it would probably be years before poor O'Brien would take the final step.

Hastily running across the landing to her bedroom, she dipped the corner of her towel into the ewer of water on her wash-stand, Bedelia rubbed her face all over and darted a look into the mirror.

Smart and all as she was, Liddy might be old enough by the time her beau was in a position to lead her up to the altar!

She ran down the stairs.

It was when she was at the bottom of the stairs that another aspect of the situation struck Bedelia.

It was all very well for Daniel and herself to be making a home for Liddy when they regarded her as a child – but how would things be after this!

Even if this had never occurred it might have been more awkward than she realised to have another person in the house with them right from the start – and another woman above all.

For the first time in her life, a bashful feeling came over Bedelia at the thought of the night that Daniel would move out of the little return-room on the back-landing, where he had slept since he was a young apprentice, and with his old alarm clock under his arm, take up his position in her room.

It was only then – only at the last minute, with her hand on the knob of the parlour door, that it came over her that things might not be so bad at all. And in any case what could she do about it? If they were bent on getting married, who could stop them?

It was all settled. It had taken less than five minutes, and yet all was arranged. Daniel had even been sent for and although he was as much taken by surprise as anyone, he was more or less brought around to Alphonsus O'Brien's viewpoint.

That was what came of being a solicitor, Bedelia supposed. They were so able. But I'll never like him, she thought. He could build a nest in my ear.

And that was tantamount to what her new brother-in-law proposed to do.

It seemed that Liddy had told him about the little house at the end of the street that they owned; it was unoccupied, tumbling down in fact, but it never seemed worth while repairing, for the small rent they would get for it.

It would be just the thing for them, Alphonsus said. With a bit of paint, and something done to the bad spot on the roof it would do until they had time to find something better: something more suitable.

'And it's so pretty,' cried Liddy. 'I always thought it was a dear little house! I used to peep in through the shutters and wish I could go and live in it' – she turned and smiled at Alphonsus – 'all by myself,' she said.

But Bedelia had enough without that. Such soppiness: and in front of Daniel. Well, Liddy might like to play the love-bird, but there was no getting away from the fact that the romantic Mr O'Brien was almost grey – whereas Daniel had a head of hair like an infant. She turned around to Alphonsus on an impulse.

'It's a wonder you never married before now, Mr O'Brien,' she said, and she looked archly at him to conceal the malice in her voice.

Perhaps he saw through her, because he put out his hand and drew Liddy nearer.

'I suppose I was waiting for Liddy, here,' he said, and it was impossible to know whether he was serious or whether he was joking.

And it crossed Bedelia's mind that that was the same mixed way in which he had wormed himself into Liddy's affections: by mixing up sentiment and mockery. It was a kind of cheating, she thought.

Nowadays people didn't go on with nonsense like that about waiting for the right person – and being the only one in the world for
each other. There was nothing like that between herself and
Daniel! Daniel certainly didn't go down on his knees to her! She
would have thought he was daft if he did.

But all the same, as she looked at Alphonsus, she felt that he was
the kind of man who could fall down in front of a girl as a kind of a
joke – and she'd know he was joking or partly joking – but all the
same it would bring a kind of sweetness into her life.

But Bedelia brought herself to order again.

Alphonsus had reached for his hat and they had to see him to
the door.

Bedelia made the first reference to what had gone before.

'Well, everyone to his own taste,' she said, after the door was
closed and they were back in the downstairs parlour. 'Although I
must say I don't know how on earth you can bear that sloppy
manner.' Liddy looked up nervously. 'You know what I mean,' said
Bedelia impatiently. She tried to think of something sloppy he said,
but it was like trying to remember a smell – she could only remember that it was sloppy. But at last she laid hold on one phrase he had
used. 'You know – all that rubbish he went on with – about you
being the only one in the world for him – and that he was waiting
all those years for you. How can you stand that kind of talk? It's so
meaningless.'

Liddy had caught up the tablecloth and was just about to spread
it, but instead she lifted it up high, high as her face almost as if it
were a veil behind which she smiled, a little, dreamy, secretive
smile.

'Oh, Bedelia, I knew what he meant,' she said, and then, over the
edge of the cloth, her eyes seemed to implore something from
Bedelia – but Bedelia turned aside: really this sentimentality was
more than she could bear. Her eyes narrowed.

'Liddy,' she said sharply, 'I hope' – she paused – 'you know how I
have always felt towards you, like a mother' – she caught herself up
– 'well anyway, like a guardian,' she corrected, 'but perhaps lately
with my own plans taking up so much of my time I may not have

given you as much supervision as I used – as much as you should have had perhaps – I can only hope that you haven't abused your freedom in any way?'

But Liddy had spread the cloth on the table and was bending across it smoothing out the folds. Had she been listening at all? Bedelia gave a clap with her hands.

'What I mean is that I hope you haven't made yourself cheap in any way? Men don't usually speak so sentimentally, unless – well, unless a girl has let them become – well – familiar!'

After she said the word she was a little daunted herself by its force, but to her surprise at first, and then to her unspeakable irritation, Liddy didn't realise its implications at all.

'Oh, but that's just it, Bedelia! I wanted to tell you! We've become *so* familiar really. Isn't it funny and to think that we only know each other for a few weeks, and that this is the first time we've ever been together inside in a house.' She gave a little high-pitched laugh. And yes – Bedelia could hardly bear it – she hugged herself. 'And yet I feel as if we knew each other for years and years.' A rapt look came into her face. 'Bedelia! you don't mind my saying it, do you, because you want me to be happy, don't you? But I feel more familiar with him than with you! I do, really! I know it sounds queer, but it's true –'

She paused as if she was trying to think of some way to make herself clearer. Then her face lit up. She didn't see the danger signals in Bedelia's face.

'Do you know what I was thinking last night?' she cried. For a minute she paused – to take courage? – and then she rushed on, 'In bed,' she said softly. 'I was thinking about when I was small and used to sleep with you in your big brass bed. Oh, I used to love it, you know that! I used to be lonely when I got a room of my own: I was never able to go to sleep for ages, and I couldn't warm up for hours! But all the same, even when I loved sleeping with you – you don't mind me telling you this, do you? I used to hate if your – I used to hate if my – I mean I couldn't bear it if our feet touched!'

But here, Liddy's faint heart failed her again, and she had to rush over to Bedelia.

'You don't mind my telling you, do you?'

Bedelia drew back. She did mind. She didn't want to hear it. It sounded a lot of rubbish to her, but still, in spite of everything she was curious.

'I must say I don't see the point!' she said coldly.

Liddy brightened.

'Oh, I'm coming to the point,' she cried. 'It's that although I never saw Alphonsus without his shoes and stockings on, of course, it came into my mind – last night in bed – that I wouldn't mind a bit if our feet touched – his and mine, you know – after we were married I mean!'

It was said. She had said it. For a minute her face was radiant. Then she looked at Bedelia.

'Oh, Bedelia! What's the matter?' She couldn't understand the look on the other's face. 'You're not hurt, are you?'

'Hurt?' Bedelia put out her two hands. 'Keep back from me,' she shouted. 'Hurt indeed. Disgusted would be more like it! Such talk from a young girl. Do you want to know what I think? Well, I think you're daft!'

The sisters were both married six months when Liddy came back to the old house one afternoon and passing through the shop with only a word for Daniel, went straight upstairs to Bedelia's room over the shop.

'I want to ask you something, Bedelia,' she said, straight away, without preamble. 'Will you let us off your share of the rent of the little house – it's such a small sum to you and – well, it's not so small to us – and I know you were only charging us something as a formality – to make us feel independent and all that – but the fact of the matter is–.' Nervously she had run on without stopping ever since she came into the room, but as Bedelia, who was sitting at the window, stood up, she broke off – Bedelia was looking so queerly at her.

'Why, Liddy,' she said, 'I must say this is very surprising. Not that the rent means anything to Daniel and me – you're quite right about that – as a matter of fact Daniel was saying only the other day that no rent would compensate us for the loss of store-space – though mind you, Liddy, I would never have mentioned that if you didn't bring up the matter yourself – but as I was saying, it isn't a question of money – you know that – you know the standard of living in this house, and your little contribution wouldn't go far to maintain it – you know that! And it hasn't changed, I can tell you that, although I must say Daniel is very particular about my keeping accounts–.'

But marriage had quickened Liddy's perceptions.

'You're not going to let us off?' she whispered, not caring that she was interrupting.

Was she going to run from the room? Bedelia put out her hand.

'Wait a minute, Liddy,' she cried. 'Don't be so hasty. I didn't refuse you, did I?' She saw with relief that Liddy had come back into the room. 'I was taken by surprise, that's all. It's such a wretched little house – I thought perhaps that you were going to tell me that you'd found something better – you know it was never supposed to be anything but a stop-gap. I thought you'd be out of it long ago, but of course, if Alphonsus hasn't been able to better his position – if indeed as it seems – he's come down a peg instead – well then I think the least he could do would be to come and see me himself and not leave you to do his begging for him.'

'Begging! Oh!'

For a minute it was Liddy's stricken face that swam in front of Bedelia, but the next minute she could hardly believe that it was her own little sister who drew herself up all of a sudden, her eyes blazing, her voice a scorpion.

'I'm very glad he didn't come to you, Bedelia,' she said. 'I wouldn't like anyone, much less Alphonsus, to be hurt like you've hurt me. But before I go, I want you to know one thing – Alphonsus didn't send me. He didn't even know I was coming. And he had no idea of what I was going to ask you.' She softened for a minute. 'I was going to pretend you suggested it yourself,' she said, almost in a whisper. Then she drew herself up again. 'I'm sorry I bothered you, Bedelia. Forgive me.'

At the door she paused.

'Please don't say anything about this to anyone, Bedelia. After all, we are sisters.' She half turned away and then she turned back again. 'And just in case you might change your mind, I want you to know I couldn't accept now.'

It was that last cut that hit Bedelia hardest, because it was just what she was going to do. She already regretted her attitude, and she was at that very minute planning how she'd scribble a note when Liddy was gone and send it up the street after her; to overtake her before she was inside the door of the wretched little house.

But as if she read her mind, Liddly looked at her sadly.

'You see, I couldn't ever pretend now that you had done it of your own accord. It would be telling him a real lie now, not just managing things a little bit, making things easy – like I meant it to be!'

She was gone.

'Liddy!'

Bedelia made her way clumsily to the door after her, but she could hear her light feet on the stairs. The next minute she heard the door clapped shut. There was no question of going after her. Bedelia was heavy with child.

It was two months later. Bedelia was once again sitting in the big parlour upstairs, and she was thinking of Liddy. Except when she caught glimpses of her in the street, she had not seen her since she ran down the stairs, and out of the house, her pathetic request ungranted.

Oh, how could she have refused that miserably small favour? How could she have refused her anything: Liddy, her little sister. Only, of course, it wasn't really Liddy she wanted to refuse that day, it was O'Brien. It was him she wanted to humiliate. Oh, how she had grown to hate that fellow. How had she ever consented to his taking Liddy away from her, because, after the tepid experiences of marriage with Daniel, Bedelia had begun to feel, no matter what, no one can ever be as near to you as your own flesh and blood. And although poor Liddy didn't seem to have discovered that fact yet, it only made Bedelia feel more drawn to her, and recalled all her old feelings of motherliness for the child! For to Bedelia as she herself grew heavier in pregnancy, Liddy, when she glimpsed her in the streets, seemed as childish as ever – thinner, if possible, than before she was married.

Oh, what had possessed her that she didn't make more effort to keep her at home?

This was the question that Bedelia asked herself over and over again, and not only did she completely forget the last minute impulse of selfishness that had activated her decision, but she was beginning to think she had erred by being too selfless. And they were both the losers. Liddy's loss was only too obvious, but it was very hard for Bedelia to sit and think of all the help the girl would have been to her in these last few months. To think of the way she could run up and down stairs, and stretch for things, and stoop for things. It would be so different from asking the maids to do things: they were so curious. It nearly drove her into a rage when she caught them covertly glancing at her swollen abdomen.

Vain regrets weren't much use, however, and the most she could hope was that something or other would break and soften Liddy, and that she would call now and again like she did when she was first married. It wouldn't be the same as having her at hand all the time, and it was irritating the way she kept looking at the clock, but it would be better than nothing. But Liddy's last fling as she ran out the door was to the effect that she'd never set foot in the place again.

It was just as she was thinking of those bitter words that Bedelia heard footsteps on the stairs, the unmistakable light little steps of Liddy.

There was something wrong though. She sat upright and her hand went to her heart. Always, she was susceptible to wild premonitions of trouble when she heard those flying feet, coming along a passage or as now, upon the stairs. But as she strained to get to her feet, she suddenly sank back again into the chair. For just as the protective waters within her lapped around her embryonic son, securing him from hurt, so in her heart and mind a protective instinct warned her against giving way to shock or distress.

Whatever it was that was wrong, it was not her concern; unless indirectly. She must not let herself become upset. She sat still.

'Oh, Bedelia!'

It was an exclamation, not a greeting; it was a sigh, a gasp, as the young woman entered the room, and closing the door, sank back against it as if exhausted. But the next minute she drew herself together, and even gave a self-critical little smile.

'I never thought I'd set foot in your house again, Bedelia,' she said, and to Bedelia there was something preposterously conscious and independent in the words, but the next minute Liddy's voice broke, and the familiar dependent note that she knew so well came into it.

'But I had to come, Bedelia,' she cried. 'I had no one else to turn to – no one.'

Oh, what satisfaction that last word gave Bedelia.

'Well, what's the matter,' she said briskly. 'But don't stand there – come in – sit down.'

Obediently Liddy moved forward into the room and sat down on the edge of a chair, but almost at once she stood up again.

'It's Alphonsus,' she said. 'We're in such trouble, Bedelia.'

Bedelia tried to look more surprised than she felt.

'It was all my fault, really,' cried Liddy. 'Only for the way he's always trying to make things easier for me it would never have happened.'

Bedelia always hated vagueness.

'What wouldn't have happened?' she asked sharply.

But it was clear Liddy didn't know how to begin her story.

'Well, you see,' she said falteringly, 'when we got married Alphonsus wanted to do everything he could to increase his income and so he took on an insurance agency – temporarily, of course, although lots of solicitors do it. He thought he might work it up a bit and that it would bring in a little regular money until his practice grew – you needn't look so contemptuous, Bedelia' – she interrupted suddenly – 'the commission wasn't very much, but Alphonsus's idea was to get as much as we could and last month' – here a weak note of pride came into her voice – 'last month he collected eleven premiums totalling forty-seven pounds.'

Weak and watery as was that little note of pride, it angered Bedelia.

'I presume the forty-seven pounds was the amount of the premiums, not the commission,' she said.

'Oh, the premiums of course,' said Liddy, somewhat flatter, 'the commission was only –.'

But here she paused, and almost as if some inspired voice had given her the cue she needed, just at the moment when it had seemed utterly impossible to go on with the story – she threw out her hands and rushed on eagerly.

'That was the beginning of it all,' she cried. 'The insurance company gives a percentage on each premium but the agent is supposed to make out the amounts himself, subtract his commission, and forward the balance to the head office – it's not fair you know, really – they have such a staff up there and everything, while poor Alphonsus has no one to do anything for him – not yet, I mean.'

At this point the voice of the celestial prompter grew faint. Liddy hesitated, 'And so he got things a bit mixed up – only in arrears really, but –.' Here, however, the voice of the celestial prompter failed utterly. But Bedelia had heard enough.

'Do you mean to tell me he laid hands on it all – the policy money as well as the commission?' she cried, and in spite of nature's elaborate provisions against such contingency, Bedelia's heart began to palpitate, and a pulse began to beat in her temple. She wasn't so indirectly affected at all. She thought it was some trouble that would affect O'Brien only – or at worst the two of them. But if the fellow had converted this money to his own use – newspaper phrases flashed to her mind – well then he might easily bring disgrace on them all.

'Well, answer me! Did he?' she cried.

Although she herself was in a fury, she didn't like the way Liddy's face was quivering.

'I'll have to know sooner or later,' she said, more kindly, 'you may as well tell me.'

But Liddy was crying.

'It's the way you put it,' she stammered. 'As if he was a thief–.'

Bedelia bit back the retort she would liked to have made, and instead she shrugged her shoulders.

'Well,' she said then, 'what do you want me to do?'

As if she had been running blindly down a wrong pathway and suddenly through the blinding branches had seen another way, the right way, Liddy ran back to Bedelia.

'Oh, Bedelia, all we need is to get an advance on the money – it isn't as if we had to ask you for it out right – it's not even a loan really, because the minute the premiums become due again we'll hand the commission straight over to you – of course it will take a little while, I expect, for it to accrue into the full amount, but you can see, can't you, that it's hardly a loan at all – just an advance.'

'Advance – accrue! You've got very glib with financial phrases, I see.'

Liddy smiled, or tried to smile. She had fore-known that it would be part of her purgatory to humour Bedelia.

'I've become quite a book-keeper,' she said, but as Bedelia said nothing, she looked at her sharply, and then drew back. 'You're not going to give it to us!' she said. 'I can see by your eyes you're not,' and she began to back away from those cold eyes, as from something destructive.

But she didn't go further than the door, against which she shrank back exhausted. For where could she go?

Bedelia, however, had risen to her feet.

Although she didn't believe the other had strength or spirit left to do what she did last time, flounce away in a temper, she just wasn't going to take any chances this time, and going over to a chest of drawers she took out a black tin box.

Liddy knew that box. There was no need to say anything: Bedelia left it down on the table and let back the lid.

'How much did you say?' she said.

But Liddy was crying; silly hysterical tears.

'Forty-seven – oh, and the commission – I forgot that – but we might be able to make that up ourselves – Oh, Bedelia, I knew you wouldn't fail me – I was only afraid on account of that other time I came about the rent – and that's another thing – I wanted to tell you – you were right about that too – I told Alphonsus and he said you were right, that I shouldn't have asked you: not without telling him, anyway. Oh, you're so good – so kind –.'

But Bedelia plunged her hand into the box.

'I'd like to get this settled,' she said. 'I want to lock away the box again. How much did you say?'

'Oh, dear – how much?'

Liddy tried to wipe away the silly tears, tried to think, to calcu-
late. On her fingers she counted up a few figures and then she
threw up her hands.

'I'll have to ask Alphonsus,' she said. 'You see, there's no immediate hurry: the inspector won't be here until the afternoon: I'll
have plenty of time to get Alphonsus to make up the amount.' She
paused. 'I'll get him to write it down so I won't forget it,' she said.

She wanted Bedelia to see that she was going to be efficient
about the whole thing right from the start.

'Liddy, I want to talk to you. Sit down.'

Bedelia's voice was so odd that Liddy's eyes flew to the table, as
if in doubt of all that had gone before, but no: the box was still
there, with the bundle of notes in it held with tape. And to corrob-
orate her previous words, Bedelia was stripping off note after note
and counting them, forty, forty-five, fifty. But still, there was that
strange, cold note in her voice.

'Sit down,' she said again.

Liddy sat down.

'I want to ask you something, Liddy. If I didn't give you this
money, what were you going to do?'

For a minute there was silence, then Liddy spoke so low Bedelia
had to bend her head to hear her.

'Alphonsus would have to go away,' she said in a little dead
voice, 'until he gathered up the money somewhere,' she added with
a little more, but not much more, life. Then she looked up straight
into Bedelia's eyes. 'He would have to go on the four o'clock train
this afternoon,' she said.

'And leave you to face the music?'

Like a weal from a whiplash the red ran into the younger
woman's face. But it was the flush of courage, not shame.

'They couldn't do anything to me,' she said, and then she sprang
to her feet. 'Why are you torturing me like this,' she cried. 'Are you
going to give it to me or not? Because I don't care! Do you hear
that! I don't mind the disgrace. It couldn't be much worse than this.
And in any case you'll come in for your share to. Do you think
people won't know you refused us!'

'Hush, hush. Stop shouting! Who said I refused you? I didn't refuse you anything. I'm giving it to you,' and without finishing the counting, feverishly, anything at all to stop her, Bedelia began to stuff the notes into her hands. 'It's only that I want to do my best for you, Liddy. Surely you must know that,' she cried, and as she felt the other soften again she led her over to the chair once more. 'Liddy,' she said softly, tenderly. 'Liddy, I want you to ask yourself something. Do you believe in your heart of hearts that Alphonsus would never do this again?'

What is weakness? What is strength? Liddy had stood up to every taunt and villification, but she wasn't proof against this tenderness.

'Oh, Bedelia,' she cried, and she began to cry again.

So many tears; she had shed so many and so many kinds, silly tears, tears of temper and tears of bewilderment, but these were tears of defeat. 'I don't know,' she said.

'Well, look here!' Bedelia took her hands. 'This is the way I see it – I'm going to give you this money, but it's not enough to do just that, I want to do more for you. I want to help your poor husband if I can – help him to help himself, I mean.'

Liddy didn't follow.

'Now, listen carefully to me,' said Bedelia. 'You spoke when I first agreed to help you of conferring with Alphonsus; well, that, I am afraid, I can't allow. This is going to be a matter between you and me' – she paused – 'between you and me and the insurance company. I mean Alphonsus is not to know anything at all about it. In fact' – here her voice became so cold and measured that it was as if she were carving the words for ever into the mind of the other – 'in fact – he won't know because he will be gone on the four o'clock train. Do you follow?'

No, no! She didn't follow it would seem from the way Liddy pressed her hands over her face. But when she took them down again it was clear she partly understood.

'But why?' she cried.

'It will test him out, Liddy. Can't you see that?' she cried. 'The other way would be making things too easy for him: it would be doing him harm; moral harm. But this way you save his name – you hand the money over to the company, with some excuse – you

might even consider having the agency transferred to your name –
but that's another matter – but you let Alphonsus think that it has
to be paid back – let him think that he has to send back the money,
bit by bit, if necessary, until the whole thing is cleared. And in that
way–.'

But as at that moment the clock struck three, the sisters both
started.

'Is this the only condition on which you'll give the money, Bedelia?' said Liddy quietly.

Bedelia's eyes ran over every cranny of the other's face. For a minute she was almost afraid of what she was doing: afraid of the
strain she was putting on the woman in front of her, so thin, so
white; so beaten-looking.

But when she had got rid of O'Brien, for a while anyway, and
had taken her back into her own care again, it seemed that she
could make up to her, make more than amends for what she had to
do now. Why, if there were nothing more gained than the opportunity – even for a few months – of feeding her properly and seeing
that she had warmer clothes – there would be something to be said
for her action.

Why, she could come home again, for the present. And with
that thought Bedelia became so pleased that all vestige of doubt
vanished from her mind, and she sank back into her chair.

And when, at that minute a button popped off her dress and
rolled under the table, she caught herself up in the act of stooping
for it. Liddy could do that.

It was two hours later when Liddy came back. The train had
gone. Bedelia heard it give a short whistle as it went under the railway bridge at the end of the town, and then a long clear blast as it
cut its way into the wide open country beyond the town.

Only a few minutes afterwards there was a noise outside the
parlour door, a sound of something heavy bumping, now against
the stair treads, now against the banister.

'In the name of God, what is that noise?' cried Bedelia. She
thought it was one of the servants.

It was Liddy, and dragging after her, as she came in the door,
was their father's big portmanteau that she had taken to carry her

things when she left to be married.

'What on earth have you got in the portmanteau,' cried Bedelia. She hadn't thought Liddy would have taken her up so quickly about coming back.

'You're welcome, of course,' she said, when Liddy, taken aback, began to explain. 'I hope there's a bed ready for you, that's all,' she said. 'You know I can't do anything. I'm doing more than I ought already.' But as she saw Liddy's face fall, she tried to be warmer. 'It's all right, you know,' she said, 'it's all right. I meant you to come, only I thought you'd have to make arrangements. I thought it would take you a few days to settle your things, but I dare say you wouldn't have much to attend to in that little poke-hole of a place –.'

'Oh, I have lots to do,' said Liddy proudly. 'I've nothing done at all, I'll have to go back during the daytime, but –' she paused, and involuntarily her glance travelled towards the high window in the gable where the clouds could be seen fore-gathering in heavy masses on the western horizon.

Bedelia understood, but some unanalysed association of ideas irritated her.

'I thought it was only spinsters that were afraid at night!' she said, but at the same time, prompted by a movement in her body, she knew she must not make those remarks.

If she was to get anything out of the situation; if she was to get some return for taking her back into the house, she'd have to learn not to show those petty vexations.

'Put down that heavy suitcase,' she said abruptly.

Was she a fool that she was still holding it all the time, dragging her down to one side.

'Come over to the fire, can't you?' she said, 'and sit down. You're tired, I expect. You're very white-looking. When did you eat anything? Are you hungry?'

She was trying to be considerate, but all her questions were irrelevant compared with the one expected question that she could not bring herself to ask. Ask it she must however.

'Well – how did he go off?' she said abruptly.

For her only answer the tears welled into Liddy's eyes.

'Oh, come now – it's not as bad as all that. You took the only course open to you, you know that!'

But as Liddy's tears still fell silently, Bedelia stood up and looked down at her.

'Oh come, now,' she said more kindly. 'You'll be hearing from him in a few days: you may have a letter tomorrow if he gets to his destination in time to catch the post tonight–.'

As she spoke, however, a new aspect of the thing occurred to her.

'By the way, I didn't ask where he went? Has he any people; any friends or relatives? We never heard of any, I know that,' she added quickly, 'but I suppose everyone in the world has somewhere to creep when they get into trouble. What's that?'

Liddy had spoken at last, but so softly; only a whisper, that the other had to bend down close to hear her.

'Like I crept back here,' that was what she said.

Bedelia looked at her. Was she being clever; trying to get out of telling his whereabouts?

'You didn't say where he was going,' she persisted doggedly. 'Are you afraid to divulge his whereabouts in case something else comes to light about him? I'd hardly give him away – now!'

It was cruel, but it wasn't cruel enough to make Liddy open her mouth. Bedelia stood over her.

'Perhaps you don't know yourself,' said Bedelia, moving nearer to her until she was directly over her like a prosecutor.

But she had to stand back suddenly as Liddy got to her feet unsteadily and swayed forward with her hand on her stomach.

'I think I'm going to be sick, Bedelia,' she said, with a mawkish irrelevance.

It was such a shock. Bedelia gave a shout.

'Not on the carpet,' she screamed, and frantically she pulled out a handkerchief from her sleeve. 'Here, take this – try to swallow. Breathe – take a deep breath – it will pass off in a minute.'

So it did; it was only a gust of nausea.

Liddy handed back the handkerchief and tried to smile bleakly through her tears.

'I'm all right now,' she said.

It was Bedelia who looked bad now; she sank down on a chair.

'I must say it's a queer way it took you!' she said crossly, and she placed her hand on her own stomach. 'You gave me such a start.'

Liddy saw the enormity of her offence.

'It must have been the portmanteau,' she said apologetically, 'the weight of it, I mean,' she said, and then gulping she came to a quick decision. 'I didn't tell you, Bedelia,' she said, 'but I'm not supposed to lift anything heavy just now –.'

'Good God!'

Heavy and all as she was, awkward and clumsy, Bedelia was on her feet again in an instant.

'You don't mean –' Oh, but it was absolutely – oh, but absolutely unbelievable. It was the last straw. Why, she felt as if she had been tricked – as if between them they had made a fool of her, Liddy and O'Brien, both of them. 'Why didn't you tell me this before now?' she screamed and as she screamed one question, others swarmed in her mind. What use would the creature be to her in this condition?

This condition: it revolted her to think of the two of them – two of them! – in the same condition, in the one house – one as useless as the other as the days went on.

And this other brat when he was born – what was going to become of him? Would she and Daniel have to rear him too, as well as their own? And for how long?

Before her mind's eye, she saw the face of Alphonsus O'Brien but it was as ever inscrutable.

She swung around. She forgot all her other questions.

'Might I ask one thing,' she cried. 'Did he know about this when he embezzled the funds, or did it come as a glorious surprise to him afterwards?'

Liddy hesitated for a minute before she answered, but her tears had dried, and she was looking steadily into Bedelia's eyes.

'He didn't know,' she said calmly. 'He doesn't know even now! I didn't tell him at all!'

'You didn't what?' Bedelia's voice had gone; she could say nothing now except in a shrill scream.

'I didn't tell him,' Liddy repeated quietly. Her voice was growing

in confidence. 'I was going to tell him the very night – the night he
had to tell me about the money and so I didn't tell him after all!'

'Why?'

'I wanted to keep it till –.'

Anyone – anyone, even Bedelia, could see what she waited for;
the hope that the clouds would be dispelled and the sun would
shine again, and her secret be given its golden due.

Even Bedelia could see that was why she waited: could see but
could not endure the sight.

'You fool' she cried. 'There may be a time for sentimentality of
that kind, but this wasn't the time! You let him get away without
knowing the full extent of his responsibilities. What in the name of
God were you thinking about?'

Liddy's mind, however, was in no confusion.

'I knew what I was doing, Bedelia,' she said. 'I wouldn't have told
him for anything. I wouldn't have made things harder for him. He
mightn't have been able to make up his mind if he knew – or not so
quickly, anyway.'

Just like the day she announced that he wanted to marry her
there was a radiance and glory about her that Bedelia could not but
perceive. Nor could she see whence came this ambience, or why it
should be her due.

'I must say it's easy to be noble at the expense of others,' she
said. 'Have you thought about us – about me and my husband? It
was one thing to have you here – for a while – by yourself – till he
sent for you – you might even have been some help in the house –
Daniel would have been only too pleased, but how will he take it
now – when I have to tell him we're saddled with rearing another
man's brat! And for how long? That's the question.'

It was the all important question.

Yet Liddy never seemed to have pondered it at all. Her body,
beautiful, frail, even in its fertility, was still a vessel for some secret
happiness Bedelia never knew, and although she hadn't known it,
what she wanted, all the time, was to break it. She thrust herself
forward, she thrust her face, that was swollen with the strain she
had undergone into the face, still so serene, in front of her.

'Do you know what I think?' she cried. 'I think you've seen the last of him – do you hear me – the last of him!'

But she couldn't make out whether Liddy had heard or not. Certainly her reply, which came in a whisper, was abolutely inexplicable.

'Even so!' Liddy whispered. 'Even so!'

Pilgrimage

Mary Beckett

Mary Beckett was born in Belfast in 1926. Her short fiction has appeared in periodicals such as *The Bell* and *Threshold,* on RTE and the BBC. Beckett stopped writing while raising a family, but has begun to write and be published again; a first collection of her short stories, *A Belfast Woman* (Dublin: Poolbeg Press, 1980) has recently appeared. A former teacher, Mary Beckett has lived in Dublin since her marriage.

Like most of Beckett's writings, 'Pilgrimage' is set in her native city. The combination of lyricism, wry humour and shrewd insight is a distinctive quality of her work. No critical appraisal of Mary Beckett's work has yet appeared.

FELICITY LIVED in a street with poor little stunted trees not far from the mountains. Her house was a red-brick house with a square concrete verandah where the old dog could lie and wag his tail in the sun. In the evening the sun came round to the kitchen window and the lustres made dancing lines of green and orange and blue on the wall. There were times when it rained, but the green of the hedge and the green of the trees made the rain glint like splintered green glass.

When Felicity was a child she used to laugh and dance up and down out there, flapping her arms in the air clumsily, like a fat little fledgling bird. She used to push her fingers through her straight brown hair and tousle it and toss it all over her face. But then she grew up and married a man who worried and groused and complained. She did her best to make him glad but though her happiness bounded bright and hard in her breast he continued to frown on the world. So to please him she cooked golden fruit pies and because she liked to feel the crunch of white sugar through her broad smooth hands she made them sweet. And he made a face and said they cloyed his tongue and the back of his throat. He'd rather have cheese from a shop.

She would give her happiness then to his children and hers; she would hide it away like grain in the folds of a winnower's clothes to spring up and bear fruit later on. But they would take no more than life from her; they were solemn and earnest and dull. 'There is no happiness in any corner of the world,' they said. 'There is only pain and sin and hurt and desire,' they said. And Felicity tried to tell them: 'I have happiness inside me, in every part of me from the grey hair on the top of my head to the brittle nails on the toes of my feet.' But her tongue stumbled over the words and they were embarrassed and would not hear. She would have made a song for them; to give them joy but her voice was weak and no tune would come into her head.

So her children went sadly out into the world and met and talked with the people there. And the people said: 'Your children are good. They are not so beautiful, perhaps, as we would like and now and then we grow a little tired of them. But they are honest and they tell the truth. There is nothing in the world but poverty and anguish and 'crabbed envy and disgust.' She longed to cry out they were wrong but she was afraid of their mocking so she asked instead: 'Have none of you felt in your lives one moment of bliss?' They shouted and stamped. 'Are you blind? Look around you. We're poor. Give us money and we'll love the poor that are left. People are stupid. Nobody wants us. You've never suffered because you's never tried to live. Go out and look at the world.' And they left her alone.

She went out into the green grassy garden to lie on the ground and think of what they had said. But the sun warmed her through her skin and her veins and she stretched like a cat and buried her face in the crook of her arm to sniff the scent of the sun on her skin. She looked up the sage slopes of the round sheltering hills and at the stillness of the rowan leaves cut out against the sky. And she was more precious even than these. But it wasn't right to lie and laze when the world suffered and sought more pain. She must go out, they had told her. She must find a chain and a weight without sweetness or light or else learn of those who had joy like her own, how to give it to others.

So she looked in the mirror and put on her best hat. A month she'd spent to find it, last year. 'A month of waste, and the world in fear of an atom bomb and of famine and debt and disease!' her husband exclaimed. It looked very well just the same. But a mirror wasn't the world.

She'd begin in the church – a red-brick church in a red-brick street with a brick round tower that wasn't meant to be a joke. But inside was God. She knelt down at the back to say her prayers but her mind wandered off to a woman's rheumatic hands and a man with a lump on the back of his neck. She looked at the walls: they were flaky and scabrous with swirling stencils of grapes and a leaf. The statues were sickly with prim painted mouths and forms without bones. 'Because I have loved, oh Lord, the beauty of Thy house,' she remembered and replied: 'There is no beauty here.' 'Here is sadness,' she thought; the words are not true. I can go home and agree with the rest. Then a boy came out with a cross in his hand, a processional cross and it clanged against the ring of the lamp, and it swung and was Aladdin's cave of amber oil and golden sun and ruby glass in great arcs until the sexton steadied it. Children sang and the girls were sweet and restrained and the boys were earnest, whole-hearted and rough in the end. A priest prayed and offered, blessed and preached about work by the sweat of the brow and the sorrows of women in this vale of tears. 'Poor man!' she thought. 'Has he never heard of man's satisfaction in work, of a woman's fierce joy in pain?'

Then a thought came into her mind that she should perhaps have given it up, this richness of hers, that others might share in her dividend if she'd shut herself in and hidden away among bevies of women in black. Now her children were grown she could go for her husband wouldn't refuse. 'I don't want you,' God said. 'I gave you a pearl of great price, to show a soft gleam to those in the world who will see. The nuns have a blaze of their own.' 'But no one will heed me,' Felicity said. 'For the house-tops are high and the light of a pearl needs the sheen of velvet or beautiful skin to reflect it.'

The convent was brick too, and bare and her shoes squeaked and slid on the floor till she found a chair, hard and straight by a table against a wall. A postulant flapped her white coif and eased it away from her rosy cheeks and smiled shyly and bowed. 'Very happy,'

she said. 'Very happy, thank God. There is peace here and prayer.
I'll be used soon enough to the cold.' An old nun bustled her on. 'If
you stand till you're cold in this world you'll have to be warm in the
next. I'll stay and talk to this lady here for God will be glad of any
gossip that is to be had. Happy? Content? Indeed I am,' and she
shook her long tooth and waggled her chin in a chuckle. 'And you,
child? Are you married? With children? That's good. What a
pretty blue dress! But there goes my bell. Where's my cloak?
Good-bye. Come again.' Then they all flitted past on their patched
black shoes, full tilt towards the church where their blessed content
would soar and aspire to the sky.

In the eddying wind that they left in their wake Felicity laughed
and held on to her fluttering skirts. 'It's all lies that they told me at
home. Here is bounding joy gleaming like a trout in a stream.' But
she knew that they'd sneer: 'They are not in the world. They have
all run away and blinded their eyes with their incense and myrrh.
It's not fair to judge them as the world.' She had further to seek but
the breeze on her cheek had been sifted through silk, and a cobweb
broke on the bridge of her nose as she went to a school. There she'd
see what it was to be young with free books and free will but no
freedom. 'Ach it's great,' they said. 'Far better than home; there's
no child to mind and nobody's cross when we're good. There's a
wireless and all but it's cold and we're crushed and we're fear'd of
the rats in the press.' The teacher sighed. 'They won't learn, and
they never were trained to do what they're told, and it's cold and
maggots breed and feed white in the dirt in the entry beside us.' A
chill struck in through Felicity's bones till the teacher cheered up.
'Now and then it's good fun. But I wish I'd a home and a child of
my own and the warmth of a fire.' Then she turned to her class:
'Back to work now. That's enough of fuss about nothing at all. We
can't very well have what we want.'

'Then why am I given so much?' Felicity wondered and wandered out through the yard and on to a bus. There, office girls
gossiped in pairs, about a boss who found fault and a dance where
the men sized them up like pigs at a fair and then smoothed their
hair and sat down without dancing with one. They complained
about men they had met who were scared of being caught, and

shied away when they passed in the street. They pinned their faith in the week's horoscope and smiled when it said a good time was ahead for some, but one of them said: 'Woman's free these days to do what she likes so long as she doesn't expect love or care or respect. She is free to grow withered and old by herself. But it's pay-day tomorrow and I'm off to book a perm.' 'Well that's good,' Felicity thought, 'though her head will be lost in a frizz for a month or more. But it's marriage they want. Well then, I'll find a quick lighting joy in the faces of those who have husbands.'

She noticed a line of poor ragged women in bright cotton skirts and black shawls with hidden bundles to sell in a shop with three winking balls that echoed the brass of the sun. She joined the queue and the women in front flicked her face with a swipe of her shawl, and a cloud of dust and of snuff and of dirt made Felicity move back a step where a woman, just come, pushed her on with a shout: 'Are you going or not? For goodness' sake move up or get out of the queue.' 'I have nothing to sell,' Felicity said and she smiled, and the woman's heavy-mouthed face opened up and she said: 'If you'd speak in this ear, Mrs dear, I might hear. The other one's not so good since my man hit me a clout in a rage. For he drinks all his dole and puts it on dogs and me and the childher's in rags. And then says he: "Won't you thank God I'm in health and fit to go out and not sick in my bed." And says I: "Come on childher dear, down on your knees and thank God that your da's only sick when he's drunk and doesn't know what it's like to be sick of your man." So he hit me and kicked me and I'm deaved on one ear but he heard what I said. Says I: "You couldn't stiffen quick enough for me, you ignorant thick-fisted galoot. The cold money I'll spend with most glee in my heart is not on a race at the dogs, but on the blind staring eyes of your corp!"'

Felicity's blood beat the breath from her lungs at the sound of her hate. She asked: 'Could you not tell the police? That's a crime fit for gaol and you should not let him off or he'll kill you some day.' 'Ah, go on out this! Sure I moped for a year when he left me before, for I couldn't get used to the peace and quiet,' the deaf woman said and the others scoffed at Felicity: 'If you'd a man at all you'd know what it's like to put up with the shouts and screech back when he quits. It's what comes with a ring and a room of your own.' And they burled Felicity round and pushed her out of the queue. 'Come here just to gawk and to gape with your uppity face and your pitying mouth. Our men are the best in the world. They get drunk but we all have our faults. The pity is, it takes up all the dole,' and their lips drooped again and they hugged their bundles up tight under crossed arms.

Felicity's cheeks stung pink with their scorn as she picked her steps on the cobble-stones with black slime in between. Perhaps if she talked to the men themselves she'd see if they found any well-being in drink or more joy than their wives found in hate. She found them at a corner with a greyhound at their knees. From lads to old men they ranged, with white dangling hands at their sides and nails bitten short to the quick. She was about to draw near when they saw her and whistled and peered. She stopped and saw deep in their eyes the urge to befoul, destroy, desecrate what they could never possess. She hastened away, her soul shrinking in shame, as their hate of a world that denied them men's work was poured molten on her.

She was hot and the street smelt sour but down at the mill there were men of a different kind. They were building, and just knocking off for the day. They'd be glad their work was done and done well; she'd find satisfaction, contentment. They shook their heads. 'We're building a chimney,' they said. 'We've built them before, here and there, with the bricks making hot welts on our hands and cement mixed with sweat in our hair and our ears. We stand back when we're done with our hands on our hips. We stand back to look up and admire what we've built, and they run up a flag that offends us.' There were others that swarmed off a tram with shining lunch tins in their hands. They talked instead of the lick of red lead on the side of the ship. 'Well isn't it good? Felicity said. 'Not bad,' they agreed. 'But the smell makes you sick and the pay's not so great. We have no chance to get on, and we never know when the others will turn, egged on by the lodge, and sweep us all out.'

The sun poured its light from the west on the orange tram tracks and square sets and Felicity walked nearer home. There, women like her with their children and husbands and homes would surely admit that their lives were full. Her heart reached out to the red houses with conservative paint and neat tidy flowers at the front. But the women she spoke to were meagre and grey. 'I worshipped my son. I have one. He went off and married a girl who thinks I've no right in his life. She won't take my advice and insists on having a family now when they haven't even a car. She's selfish, that's all. She should wait as I did until I could give him all that he could desire. But he's gone and I'm left, bereft.' 'My children have gone into the world and they stand by themselves,' Felicity said. 'They need me no more, but that adds to my pleasure.' 'I don't understand what gave you such joy at the first.' 'I was born.' 'So was I.' '–and baptised?' 'That too. And last year we bought a sitting in the church. We go on Sundays when it's fine but it means that the house has to go without cleaning for the day. And on Monday I could cry at the state that it's in.'

Felicity went home. The hills were enormous and pale in the mist and the sun was a red gash in the gathering dark. Dew beaded the snapdragons' wine velvet jaws and a few russet leaves were fissling round the milk-bottles. The old dog on the seat thumped his tail and a blister of paint broke, showing green underneath. She patted his head and he followed her into the house, and she took off her hat.

'I have looked at the world,' she said to them all sitting round. They looked up, unease and regret in their eyes. 'Well weren't we right?' they demanded. 'Not quite,' she replied. 'There were some with a grain of gladness but it was buried too deep under fear that it shouldn't be there, to rejoice in it. But you're right in a way. I have seen an old woman cry with no space for her grief in a room crowded with children at play. She turned on the cat when it jumped on her knee and hurled it down to the floor. And a child whose body shivered and twitched with disease, cowered away when her mother came near. These things have given me pain.'

She closed her eyes, for her body was tired and they sought to console her: 'Now you are one with the world in your suffering. You are joined, you are knit with the world in its pain.' 'And I'm glad,' Felicity said, and wondered to find it was true – that her joy was re-created, renewed, fuller and deeper than ever before. She sat very still to feel what had become of her pain and she found it absorbed and contained in her joy in being the woman she was. Unable to bind and keep hidden such bounty she leaned back her head and she laughed, and startled resentment in them. Then in the depths of her laughter there grew up an ache, for how is a woman to live with joy in her heart that so few in the world will share.

The Tragedy of Eight Pence

Geraldine Cummins

Geraldine Cummins, who was born in Cork in 1890, came of Anglo-Irish stock. She was very active in the suffrage movement, and like Edith Somerville (a close friend) and Violet Martin, she served as an officer of the Munster Women's Franchise League.

Cummin's writing career began when she collaborated with Susanne R. Day in writing plays for the Abbey theatre. *The Land They Loved* (London: Macmillan, 1919) and *Fires of Beltane* (London: Michael Joseph, 1936) are her best-known novels. Like Edith Somerville, of whom she wrote a biography, *Dr. E. Œ. Somerville* (London: Dakers, 1952), Cummins was deeply interested in parapsychology and psychical research, and she wrote a number of books about her experiences, among them her autobiography, *Unseen Adventures* (London: Rider, 1951).

'The Tragedy of Eight Pence' is one of the best stories in Cummins' only volume of short fiction. It is an account of a conflict between two ways of life, of bitter-sweet marital happiness, and, above all, a study of a caring woman – a type of character which is not dealt with sympathetically, or extensively in Anglo-Irish literature on the whole.

Geraldine Cummins died in 1969. Her work has been forgotten.

AFTER FIFTEEN years of married life Colonel and Mrs Moore were still inseparable though no coercive methods were used by either party. The group of semi-detached couples in Patrick Moore's regiment considered such behaviour ridiculous. But when social relations were resumed following the First World War the Moores' anti-social unit, their apparently permanent honeymoon had a souring effect upon the officers' wives and were a subject for spiteful remarks. Polite but uninterested in manner, they avoided intimacy with others, being sufficient unto themselves.

Perhaps it was Patrick's delicacy and the absence of children that furnished Kate with cogent reasons for remaining on more friendly terms with him. She was a motherly soul, and the love she might otherwise have lavished on children or dogs remained concentrated upon her husband.

A great deal of persuasion had been necessary before he had succeeded in acquiring Kate Curran as his wife. That success and not his V.C. was in his opinion the supreme achievement of his life. His thronged wedding was his last large social gesture. The little affair on the Somme that earned him the Victoria Cross had exacted a lesser output of courage.

Patrick Moore was gassed and seriously wounded near the end of the War and never really recovered from these injuries. Suffering from a weak heart, asthma and damaged hip, he was glad to say good-bye to his career in 1925 and settle in a small house on a hill some miles from the town of Garryvoe.

The Moores couldn't avoid society as long as Patrick was commanding his regiment; they were now determined to be entirely unsociable. Eventually they won through to their freedom, but quite two years passed before they succeeded in gently snubbing their neighbours into submission. At last even the amiable rector of Kippagh was defeated, and Reenascreena and its occupants were left to themselves.

The Moores were not by any means angels. The Colonel, a small, thin, grey-haired man, had his hours of peevish depression when his blue eyes became fierce with melancholy while his face wrinkled up with pain, so that he looked sixty instead of forty-six. Then Kate was occasionally nervy, and in such a mood could be extremely satirical, but she had a kind of infectious brightness that took the edge off criticism and prevented any differences of opinion from becoming quarrels.

After an attack of pneumonia Patrick became almost entirely dependent on his wife. His weakness and his condition as a semi-invalid only seemed to refine the character of their happiness. Their pretty little house and the grounds with their magnificent view of river and lake, were to them a kind of miniature garden of Eden. All they needed to complete their bliss was a vigorous Tree of Life which unfortunately did not grow in the Reenascreena acre of land. One carefully hidden fear, the fear of death, took the edge off the perfection of that gay and beautiful time for Kate; but as she watched Patrick from hour to hour there came more assurance, and she was happily aware that he lived in the day, and in spite of illness and weakness, had found perfection, giving no thought to the menace to himself of a blank tomorrow.

An acid touch of realism broke up the tranquillity of this enchanting existence one summer morning as the two breakfasted in their dressing-gowns on the veranda. The post had brought a letter from Angelina Hussey, the Colonel's step-sister; it announced her arrival with her husband at Reenascreena one day in the following week. They owned house-property in Garryvoe and were coming from England to see a solicitor about its sale. Characteristically, Mrs Hussey invited herself to stay with her brother. She assumed that his home was hers when she wished to save the expense of an hotel.

'You know you can't bear Angelina,' protested Kate.

'She'll have to be borne,' replied Patrick; 'and I feel in pretty good trim for standing her racket at the moment.'

'Racket! She has a tongue as long as today and tomorrow. She'll wear you out.'

'Oh, well, one crowded hour of nauseating life is worth an age of offensive and abusive letters. As a matter of fact she'll be quite amiable when she's saving hotel expenses for two.'

'But they'll stay at least a fortnight!'

'My dear, to please me.' Patrick stretched out the hand from which four fingers were missing; they had been amputated after the battle of the Somme. It now rested caressingly on Kate's bare arm. He was taking advantage of a weakness of hers. She could never resist the pathos of that hand. So she grudgingly agreed to entertain Angelina and Claude Hussey.

Having won his point, he stared appreciatively at his wife's red hair flecked with grey, at her plain good-humoured face, its attractive irregular features; and he appeared to add insult to injury by remarking in the tones of a lover, 'You're looking prettier than usual today, Kate.'

'Your aesthetic values seem a bit wonky, Pat,' she retorted; 'I'm looking every month of my forty-five years.'

'Oh, that reminds me,' was his irrelevant answer, 'that Claude's a mycologist. He's writing a great work on the aesthetic values of the higher fungi. I believe it's a kind of escape from his wife's values.'

'What are they?'

'The beauties of thrift. Angelina's a poor woman who is very rich. She and Claude are both misers. Promise me when you go about with them always to pay for yourself.'

'I will of course.' Kate lightly kissed her husband as a sign that she was reconciled to her fate. But later her aesthetic values as well as her composure were sadly shaken when she welcomed Angelina to Reenascreena. For her sister-in-law's black boot-button eyes, classic features, thin mouth, grey woollen dress buttoned to the throat and her lanky husband with his bald head and oily, sickly complexion all suggested that the two had lived in cellars barred from the light, and that they belonged to the higher fungi. Their annoying unattractiveness had a painful fascination for Kate, ugliness as well as beauty can be a spell binder, and their personalities presented the perfection of all that was sinister and of the earth earthy.

They were, as Patrick had predicted, exceedingly amiable, almost too amiable. On the first evening of their stay Angelina announced that they did not care for the wireless and did not play bridge; and it soon became obvious that she only liked the sound of her own voice. Resignedly the Moores settled down to listen to its metallic clatter.

Kate was proud of her pretty drawing-room with its rose curtains and black Chinese furniture. Angelina valued every stick of it and reproached her hostess for locking up so much money in carved wood.

Thinking of the great work on the higher fungi, Kate replied, 'but it has its aesthetic value for us.'

'Tch – much better to have the value and use of four hundred pounds. That is about what it's worth. You're losing fifteen pounds a year interest. It's little things like that that mount up as the years go by.'

'Do they matter?' inquired Kate.

'Of course. Take care of the pence and the pounds will take care of themselves. When we were at Bournemouth last summer I walked two miles every day to get apples tuppence a dozen cheaper. We eat a great many apples because an apple a day keeps the doctor away. Chemist's bills are enormous you know. Illness is a luxury poor people like us can't afford in these difficult times.' Angelina gave her brother a reproving glance. 'Your bills for medicine must be ruinous. Now to show you what can be done in little things, Claude and I had our remaining teeth taken out so as to save dentist's bills.'

'That must impair your apple bite.'

She ignored Patrick's facetious comment, fixing him with her button eyes, inquiring earnestly, 'Are your teeth your own?'

'No they're my wife's. I have them on loan.'

'Don't be stupid. I mean are they false?' Then shrugging her shoulders she turned to Kate who had begun a conversation with Claude on the subject of toadstools, his speciality.

Ruthlessly she cut across their discussion of this entrancing theme with the inquiry: 'Have you thought, my dear, what can be done with servants? When we lived in Barbados I had a raised concrete platform in the kitchen from which every morning I instructed the domestics in economy. Niggers, you know, are very wasteful. Day and night they must be watched. I had to lock up all the household requirements and give them out each morning. I counted out pieces of wood for the fire – three for soup, two for meat, one for plum pudding.'

'Eighty in the shade at the lowest. Hot spot for plum pudding,' murmured Patrick.

'Oh, we're not heathens. We always kept Christmas and we always had late dinner because it maintains British prestige with the niggers.'

Strangely enough the niggers suggested the Oxford Group Movement. Angelina talked for an hour about the many good and holy people it had produced, and with great gusto she reeled off the names of those members of it who were of the aristocracy.

'You talk as if there were no good people anywhere else, but in Oxford,' Kate remarked, trying to divert her guest's attention from Patrick, whose face had become haggard with fatigue. He was huddled in his chair, wilting visibly before this devouring woman.

'Oh, I suppose there are some holy people in Ireland,' the oracle responded, 'but those in England are so well connected.'

'Then I'm hardly suitable company for you.' Kate bit her tongue in her effort to avoid making this retort and instead of it called a closure to the evening.

That night in her prayers she thanked God that she was not in the power of this woman – financially or otherwise. And she added a biblical reference, 'As, God, you look after the sparrows I know You'll look after me later on.'

The Moores were badly off. Patrick only had his pension and his was a precarious hold on life. But at present he was not worried over his wife's future as their cousin Arthur Moore had not merely promised to provide for her; six months ago he had written saying that he was arranging a settlement of a capial sum on Kate. This would save death duties and relieve his conscience of an old debt. It was Patrick's kindness years ago in extricating him from an entanglement with a woman that had led to his becoming a rich and happy old bachelor with no impedimenta in the way of poor relations, or nephews or nieces. In these circumstances Kate agreed that the money could be accepted.

Beyond a brief note that it was all going through in the correct red tape manner, Patrick had no further news of the settlement. About two months later in reply to his inquiry Arthur Moore's housekeeper had written saying that all correspondence was withheld from him as he had been ordered a rest cure for his neurasthenia. This statement satisfied the Colonel since the notes stated that all had been arranged for his wife.

But Kate's benefactor was not in her mind on the morning following the first wearisome evening spent with Angel and Claude. After bringing Patrick his breakfast she was in a gay mood that was not even dashed by the sour expression on her guests' faces as they eyed the laden dishes in the dining-room.

'You must be starving!' was her apologetic exclamation, and she hastened to provide them with nourishment.

But their curdled facial expressions did not alter even after Claude had consumed a plate of stirabout, two eggs and bacon.

He thereupon abruptly announced that he had become Arthur's

solicitor, and clearing his throat added with the air of the chief mourner at a funeral,

'I didn't like to say anything before your husband. But I have very sad news for you, Kate. Arthur has lost practically everything.'

'His money was in molasses,' interrupted Angelina. 'Wicked I call it to invest in speculative shares.'

'My dear, one moment,' pleaded Claude; 'I want to explain to Kate why there will be no provision for her future. Arthur has invested the remainder of his money in an annuity.'

'I know,' Kate replied lightly, 'he wrote to me about it, and I've made him promise not to tell Patrick.'

'Most mistaken,' returned Claude. 'Patrick must be told, as I understand – poor fellow – that his days are numbered.'

'For that very reason he must know nothing.'

'On the contrary,' began Claude.

Kate drew herself up, and the wistful tenderness that brightened her face was like a lovely light at sunrise, as she said, 'I want Patrick to be perfectly happy in the little bit of life that is left to him. He's often in pain. Why add to that pain? What good would it do?'

'Every good,' broke in Angelina, 'you ought to economise, to save every ha'penny. You've got to live in a much smaller way. Sell that drawing-room furniture – leave this house –.'

'And live in a tenement?' Kate drily replied. 'No I won't tell Patrick or make any change. I'm giving him a beautiful time. Why wreck it?'

'But you'll be left a beggar. I understand he has only his pension.'

'That doesn't worry me in the least. I can always work.'

'What at?' inquired Claude in his best sepulchral voice.

'With my talent for food I'll never starve. I'll get a job as a cook. I have it all planned.'

'Impossible!' exclaimed Angelina, her eyes almost starting from her head with horror. 'What would people say?'

'Thank you and pleased to meet you of course,' laughed Kate. 'A good cook – is as rare as a museum piece in England. I shall be a social success over there.'

'Such a position is unthinkable for a woman of our class,' barked Angelina. 'My husband must speak to Patrick tomorrow.'

There came a queer breathless pause. In the silence Claude's boots creaked uneasily. Then wrathful and beside herself, Kate cried out:

'He shan't – he won't – I forbid it.'

'You can't prevent him, my dear,' sweetly responded Angel. 'It's his duty, and he is no shirker.'

'But it will make Patrick ill. It will shorten his life.'

'Nonsense. He'll be grateful – glad to know the truth. He hates deception.'

The two women were now on their feet, facing each other, preparing for argumentative battle. But gazing at this relic of a lamentable Victorian era, Kate realized that she and Angelina were of different periods and so of different worlds, that there was no point of contact between them. No pleading could change this woman's petty snobbish outlook. She was only thinking of herself, of what her relations would say if the rich Husseys allowed the widow of a distinguished soldier to work for her living in the manner proposed. To Kate, Angelina's outlook was grim with potential tragedy. It would, if not defeated, steal all Patrick's happiness away. She felt she must play for time, and this thought steadying her, she said craftily, 'There's no hurry about telling my husband. Wait a few days. You know he may ask Claude to provide for me if you speak to him now.'

That was a shrewd thrust. The two Husseys were momentarily staggered: but Angelina was quick in recovery, replying, 'Of course, my dear, Claude will always be delighted to help you with his advice. Unfortunately financial assistance is out of the question. I am afraid we've barely enough for two as it is and –.'

'Oh, I wasn't suggesting anything. But Patrick will naturally look to you,' replied Kate, while inwardly she registered the reflection, I'd rather be hanged, drawn and quartered than accept a penny from you, you old devil.

But she recovered her composure and her sense of humour and even emitted a husky chuckle of relief when Claude came to his wife's rescue by saying, 'Kate has very sensibly remarked that there's no hurry. Of course, if it seems necessary – ahem – on the eve of our departure, Angel, I might hint – I might even in a few tactful words make the position clear to Patrick. *Festine Lente* – in vulgar parlance, make haste slowly is a very sound motto. . . *Festine Lente,*' he sighed.

Kate was under no illusions. She had gained time but not victory. The Husseys intended to speak to Patrick just before they caught the train for Dublin and not before. It would be less awkward and disagreeable to refuse his anticipated appeal to their generosity when they were bidding him goodbye. Angelina would lecture him on thrift; and then with a clear conscience, they would leave him crazy with anxiety, determined to cut down expenses and live in squalor.

In the circumstances it wasn't easy for Kate to be polite to her guests. But she derived, even in this crisis, a morbid amusement from observing the chronic state of worry in which they lived. They began the day with the study of the financial columns of the newspaper. Dolefully they shook their heads over its revelations. They looked harrassed and alarmed when they learned that their cheap hot water bag had burst when the maid was filling it. Kate bought another one, and with delight, noted Angelina's obvious qualm of conscience when she accepted it saying, 'Of course it was your maid's fault. You must deduct the price of it from her wages. It will be a lesson to her.'

Kate refrained from saying she would do nothing of the kind. Such a rash remark would only have involved her in an interminable argument.

For Patrick's sake she must keep Angelina in a good humour; but she failed to avoid quarrelling with him when they were alone together. He objected to her biting criticism of his sister, told her she was as sour as a crab-apple that morning, reduced her to silence and almost to tears.

'Merciful God, preserve me from in-laws,' was her voiceless prayer each day as she drove them fifteen miles into Garryvoe. Claude had said that Angelina couldn't walk to the bus. He really meant that their inadequate income of two thousand a year did not permit them to run to the expense of a two-shilling bus fare. But however irritated she was at waiting about for them, she derived some cynical entertainment from Angelina's face glowing with the light of battle and approaching victory when she and her husband emerged from the house-agent or the solicitor's office.

Theirs was a successful business deal, for house-property had trebled in value; and on the afternoon the last documents were signed, they actually ventured on the expense of a cinema and tea afterwards, at a restaurant.

Kate offered to pay for her share. With an air of extreme reluctance Claude accepted the money, on the principle that it is more blessed grudgingly to receive than to give.

That evening Angelina talked interminably. Patrick had an air of extreme exhaustion. But ignoring his look of entreaty Kate had left him to his family, and escaped to her garden in order to face her problem. It was desparately urgent now. The day after tomorrow the Husseys were leaving Reenascreena. Claude intended to make his announcement on the following evening. How on earth was she to circumvent him? No appeal would penetrate his thick hide. The problem seemed insoluble.

It was a moonlight night; but its luminous peace neither moved nor comforted her mind. This small sordid care cut her off from communion with unearthliness, from the pleasure conveyed to her so often before by the dark, solemn trees, the pale outline of the flowers, the perfumed evening and the myriad watching stars. Their light seemed to flicker wantonly, and she was merely sensible of her minuteness, of their vastness and their indifference.

The microcosm mattered so much, the macrocosm counted for so little.

Filled with a sense of fate's cruel indifference, she accepted resignedly the fact of Patrick's collapse. He spent a good part of the night gasping, his lungs reedily wheezing in the effort of breathing. The doctor came late in the morning when the attack had subsided. He was less vague than usual in his pronouncement; and that afternoon Kate sat mute in her drawing-room scarcely heeding her sister-in-law's chatter, oppressed and burdened by her fear. 'Two years if worried,' the doctor had said. 'Death at any time from sudden shock.' Or six, seven more years life if attentively looked after, and if he is free from worries.

Apart from this miserable sentence, it was not a day to inspire anyone to live gaily in the happy security of the passing moment. All the lights and colours of the landscape were obliterated by the rain that streamed against the windows and by the loaded clouds that brushed the hills. Yet, as the afternoon darkened and the wind became louder and more melancholy in its tone, Kate's face brightened, and suddenly she laughed softly to herself. Eureka! She believed that she had solved her problem. The solution was prosaic enough and inspired by Angelina's discussion of the ever absorbing topic of servants.

'When Claude and I give up hotel life I'm going to engage a lady help. Ladies are far cheaper than maids.'

The maid brought in tea at this moment, and Angelina changed the subject, speaking of her early departure the next morning. It was a reminder of duty unfulfilled, led up to that crisis which Kate had been anticipating all the afternoon. Brushing the cake crumbs from her skirt, Angelina sat comfortably back in her chair and delivered her ultimatum.

'When Claude sees Patrick after tea he will tell him everything, Kate dear. The serious financial position, your prospects as a penniless widow –.'

'Very awkward for Claude. Pat is sure to ask him to provide for me.'

'I'm sorry – that's out of the question, and –.'

Kate interrupted her sister-in-law quietly but firmly: 'I could be very useful to you, Angelina, as – as a lady help when I'm a widow.'

'But I thought you'd decided –.'

'To be a cook,' Kate finished the sentence. 'Not necessarily. It all depends on you.'

'What do you mean?'

'If you promise to say nothing to Patrick about Arthur's failure I will be guided by your wishes later on. You know I can cook, clean, sew, do every mortal thing in a house, and I'm wonderfully healthy.'

Instantly, the boot buttons were fixed appraisingly on Kate who read the careful calculations of Angelina's mind and perceived the dawning delight on her face as she realised the financial advantages of possessing a poor relation. It might mean complete possession and credit as well with her cronies. She would work Kate like a galley slave and boast of her own generosity in supporting her brother's widow.

'I agree,' she said; 'we'll say nothing to Patrick. Claude and I will be very pleased to give you a home. Only of course we won't be able to afford a maid, so your help in the house would be necessary – and I think we could give you an allowance.' Here there came a momentary pause, and then the crucial question was asked, 'What about twenty-five pounds a year, and I can occasionally pass you on some of my old clothes. We're nearly the same height.'

Kate glanced over her sister-in-law's hideous woollen dress as she enthusiastically replied, 'Angel, how generous of you – how kind!'

'Not at all, I'm too delicate to cook.' Angelina licked her thin lips savouring excellent fare; 'But you are –.'

'Not a mere cook, I'm a chef!' Kate gaily interrupted.

'But we mustn't be extravagant!' was the cooling response, while the boot-button eyes gleamed with pleased calculation.

Through a hazy dawn Kate drove the Husseys in the direction of Garryvoe. She chuckled to herself as she listened to their talk. They were seated at the back of the car and unaware of the fact that their remarks were overheard. After some discussion they decided that morning tea and one slice apiece of thin bread and butter had provided them with an adequate breakfast. No need to pay for another meal on the train to Dublin. They would ask cousin Alice for lunch on their arrival at her residence at three o'clock in the afternoon. Another fourpence must be saved through employing Kate as their porter. Between the three of them they could carry their suit-cases to the platform for the mail train; it was some distance from the ticket office.

Unfortunately the Reenascreena clocks kept 'God's time' or 'old time' but not 'new time'. When encumbered by luggage the Husseys customarily made a point of arriving forty minutes before the departure of the train. On this occasion they had only twenty minutes to spare, and in consequence, there was an edge on Angel's voice that caused Claude to snuffle and look more than ever like a specimen of the higher fungi.

Kate was a little light-headed as she had not had time to drink her tea before leaving home. The sharp morning air had induced pangs of hunger, and occupied with them, she gave half her mind to the search for the machine that provided platform tickets. Five minutes were wasted before she found it, and at the same time, made the woeful discovery that she had forgotten her purse. The Husseys would have to provide the necessary tuppence. Hurrying back to them she made her indelicate demand.

Claude's jaw dropped. But he wouldn't be rushed when it was a question of parting with ready money. Another four minutes were wasted in a whispered discussion between husband and wife before they arrived at the conclusion that they would still save tuppence if they paid for the platform ticket; its purchase assured them of the services of their hostess as their porter.

On receipt of the coppers Kate fled back to the machine, hastily inserted them and received in return a bar of milk chocolate. Though fasting she was not grateful to this deceptive machine. Her only feeling was one of distress and deep concern, when on showing the chocolate to the Husseys, she perceived their tragic faces.

They edged away from the culprit, then after another protracted consultation, again approached her, and their expressions now betrayed their dark distrust of her motives. Nevertheless, Angel thrust forward two coppers that were accompanied by a look that more plainly than words conveyed their considered opinion that she was a thief and as guilty as if she had robbed them of a hundred pounds.

Time was precious; a reputation for honesty might yet be restored to Kate if the duties of amateur porter were fulfilled. Breathlessly she made her demand for the ticket through the little hole labelled first-class: but here again she met with frustration. A contemptuous clerk directed her to the third-class ticket office. The hands of the clock were moving now with what seemed incredible rapidity. With damp fingers clutching the dirty pence, Kate assumed a position at the tail of a long queue of travellers and during those fleeting minutes felt wretched and remorseful. She was a sensitive soul and hated to wound even her enemies in their most sensitive parts. But remorse soon gave place to the overwhelming fear that rather than lose the services of their amateur porter the Husseys would lose their train and then demand another night's lodging at Reenascreena, a second departure at cockcrow. Any return, even such a wraithe-like reappearance as theirs, was almost certain to give Patrick a heart attack, and the thought of it was not to be bourne. There is a condition of mind when terror becomes so acute memory and awareness no longer function. Kate experienced such a period of vacancy. She only came to as she raced up the subway and heard the guard's whistle. A moment later her scared eyes registered the fact that the train was gliding from the platform and that the Husseys were scowling at her from a third-class carriage.

They made no kindly gesture of farewell. Even a sign indicating recognition was not possible in view of the injury sustained. They had been compelled to tip a porter, pay for a bar of chocolate and a useless platform ticket. The study of accounts that evening would reveal a disastrous loss of eight pennies – a loss that must cast a gloomy shadow over the memory of their Reenascreena visit, a shadow that might never be dispelled.

When Kate's mind functioned normally again her first instinct was to fall on her knees upon the stone platform and thank Providence for her deliverance. But hunger asserted its rights. Instead of the ritual act she proceeded gluttonously to gnaw the bar of chocolate, and then exhausted by her last crowded hour of emotional life, she stumbled out of the station and collapsed on to the seat of her car.

The sick man was strolling about the garden as the old 'Tin Lizzy' came rattling up the drive. It was well that the Husseys had not returned in it. Clad only in a dressing-gown and bedroom slippers, Patrick had a carefree appearance and truculently hummed the air of *The Boys of Wexford*. Almost he swaggered as he approached his wife, and his was the appearance of one who had cast off ten burdensome years in the night.

'June 23rd – our wedding day,' he remarked, and after a pause added: 'On June 23rd twenty years ago I'd a kind of idea that I was the happiest, luckiest man in creation. Today I am sure of it.'

Thinking of the danger averted, Kate laughed a little hysterically and retorted, 'Don't be sentimental. I can't live up to it on an almost empty interior.' Then travelling as if on swallow's wings, she flew off to cook their belated breakfast.

During the meal Kate told of the Husseys's tragic loss of eight pennies.

Patrick Moore laughed till he was tired.

But when the sun rose clear and bright above them and was free of all shadows, the Husseys were forgotten in the pleasure of resumption of the interrupted duet.

In the same series:

The Ante-Room
The Last of Summer
The Land of Spices
by Kate O' Brien

The Maiden Dinosaur
by Janet Mc Neill
A Flock of Birds
by Kathleen Coyle
Bridie Steen
by Anne Crone

If you would like
to receive regular
information about
our books write to:
Arlen House
The Women's Press
69 Jones Road
DUBLIN 3